The *Archbishop*
in
Andalusia

**Also by Andrew M. Greeley
from Tom Doherty Associates**

Blackie Ryan Mysteries

The Bishop and the Missing L Train
The Bishop and the Beggar Girl of St. Germain
The Bishop in the West Wing
The Bishop Goes to The University
The Bishop at the Lake
The Archbishop in Andalusia

Nuala Anne McGrail Novels

Irish Gold · *Irish Stew!*
Irish Lace *Irish Cream*
Irish Whiskey *Irish Crystal*
Irish Mist *Irish Linen*
Irish Eyes *Irish Tiger*
Irish Love

The O'Malleys in the Twentieth Century

A Midwinter's Tale *September Song*
Younger Than Springtime *Second Spring*
A Christmas Wedding *Golden Years*

All About Women
Angel Fire
Angel Light
Contract with an Angel
Faithful Attraction
The Final Planet
Furthermore!: Memories of a Parish Priest
God Game
Jesus: A Meditation on His Stories and His Relationships with Women
Star Bright!
Summer at the Lake
White Smoke
Sacred Visions (editor with Michael Cassutt)
The Book of Love (editor with Mary G. Durkin)
Emerald Magic (editor)

The Archbishop
in
Andalusia

• A BLACKIE RYAN NOVEL •

ANDREW M. GREELEY

A Tom Doherty Associates Book
NEW YORK

This is a work of fiction. All of the characters, organizations, and events portrayed in this novel are either products of the author's imagination or are used fictitiously.

THE ARCHBISHOP IN ANDALUSIA

Diagram by Heidi Hornaday

A Forge Book
Published by Tom Doherty Associates, LLC
175 Fifth Avenue
New York, NY 10010

www.tor-forge.com

Forge® is a registered trademark of Tom Doherty Associates, LLC.

Library of Congress Cataloging-in-Publication Data

Greeley, Andrew M., 1928–
    The archbishop in Andalusia : a Blackie Ryan novel / Andrew Greeley.—1st hardcover ed.
        p. cm.
    "A Tom Doherty Associates book."
    ISBN-13: 978-0-7653-1590-8
    ISBN-10: 0-7653-1590-4
1. Ryan, Blackie (Fictitious character)—Fiction. 2. Bishops—Illinois—Chicago—(Social class)—Spain—Andalusia—Fiction. I. Title.
    PS3557.R358A78   2008
    813'.54—dc22

                                                                2008034734

First Edition: November 2008

Printed in the United States of America

0 9 8 7 6 5 4 3 2 1

Resurrection is not supposed to be easy.
—Noelle Farrell

Characters

Cardinal Sean Cronin, Archbishop of Chicago

Archbishop John Blackwood (Blackie) Ryan, coadjutor to Cardinal Cronin

Joseph John Ryan, Golden Domer, missionary, graduate student at the University of Chicago, nephew to Archbishop Ryan

Margaret (Peggy Anne) Nolan, pilot, Golden Domer, missionary, promised bride to Joseph

Cardinal Diego Sanchez y Romanos, El Moro, Archbishop of Seville

Don Pedro, factotum to Don Diego

Doña Teresa Maria Romero y Avila, Duchess of Seville and Huelva, La Doña, Teresa, widow, businesswoman, celebrity

Señorita Maria Luisa, daughter to Teresa Maria, Mary Louise, medical student

Don Leandro Santiago y Diaz, widower, attorney, lover to Doña Teresa

Señoritas Justa and Rufina, daughters to Don Leandro

Isidoro de Colon, Admiral of the Ocean Seas, *novio* to Maria Luisa

Don Teodoro Guzman, El Jefe, rejected promised groom to Maria Luisa

Characters

Don Marco Antonio Navaro y Gomes, general in the Spanish Army (retired)

Doña Inez, wife to Don Marco Antonio, *duenna* (self-appointed) to Teresa Maria, who is her distant cousin

Manuelo Lopez, Investigating Judge

Pepe Garcia, chief of detectives

A Note on Language

The actors in this tale must be imagined speaking in a mixture of good Castilian (the only kind), a Mexican dialect of Spanish, and good and poor English. It would be impossible to write a story that reflected that kind of linguistic confusion. Also the Spaniards speak Spanish while the Americans speak good English (mostly with a Chicago accent). Only Don Diego and Doña Teresa speak excellent English. To create some verisimilitude about this mixture I interject some Spanish words and verbal customs.

The word "Negro" contains no slur in the Spanish tongue. Hence the decision by Don Diego and Don Pedro to translate "Father Blackie" as "El Padrecito Negro"—"that cute little priest called Blackie"—is perfectly appropriate and says nothing more about his skin color than the original nickname and is no more a slur than the original nickname.

Many of the people in the book are named after Spanish patrons: Teresa, the great Carmelite mystic and theologian; Diego, after the Apostle James, who is alleged to have preached in Spain; Justa and Rufina, after Hispano-Roman saints; and Leandro and Isidoro ("The Farmer"), after Visigoth saints. The shift from formal names to less formal and even nicknames—Doña Teresa Maria Romero y Avila, Doña Teresa Maria, Doña Teresa, La

Doña, Tessa, and Teresa—as I understand it, is part of their culture.

Nobility in Spain ranges from the poor but proud all the way up to those who because of money or prestige or physical attractiveness or success in business have become celebrities.

All the characters in this story, clerical and lay, Spanish and American, are products of my imagination. As far as I know there is no Blessed John XXIII Hospital in Seville. However, I think there should be many such hospitals to recall the man, whom many would like to forget, who changed the Church.

LA DOÑA'S *PALACIO*

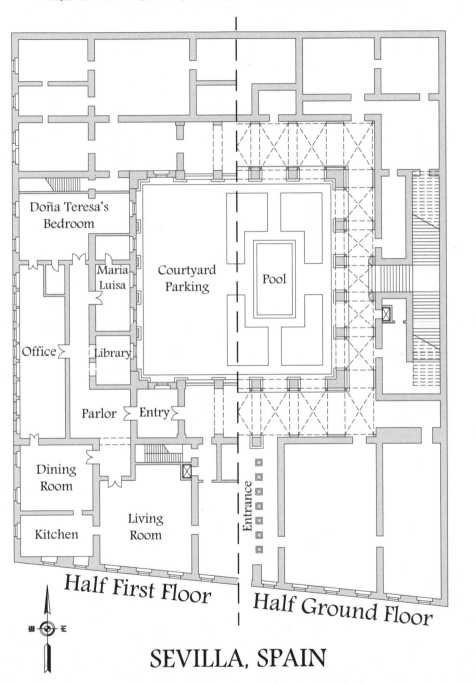

Doña Teresa's Bedroom

Maria Luisa

Courtyard Parking

Pool

Office

Library

Parlor Entry

Dining Room

Living Room

Kitchen

Entrance

Half First Floor

Half Ground Floor

W · E

SEVILLA, SPAIN

The Archbishop
in
Andalusia

I

"So, Don Juan, I am told that your presentation this morning was brilliant?"

The Cardinal Archbishop of Seville was about to invite me, with the deviousness he shared with Milord Cronin in Chicago, to a dinner that would have distinctly unpleasant, if fascinating, consequences.

He honored me with the title applied to royalty and princes of the Church in this rather odd country. Even the King was Don Juan Carlos. One would hardly address the Cardinal Archbishop of Chicago as Don Sean or even Don Juan Patricio. It would be thought a pretentious affectation, much as if one referred to the putative president of our own republic as Don Barack.

I must respect the wisdom of the dictum "When in Rome . . ."

"Call me Blackie!"

Not Ishmael surely, not in al-Andalus where it might be a fighting word.

The Cardinal, always effervescent, clapped his hands enthusiastically, though not as the flamenco groups in this part of the world clap, and permitted his dark-skinned face to erupt in a smile as bright as the Andalusian sun.

"Bravo! Bravo! Don Nero!" he exclaimed in his rich baritone. "It conveys perfectly the persona. But Nero is Italian. So we will call you El Padrecito Negro—the little priest called Blackie."

Which is what my siblings and my friends call me. Also my fellow priests, such as these may be, and my parishioners, when I had such, and my lay staff, and even the ineffable Megan, the porter persons in what used to be my rectory and now is the house where I live, and almost everyone else, save for deadly serious religious women for whom the name indicates an absence of seriousness, call me Blackie. The name fits me perfectly.

As in Boston Blackie and Black Bart and the Black Prince and the Black Knight, though not as in the Black Death and the Black Sox.

Said serious religious women choose to call me "Jack," a name that depresses me. I only vomit, however, when that is changed to "Jackie."

But what could "Blackie" convey to this tiny (at least four inches shorter than I) prince of the Church, resplendent in his watered silk crimson cummerbund, cape, and zucchetto (looking very much like "the fool" in a Renaissance painting of a royal family), as he struggled to make sense out of me.

"I do not fully understand you, Padrecito Negro. You wear black jeans, a black clerical shirt without a collar, a blue and red windbreaker celebrating the Chicago Cubs, whoever they be, and a baseball cap that depicts a fearsome *toro,* but not one of ours." Don Diego was finding it difficult to sort me out. "You do not act like a coadjutor archbishop with right to succession and a distinguished enough philosopher to be invited to a conference in Seville on American Philosophy. Still, I find the whole image charming."

I should not have put the man in such an awkward position. When Milord Cronin heard that the conference would be in Seville, he absolutely insisted that I had to live in the home of his good friend Don Diego. "You and he will hit it off perfectly. He's just like you."

I was not at all sure that I wanted to hit it off perfectly with someone who was just like me.

Don Diego sipped his superb sherry with the respect it deserved. He was a bright and quick man—he had dismissed my adversary at the morning conference as a "Dominican and they haven't had a decent philosopher since Aquino. You will, how do you say in America, crush him. That would be a good work if only he could realize that he had been crushed."

His grin was especially impish against his black face which earned him the admiring nickname among his priests of "El Moro"—the Moor.

El Moro and El Padrecito Negro.

"It is true that my ancestors were Moriscos, people who pretended to be Christian but in fact kept the faith of the Prophet. But that ended a couple of generations ago, I believe."

He laughed again, a deep, solemn laugh, somehow inappropriate for a man of his size.

"Touché, Don Diego."

We were sitting in the study of his rose-colored palace whose broad windows faced on the Cathedral Plaza. On one side was the Alcazar Royal, a network of palaces rebuilt by Don Fernando and Doña Isabella, and then again by Don Carlos, the first Hapsburg king. On the other side was the immense gothic cathedral which El Moro had claimed was the largest in Europe (a claim which my friends in Cologne would deny). Next to the Cathedral loomed the Giralda, the giant bell tower with the one-ton weathervane which had begun life as a Muslim minaret and appeared in the set of the Tyrone Power TCM favorite *Blood and Sand*.

It had been, as I told him upon return from the conference (in Carmen's tobacco factory, now the locale of the philosophy faculty), "a piece of cake."

This had delighted him and occasioned his first spasm of joy.

"You are not a serious man! That is excellent!"

"It said in the islands, which were originally populated by migrants from Spain at the end of the ice age, that for the English a situation may be indeed serious but never desperate, while for the Irish the situation is always desperate, but never serious."

He celebrated again, toasting me with his sherry.

"You are, then, a desperate man, no?"

"In the land of my ancestors that would be a high compliment. Life is too short ever to be serious."

Though my worries about Milord Cronin these days violated that principle.

Don Diego did not look like an African. Rather he had the appearance of a Moor, the folk who had run this part of the world for hundreds of years until the arrival of Ferdinand III, a pragmatist who thought that the local folk, a mix of Arabs and Persians and Berbers, were brilliant architects and builders and should not be chased away. He also believed that the Jews were clever and ingenious and sometimes even wise. Tolerance had ebbed and flowed during the half millennium in which Christians and Moors had fought over the Iberian Peninsula. Pragmatic leaders on both sides were not as tolerant, perhaps, as political correctness would require today. But in many places and many times under Moorish and Christian monarchs the three religions of Spain lived together in relative amity.

Appropriately therefore in this new ecumenical age the Cardinal of Seville (Is BE ya) would be a Moor.

Sometimes a new dynasty of Berbers would sweep across the Straits of Gibraltar and proclaim "Death to the Infidel!" But the modus vivendi would survive. Sometimes a Castilian king would surround a city like Toledo and threaten "death to the infidels," and then change his mind. However, finally, one of San Fernando's descendants, Isabella the (so-called) Catholic, toppled Granada, the last Muslim city-state, and celebrated in due course (having dispatched Cristobal Colon, the Admiral of the Ocean

Seas, to New York City) by banning all who were not Catholic from her brand-new kingdom.

It was in this very Cathedral Plaza that priests baptized Moriscos and Marranos by the thousands by the simple expedient of strolling about and sprinkling them with water while pronouncing the sacramental words. It was an act of blind folly, not to say horrific injustice, and was at least one of the causes of the terrible murders which have afflicted Spain ever since. Since there was some reason to suspect that not all of these converts were sincere, the local Holy Office of the Inquisition was set loose on those who might be heretics.

Why else would Don Diego be lifted from his comfortable chair of Philosophy at Salamanca and deposited here in Andalusia.

"But you did indeed crush that nasty English Dominican this afternoon! So I am informed by my best spies!"

"One can but try," I murmured with false modesty.

"You told him that William James's pragmatism converged with the reflections of his fellow Englishman Cardinal Newman. And when he asked you about the President of the United States, you told him that you were no more responsible for that gentleman than he was responsible for Ms. Thatcher."

"Cheap trick," I said.

"And the audience cheered like you were a matador in the bullring."

"I don't attend bullfights."

"Nor do I. Quite inappropriate."

It was a triumph that I would not dare remember for long, lest I fall victim to the temptation of morose delectation.

"Your nephew, I am told, is residing currently at the Alfonso XIII Hotel. He is the *novio,* I believe, to the young woman also residing there who flies her own jet plane."

"A *novio* in separate hotel rooms," I insisted.

My virtuous sister, Mary Kathleen, so impatient for a marriage date to be settled upon, had confided to me, "They won't sleep together, but I wish they would."

I understand nothing of these matters. I am at her own request the spiritual director of the good Peggy Anne. She had, however, on one occasion drifted away from addressing her prayer life, to explain the situation.

"We still love one another, but we have some things we have to tidy up first. Like he has to finish his dissertation and I must finish my term as president of ACE Fellowship."

ACE is the remarkable Notre Dame missionary effort to provide teachers for poor Catholic schools. They are an attractive, dedicated, and enthusiastic bunch of young men and women. The Fellowship is an alumni group, most of them still teaching in Catholic schools. About a third of them marry one another. A new form of a religious order? Why not?

"Peggy Anne," I had said, lapsing into a vernacular I rarely use with young women, "that is, you should excuse the expression, a crock of bullshit! You both are losing your nerve."

She blushed and then laughed.

"I guess you're right . . . we don't want to give up our last bit of freedom."

I left it at that.

"I understand," Don Diego continued, "that both of the young people speak Spanish?" He took on a crafty look, like someone who had a plot. Only difference from Sean Cronin's plots is that Milord is much less obvious.

"No, they speak a Mexican dialect thereof, just like I do. None of this effete Castilian lisping for us."

"I understand also," he continued, "that they were at your lecture? I would have liked to be presented to them. Señorita Margarita and Don Jose are apparently striking people. But I was bound by the University rule that they don't want Cardinals at their academic events."

"Good rule. Too many Cardinals getting in over their heads."

"Though several times a week I walk over to one of the campuses and chat with the young people. They seem quite friendly despite the general hostility of all professors to the Church."

"A tendency for which they have some historic reasons."

"God knows." He made a reverent sign of the cross. "I would like to offer a dinner in your honor this evening. I will try to invite interesting people."

"That would necessitate my presence?"

"I fear so. Unfortunately we descendants of the Vandals eat our evening meals rather late in the day when the heat of the sun has cooled . . . perhaps nine thirty? And I would instruct Don Pedro to invite your nephew and Señorita Margarita, if that would not displease you?"

"We will be honored." I tilted my head in what was the closest I could come under the circumstances to delight. Joseph and Peggy Anne (as she is called in our family) might be too much for the locals, so it could even be an amusing evening.

"Incidentally is that Gulfstream 560 really hers?"

"Oh, no," I said, as if I were horrified at the thought. "Her personal aircraft is a modest Cessna Citation 310 Bravo which does not have intercontinental capabilities. However she recently has been cleared to act as copilot on the Gulfstream. Actually it is a company plane. She is using it to demonstrate for European airlines the merits of a new radar system for intercontinental flights."

"Interesting."

You better believe it, Don Diego.

"And she writes articles on spirituality too."

"*Very* interesting."

And in the unlikely event the conversation wanes tonight she will intervene to save the party.

"May I have Don Pedro tell them that the dinner is in your honor?"

"Certainly, but they'll come anyway."

Don Pedro, whose last name I never learned, was the perfect cardinal assistant. He possessed all the admirable qualities that I lack for such a role—charm, youth, discretion, wit, enthusiasm, and a wonderful smile. He lacked, however, two indispensable qualities which I possess in super-abundance—cynicism and skepticism.

"Now, since you have been traveling, you might wish to avail yourself of the afternoon siesta after you join Don Pedro and myself for some tapas and a sip of a different sherry, drier than this, but very interesting."

Tapas are a variety of fascinating snacks offered on a single plate, a small but vigorous version of the Swedish smorgasbord.

I confessed that his suggestion was very pleasant.

I don't believe in siestas or naps, but I do think it imperative that at certain times and on certain days one rest one's eyes.

None of the Ryan clan of my generation enjoy traveling. I think that the Notre Dame football stadium is the outer limit of my tolerance for a journey. Name all the troubles which affect the jet flyer and I have them—motion sickness, altitude sickness, jet lag, troubled digestive tract, irritability. "How long does it take you to get over an intercontinental flight, Uncle Blackie?" she demands as she aims the Gulfstream toward Andalusia (land of the Vandals, who were the first wave of invaders who attacked Roman Iberia, enjoying a brief interlude of destruction before the arrival of the Visigoths, moderately more civilized but also Arian heretics).

She laughs as she contacts the Santa Justa (pronounced Husta) Airport to announce our arrival.

The only aircraft problem I don't have is the classic fear of flying, perhaps because a crash would put an end to my various afflictions.

Nor did I particularly like Seville after less than a day. It was one more modern city with a million or so inhabitants, traffic problems, abundant graffiti, and swarms of tourists from every nation under heaven, not excluding Kazaks, Icelanders, and Micronesians, each equipped with digital cameras and sunscreen. What did the New Testament say, "Parthians and Medes and Elamites, Irish and Turks and Swedes and, oh, yes, Yanks."

The sun was bright and the white buildings in the old Jewish Quarter glowed. The gardens around the Alcazar dazzled. The gold in the Cathedral glittered until you realized it was stolen from the Aztecs. The outside of the arena where the bulls were killed looked like a set the Lyric Opera of Chicago had lent to Seville from its *Carmen* production. The souvenir shops were like all others around the world, and there was no one dancing the flamenco around the restaurants on the Avenida de la Constitucion. It was clean anyway and the cops in their gray baseball caps were polite and tried not to smile at my Mexican accent.

Seville did not conform to the image of Arturo Perez-Reverte or Pierre Beaumarchais or Prosper Merimee. No one was singing Mozart arias in the steets. My late mother, God be good to her and he'd better or he'll hear about it, used to complain that the TV version of *The Lone Ranger* ruined the story because no mortal white horse could live up to the image of the "great white horse Silver!" One would not find the cruel passion, tragic romance, ill-fated love, and fierce hatred which had allegedly marked Spain and Spanish culture since the Romans replaced the Celto-Iberians in this city with an Arabic name.

I could not have been more wrong.

2

The dinner party included one Moor and three Chicagoans. All the rest were Castilians, an extraordinary handsome people with pale skin, thick black hair, and striking El Greco faces. This was the ethnic group which rallied to drive back the Muslim hordes. They were courteous, refined, and proud. Clustered originally beneath the Pyrenees, they had gathered a kingdom which had slowly spread over most of the remnants of Christian Spain and then taken advantage of the internecine conflicts among the Muslim principalities as the Muslims had exploited the disunity of the Visigothic kings, all fifty of them. They were also stalwarts of the Inquisition. My weary brain insisted that their infinitely polite refinement concealed, though just barely, dangerous emotions which might erupt at a hint of dishonor and would fill the room with drawn swords. They looked like Black Irish lords and ladies sitting around a table in a rocky keep on the western edge of the island, each one of them with a jug of stout in their hand and fully prepared to throw over the table and have at one another with terrible curses, as thunder and waves roared in the background, rain beat against the walls, and lightning danced across the sky.

When I am trapped in jet lag, my imagination turns violent.

Yet this troop of elegant and attractive aristocrats in white dinner jackets and black gowns, with black lace mantillas covering possibly bare shoulders, scared me when they entered Don Diego's dining room. The barbarians were at the gates again and this time they were Irish. Were the Neolithic tribes who had walked from Iberia to the British Isles, over the land bridges that united the continent and the islands as the glaciers from the last ice age melted, been cousins of the ancestors of these people? Or were the Black Irish, as was often claimed, descendants of Castilian survivors of the Armada? Did they recognize in my stalwart nephew Don Jose a possible distant cousin?

Foolish speculation. Instead they seemed boring and bored and had created a vacuum into which the Chicago Irish would surely rush, even if it was a vacuum into which the very angels would fear to tread.

At such gatherings where there are strangers, I try to organize the relationships in the group by creating a mental road map based on the women. This one was rather easy because the three Castilian women were striking beauties in various points in the life cycle and the men were much less interesting save for the youngest, a bright-eyed, smiling young man with flawless white teeth, called Don Isidoro de Colon. He was paired with the youngest of the women, Señorita Maria Luisa, daughter and virtual clone of the most dazzling woman in the room—Doña Teresa Maria, Duchess of Seville, a woman in the prime of her beauty and a disturbing presence next to me. She was paired it would appear with an overweight middle-aged man called El Jefe, in a military uniform laden with medals whose white dinner jacket was at least one size too small. The third woman, maybe twenty-five years older than Doña Teresa, was Doña Inez, accompanied by her husband Don Marco, a retired general perhaps in his middle eighties with white mustache and beard to match his jacket and in contrast with the red sash covered with decorations that stretched across his somewhat sunken chest. The three women, each in their own way, attracted probing male eyes, especially my dinner partner, Doña Teresa, the Duchess of Seville.

"Blackwood," Milord Cronin once remarked in a rare playful moment, "attracts dogs, little children, and dangerously beautiful women." There was considerable exaggeration in his allegation. Such women scare me. However, there was no question that my radiant dinner partner was a beautiful woman. Indeed, her appealing smile and her soft seductive voice hinted at deep and powerful sexuality. Delightful. And dangerous.

"Don Diego tells us," Doña Teresa whispered gently to Don Jose and Señorita Margarita, "that you both have done mission work for our Church."

Doña Teresa was in charge though a generation younger than her cousin, Doña Inez. Like her mother, Señorita Maria Luisa was a slender, ethereal woman, a radiantly beautiful noble, excerpted from a Murillo painting.

"Not mission work," my presumptive future niece-in-law replied with equal restraint. "We don't attempt to make converts in ACE—Alliance for Catholic Education. We want only to serve the Church and the young people who attend Catholic schools in impoverished Catholic communities. I taught in the Lower Ninth Ward in New Orleans, where the hurricane hit the hardest. The kids were great. It was fun."

Her smile and enthusiasm should have melted these Castilian glaciers.

"And I," my nephew continued, "worked for the Peace Corps in Costa Rica, the most salubrious country in South America. I taught English and basketball. It was fun. I loved the kids."

"Basketball!" Don Isidoro, the youngest of the Castilian males, suddenly came alive. "Did you play at Notre Dame?"

The heir to Cristobal Colon, as I assumed he was, had the compact build of a young athlete, the quick wit of a salesman, and the intelligent eyes of a man who would not be taken in by fools, even the brightest of fools.

"A little," my nephew replied smoothly. "Mostly intramural stuff."

Once characterized by his mother as a galoot, Joseph (no longer Joey Jack) was now, when he chose to be, a tall and sophisticated man of the world.

"My *novio,*" Señorita Margarita set the record straight, "led the Golden Dome to a National Invitational Championship. He scored the last twenty points in the final game and he's finishing a doctoral dissertation in theology at the University of Chicago."

The Cardinal, as bored as I had been, came alive, interested as we academics must be in a possibly important junior colleague.

"With the legendary David Tracy, I presume?"

"Naturally."

"Excellent." El Moro rubbed his hands together. "And what is the subject matter of your dissertation, Don Jose?"

Don Jose's eyes twinkled as the mischief of his Joey days returned.

"God in the movies," he said, as though it was a commonplace matter for theological reflection.

"God in the movies!" exclaimed El Jefe. I wondered what he was the chief of. "Absurd!"

"Not at all," Joseph replied. "God as he appears in many films is a God who pursues his people with passionate and forgiving love, which is how Jesus described him in the Gospels."

"Sometimes," Peggy Anne joined the conflict as women must when their *novio* is under attack, "an actress plays God like Jessica Lange or Audrey Hepburn."

"Nonsense!" exclaimed Don Marco, the elderly general with the beard and the sashful of medals. "God has always been a man."

"God," the Cardinal intervened as the acknowledged expert in the field, "as the wise man and holy Cardinal Niccolo de Cusa taught several centuries ago, is a coincidence of opposites both male and female and neither male nor female. Those characteristics we see in men and in women are combined in God. We can imagine God either way if we want."

"Our father and mother who art in heaven?" Don Marco protested. "If you would look it up in your theology books, Don Diego, you will find that God is only one person and that is male. I think you should write the Holy Office about this pernicious idea."

"I think you'll find, Don Marco, that the Catholic theology books, the orthodox ones which are the only kind you would have, hold that there are three persons in God—the Father, the Son, and the Holy Spirit."

"That's not polytheism," Don Marco sputtered in reply.

"The Prophet thought so," Don Diego replied.

"This is not an Islamic state," Don Marco fumed, his face turning red.

"Not yet, anyway," agreed El Jefe, the fat man in the dinner jacket. "It's not a Catholic state anymore either."

"They have taken it away from us again," Doña Inez, the elderly wife of Don Marco, said sadly. "Just like they did in 1936."

"The Army will not let them do that," El Jefe insisted. "It stands ready to act whenever the King tells us to act."

"You know, Teodoro, that will never happen," Doña Teresa intervened. "Why start a civil war when you know you will win the next election or the one after that?"

As she spoke, Doña Teresa seemed to take charge. The radiance of her exquisite beauty filled the room. The transformation was striking enough to catch the breath of any aging celibate from the South Side of Chicago who might be present.

"There are no real Communists, no anarchists," the Cardinal added. "The Spanish state is prosperous. No one is starving. The Reds today are not killers. They simply want to rewrite some history and put the Church in its place."

"Historically revolutions are infrequent in prosperous democracies," I said.

"My grandmother," Don Isidoro said, "was a Communist, an avowed member of the party. She went to Church every day nonetheless. When the anarchists seized our town she was coming out of Church after Mass. They raped her and shot her. Then they killed all the priests and raped and killed all the nuns. Later the Generalissimo's Moors killed them. We Spaniards are crazy people. We love to drink the wine of revenge."

Doña Teresa rejoined the argument.

"We still want revenge for what happened hundreds of years ago . . . for all the people who my sainted ancestor forced to become Christians, Diego, out there in the Plaza. You and I say that it will not happen again. How do we know that we're right. You want us to trust the Spanish people? Or the Spanish Church?"

"Yes, Teresa . . . but cautiously."

Teresa and Diego—good friends! Well, that was all right!

"Isabella the Catholic should be canonized," El Jefe insisted. "It will strengthen the faith of Catholic Spain."

Fat, pompous, and pious.

"It will not please the followers of the Prophet, Teodoro," Don Diego replied. "Nor the followers of Abraham, Isaac, and Jacob."

"The Church ought not be concerned about them, Eminencia!"

"Wrong century, Jefe. We are very concerned about them."

"The Civil War ended almost a century ago," Señorita Maria Luisa spoke for the first time. "You can't expect my generation to worry about it."

"Be silent, child," El Jefe snarled. "You understand nothing."

"I understand that you are a pig," she shot back.

On the other side of me, the valiant Doña Margarita, aka Peggy Anne, smiled approvingly.

"That is no way to talk to your promised groom," Doña Inez reprimanded her young cousin.

"It was no way for him to talk to me," the young woman fired back.

That blustery overweight fascist was her affianced! This was not good news.

"As a scholar," Don Isidoro murmured, "I do not admire the Falange. But I think we must say that on balance it was good that Franco won the Civil War. If the Reds had won, Spain would have become a Soviet state. As we have learned recently it requires at least a half century to get rid of such a state and much longer to repair the damage. We can argue now about the Civil War. If the Republicans had won, there would be few arguments about anything. I see no signs that the PS is trying to take away freedom of discussion. Considering our nation's long history of oppression, this is a very good sign."

The PS was the Socialist Party, the PP was the People's Party.

"Whom do you vote for?" El Jefe demanded.

"In the last election the PS. I thought the leaders of the PP had become arrogant and incompetent. In the next election I will vote against the PS because they have gone too far in recalling the memories of the past."

"Like all young people," Don Marco said, rubbing his beard, "Isidoro, you do not grasp how things work in our society. If it had not been for the Generalissimo your father's company would have never become successful. You wouldn't be able to attend the University and write your pallid little tracts. You have no sense of loyalty to the past."

"That is true, Don Marco," the young man replied respectfully, "and yet it is not the whole truth. It is certainly true that in the final years of the regime, Spain's economic growth increased and our little boats became popular. But the current prosperity is the result of our membership in the EU. Even the Irish want to buy our boats."

He glanced at me and winked. Doña Maria Luisa flushed and smiled. So that's the way the wind blows.

"That's the trouble with your generation," El Jefe complained, stretching his tight dinner jacket so he might look fierce.

31

"You are concerned only about materialist issues. You don't value principles and ideals. We who have memories also have much purer values."

"Perhaps, but we know that the EU has been our salvation."

"Our Lord and Savior Jesus Christ is our salvation," Doña Inez said solemnly.

"Cooperation across borders," my dinner partner said, "is what the peacemakers have created in Europe. I believe Jesus said that the peacemakers are blessed."

"And," I added, "the Children of God."

Smart woman as well as lovely. She was in charge of the dinner. No one was ready to take her on, least of all the jet-lagged, harmless little ecclesiastic from Chicago whom she had quite overwhelmed.

The conversation turned to other matters, mostly concerning the United States. I revised my guidebook. Don Marco and Doña Inez were grandees representing those who enjoyed the booming prosperity of Spain, but lamented for the days when the Falange ruled—fascism with a competitive face and a government of technocrats trained by Opus Dei. Doña Teresa and the Cardinal stood for a more pragmatic Spain, one not inclined to destroy the prosperity by risking too much conflict out of the past. El Jefe was a soldier who had never fought anywhere but was willing to start another civil war if the King ordered it. Which Don Juan Carlos would never do. Señorita Maria Luisa, Doña Teresa's daughter and Doña Inez's cousin, was somehow betrothed to the goof El Jefe. Don Isidoro, however, was the real *novio* of Maria Luisa, invited perhaps because she wouldn't come unless he was there. They were the new, incredibly prosperous Spain who wanted to hear no more about the Civil War. A dysfunctional family, Spanish style. However, one point was clear. By sheer power of her personality, Doña Teresa was in charge.

Outside under a sky of stars the nightly *paseo* was occurring—a slow and solemn procession of men and women taking their ease (and perhaps in this day and age getting their exercise) in the cool night air. In the distance over the sounds of the duet which was entertaining us, I heard the bubble of voices—young men and women at the beginning of courtship ("walking out" as they would say in the land of my own ancestors); lovers of many different ages, oblivious to everyone else; spouses pleased with the evening tranquility in their union; tourists who thought it was an interesting if useless custom; occasional pickpockets, members of the Civil Guard in their simple gray uniforms and baseball caps (a long way from Rossini opera garb of bygone years).

I suspected that none of the guests would be part of that nightly entertainment and reassertion of community.

As she was leaving Teresa shook hands with me, not being able to find a ring to kiss.

"Your nephew and his *promisa* are very attractive, Excelencia. She and my daughter are becoming friends, are they not?"

"Call me Padrecito Negro."

She laughed.

"Very well . . . My daughter is very beautiful, is she not?"

"Like her mother," I replied smoothly enough, I thought.

"She is so innocent. I worry about her."

"I think that one can take care of herself."

"Please God better than I did."

The assembled guests went out of their way to be courteous to the two young Americans in whom they had apparently delighted. They had agreed, Joseph told me, that they were taking a ride with Isidoro and Mary Louise down to Cadiz, and if the ocean was calm enough over to Gibraltar and then across to Tangier. It would be in one of the big boats that Isidoro's company made and there would be no reason to worry about motion sickness.

I declined on the grounds that I had to be at the University in the morning for the conference sessions. I would, however, eat breakfast with them at nine at the Alfonso XIII which was across the street from Carmen's cigarette factory turned into a university. I also wanted to learn more about the fascinating and, as I thought, dangerous dynamics of the ducal family.

3

"You found the guests interesting, Padrecito Negro?"

We were sipping a final sherry of the day at an open window in the Archbishop's suite. The *paseo* had ended quickly as its participants had faded away to their homes for a few hours' sleep before they would arise in the morning to begin the day, eagerly awaiting the afternoon siesta, for which centuries of hot weather and perhaps the propensities of the human organism had prepared them. It may well be, I told my jet-lagged self, that our bodies demand a period in midday to rest one's eyes.

"Very interesting. I found it difficult at first to figure out the pairing. I rejoiced to learn that El Jefe . . . By the way, of what is he the chief?"

"Don Teodoro Guzman is the chief of the Western Andalusian quartermaster system, a relatively unimportant position for a man with such a high opinion of himself. His father was an important and equally useless general in the Falange. Don Marco has taken him under his protection because he was a friend to Teodoro's father."

"It was good to know that he was not the *novio* of the magical Doña Teresa."

"Oh, no, the Duchess has acquired an *amante* but the matter is too delicate to reveal it in public. However, all of Seville knows about it."

"So it is a delicate secret that everyone knows but it is still a secret."

He raised his sherry glass in a gesture of accepting mystery.

"It is Spain, Padrecito Negro. What would you have? . . . Incidentally, I am not that *amante,* though I trust you will understand when I say that it would be pleasant to be in that role."

"I understand both decisions."

He smiled sardonically.

"Again I say it is Spain . . . And they all live together in their fading palace in Macarena which is just above us. All except Don Isidoro. The Colon family, by the way, claims the title of Admiral of the Ocean Seas as their rightful inheritance. By courtesy the claim is frequently honored."

"He is the true *novio* for Mary Louise."

"Certainly . . . There are, you see, different apartments in the palace. Teresa and Maria Luisa share the principal apartment. They enjoy one another's company. Maria Luisa usually obeys her mother because she not only loves her but admires her greatly. She is studying biology at the University and next year will enter medical training. She is nineteen, a year older than Teresa when Maria Luisa was born. The name, by the way, is that of the princess whose gardens are across from the Alfonso Hotel. The love between mother and daughter is obvious to the whole city. All families should have such friendship . . . I assume yours does too."

"Oh, yes, we get along very well. The only problem is that they find it embarrassing to have a bishop in the family."

He hesitated about laughing but then he did.

"It is evident that those two young people find you embarrassing."

"Patently."

He was beginning to learn the game.

"Don Marco and Doña Inez also have their apartment. It is

said that Marco desires his wife's cousin and indeed promises that he will delegate his power over Maria Luisa to her mother, if in turn the mother yields herself to him."

"Dirty old man."

"El Jefe, as he likes to be called, has an apartment of his own as the designated *novio* for Maria Luisa approved by her guardians. It is, you may be assured, at a safe distance, indeed more than a safe distance. The excellent young woman has promised that she will kill him should he attempt to claim any rights over her. He believes her, which he should."

"Why would he wish to be part of the family?"

"Prestige . . . The marriage would entitle him to claim the ducal title."

"So."

"Much money could be involved. Doña Teresa has invested the family money very wisely. She is a most remarkable woman. A mix of modesty and passion which disturbs most men."

"I had noticed that, Don Diego. It was good of you to put me next to her."

"She is often referred to as a national treasure. She is an astute administrator of her family's business interests, a generous and wise philanthropist, a writer of witty articles, a fashionista, a television personality, as you would say in America, and a very unhappy woman. It is very sad."

"Yet those two grandees control her life."

"Only the right to marriage. And that probably without any legal grounds. Teresa, alas, is very old-fashioned when it comes to family rights. She is willing to wait the three years she must before she marries her *amante*."

"How can this be!"

"The late Duke, a homosexual by the way, was killed in Madrid by a bomb ignited by ETA, the Basque terrorist movement. Don Marco, El Jefe, and Doña Inez were with him as he was dying, before his wife and daughter could get to Madrid.

37

They persuaded the Duke that he had to protect his women from those who would have designs on the ducal prestige. Thus the Duke signed a will making them the guardians of Teresa and Maria Luisa. They have no control of the money but they do have the power to block a marriage of either of them, until Maria Luisa is twenty-three, which is three years from now. Moreover, the Archbishop of Seville must also approve of the marriage. There is no doubt which way he would vote. If they choose a spouse of whom the Archbishop does not approve, then he has the right to propose an alternative which they may not veto. You perceive the delicacy. And you comprehend the sexual energy that bounced around the dinner table tonight, especially as Don Marco blatantly desires his wife's cousin."

"Who is?"

"Teresa of course."

"Does Mary Louise approve of her mother's *amante?*"

"Certainly. It is said she selected him from a group of corporate executives. But that is not true. An ecclesiastic we both know recommended him to be her *abrogado.* As you might imagine he was not able to resist the attractions of such a woman."

"Patently."

"Don El tells me that you have some skills in untangling such situations."

"Don El" is a term of the highest respect, perhaps something like "your very good friend." "That one" was in context a reference to Milord Cronin who has a tendency to send me on such assignments. The equivalent for a woman, I have learned, is "La Doña."

"Yes, but only after there is a murder."

Don Diego sighed, even louder than I normally sigh.

"Oh, there will be a murder eventually. All the sexual frustration among both the men and women . . . and the money."

"Is that not unusual in these days for the nobility to be rich?"

"The late Duke's father was a canny man. He bought vineyards and mines and factories during the time of the Falange. He arranged a brilliant marriage, save for the spouse's sexual orientation, for Doña Teresa. His family owns hotels and wheat fields. She moreover has kept a careful eye on all the investments during this time of economic growth. She is a great prize in many ways."

"And she has only now found a lawyer who can free her from this oppressive will?"

"Until recently she was too proud to do so. It would have been disrespectful to her late husband whom, I believe, she loved with considerable affection."

"No more than affection?"

"One cannot always find passion, can one?"

"And with her current *amante*?"

"I don't ask, of course. But I assume so. I have hinted that one could validate such a situation privately, at least if one was an Archbishop. She does not take the hint. Spaniards are crazy, Padrecito Negro . . . you see La Doña's mother, Anna Rosa, and Inez were cousins. Their grandfather perished in the Battle of the Ebro River during the Civil War. Since there were no males in that generation they were rivals. Anna Rosa produced a daughter, Teresa Maria. If she had lived to produce a son he would have been the Duke. Inez, sad to say, has no children. The line passes on to women if there are no males in a generation. Should it pass on to Señorita Maria Louisa and should she marry her *novio*, it would bring together a descendant of the Admiral of the Ocean Seas and a descendant of Isabella the Catholic."

"Sounds very . . ." I almost said "Byzantine."

"Spanish," he finished before me. "We are an old country with a long and twisted culture. And as a state we have existed only since 1975 when General Franco died."

In my room, under the sinister stars of al-Andalus, I called Milord Cronin on my cell phone. It would be middle evening there.

"Cronin."

"Blackie."

"Spaniards are crazy."

"I will not dispute the point . . . You're getting along with Jimmy?"

"El Moro."

"You need capes and white horses." His voice was weak.

"And swords."

"He tell you about his problem and the implications?"

"The Visigoths are at the gate."

"They're heretics, Nestorians."

"Arians . . . But how can I solve a murder before it's committed?"

"Jimmy is a good guy. He needs some help. That woman is a celebrity and a generous contributor. See to it, Blackie."

"I'll have to find my white horse."

But he had hung up. I did not like the weakness in his voice.

I rose early the next morning, awakened by the sun, and stumbled out of bed. Where was I? Al-Andalus, of course. What was I doing here? Milord Cronin thought I could solve a murder before it was committed. Even Holmes and Poirot and Brown, and Bosch, could not do that. I rubbed my face and tried to remember the complex story my host had told after that weird dinner party with beautiful women and menacing men. Even the apparently virtuous Don Isidoro, scion of a boat-making family, was menacing because he was too good to be true.

And the woman sitting next to me was an intensely disturbing presence.

None of them was to be trusted.

I sought refuge in a shower that was weak on hot water and then dressed in my uniform of jeans, Bears jacket, with a local black baseball cap exhibiting a local *toro*, who might be related to the Chicago Bulls.

The air was crisp, clear, and still cool. I wandered over to the banks of the Guadalquivir which before Cadiz replaced Seville as the port of return for the Indies trade had been the golden port for all of Spain. The river had been broken by an earthquake and silted up. A canal had been cut which opened the way to the main flow of the river. Overlooking it on the Paseo Cristobal Colon was a gold tower, appropriate for the place I suppose, but in my dyspeptic mood it seemed ugly, as did all the gold over in the Cathedral. Spain's greatness, I told myself, was the result not of hard work, or fruitful farms, or intelligence, but of theft. Nor did that theft benefit either the poor in Spain or the poor in the countries it had occupied. Rather the Spaniards had spent it on gross cathedrals, ugly palaces, and expensive artists.

Not that the treatment of the natives in North America had been all that different.

The Spaniards must have thought they were entitled to take whatever they had found, just as we Americans had taken whatever we found, including Spanish possessions which were of no more use to us than to them. In fact, we had probably done them a favor by assuming the burden of the Philippines and Cuba. Their explorers had opened up the world for Spain and the rest of Europe. They were entitled to some gold, were they not?

I reflected that not far off the coast to the east of us was the Bay of Trafalgar, out of which their fleet and the French fleet sallied to keep an appointment with Lord Nelson. After that Britannia ruled the waves for a century or so. And now Columbia was the gem of the ocean. Next please?

I found the stalwart Joseph and the valiant Peggy Anne waiting for me in the breakfast area of the Alfonso XIII, a pseudo Moorish castle with a pool that was unheated and might have been a onetime prison for Christian slaves if it had not been built in 1930.

They were in a vigorous early-morning mood. Isidoro and Mary Louise were to take them down to Cadiz—and perhaps on to Gibraltar and Tangiers. Wasn't that cool! I asked them if they

41

had enjoyed the *paseo*. They had, but it was not something they would want to do every night . . .

"That was a strange bunch last night, wasn't it, Uncle Blackie?"

"Sexual frustration so thick you might ice skate on it."

"Are they serious?"

"It's like they're trapped in a nineteenth-century soap opera."

"Doña Teresa is incredibly beautiful."

"Mary Louise adores her."

"They are all a little crazy," I said. "And Doña Teresa is the craziest one of them all."

"She and her friend might come with us on the trip."

"I can't wait to get a look at him."

"You will find him, Joseph, a man of intelligence, charm, and respect. He will also devour Doña Teresa with his eyes, just as your friend Isidoro devours Mary Louise."

"It's all out in the open here, Uncle Blackie. I don't see why they just don't get married."

"The 'get' is bad syntax, Peggy Anne. You mean that you don't see why they don't marry one another."

"And everyone is asking that about us, aren't they?"

"We still plan to get . . . to marry one another. The whole point of this vacation is to set a date we'll stick with, come what may."

"And we probably won't set the date here. Then we'll come home and say what the hell!"

"And do it and be done with it!"

"Then," I added, "the gift giving only begins."

They both nodded solemnly, as if they understood what I meant, which they did, about one-tenth. That was enough.

I bade them bon voyage, and suggested that they call Joseph's mother from Tangiers.

I ambled over to Carmen's University and chatted with the

participants in the conference which all acclaimed as a major milestone in transatlantic philosophizing. I remarked that doing philosophy in a cigarette factory was at least an innovation, especially since the rules required that there be no smoking inside.

Irony is usually lost on academic philosophers. It would not have been lost on my man William James. Nor his brother Henry. The American academic system produces a lot of people who write about philosophy but very few philosophers.

I slipped away before the morning session began. I have found that the essential goal of such a meeting is to be seen. Then one can slip away, as I would have slipped away from my own session if I had been blessed with the gift of bilocation, as have several Spanish saints. I managed to avoid my English Dominican adversary who wanted to continue the discussion. I did not escape the charming Italian woman who wondered why I had not worn my archiepiscopal insignia. I removed my St. Brigid pectoral cross from my shirt pocket, untangled my New Grange ring, and showed them both to her, avowing that I had to keep them in my pockets lest I lose them. I departed then, leaving her with a puzzled expression.

What else should she expect?

I then explored the winding streets of Santa Cruz, the old Jewish quarter in back of the Cathedral. It was a maze of whitewashed houses, narrow cobblestone walks, tiny squares lined with souvenir shops, some of them with elegant and tasteful prizes, intriguing little restaurants, flourishing gardens exploding in color, including flowerpots hanging from the walls, expensive and elaborate atria inside iron gates of the larger homes—a veritable vest pocket theme park of Old Spain. The effect was marred only by the American tourists, of which I was one. If there were any Jews in the quarter they were probably American tourists. I did not want to think about the lives of those who had been forced so long ago to live in the ghetto, of those who under pressure participated in mass baptisms in the Cathedral Plaza, of those who pretended to change their faith, only to be tripped up by the Holy Office of the Inquisition.

All right, the Curia had reasserted its power over the Church after the Council, but the documents on religious freedom and the Jews which the American bishops had sponsored and salvaged were still on the books and would never be taken off.

Sometimes things do get better, at least a little better.

I consumed a plate of tapas at an appealing little café next to an overwhelming garden, found my way out of the quarter (after three unsuccessful attempts), and wended my way into the Macarena district, looking for the ducal palace. It is the old neighborhood of Seville, a mix of lower-class homes with back alleys lined with laundry, old churches, a monastery (in honor of San Clemente), a new basilica, and the parliament of Andalusia, combined with expensive homes from the nineteenth century close to the Guadalquivir, small tapas bars, dubious-looking apartment buildings, and a somewhat dilapidated redbrick palace with a garden that struggled for elegance.

It was a sad and run-down excuse for a palace, but testified to the obsolescence of much of the European nobility. They used to be the military leaders of Europe. Now they were parasites living off the memories of the past. Hard to find a leader among them. Yet this family, like some of the others, had set themselves up in business and become successful. Sherry companies, farms, olive and orange groves. Why the sad aspect, why the agonies revealed at El Moro's dinner? Why did that sensitive crimson-clad churchman fear there would be a murder? Who might kill whom?

Was not my disturbing dinner partner with the lovely breasts and haunted eyes a perfect target for a murder?

And what ghosts scurried around its multiple apartments?

I liked it not, as they say in the Bard's stories.

"Palacio Ducal?" I asked a young woman who was pushing a baby buggy along the tree-lined street with two sleeping kids.

"*Sí,*" she answered. "The Duchess who is a saint is a captive in there. Evil relatives who hate her goodness and beauty. She gives to the poor, spends money on children who need hospitals—like my little boy here—and pays for the churches. She suffers terribly and is so lonely."

"Poor dear woman," I murmured.

The little boy, who had benefited from Doña Teresa's charity, opened his eyes, looked up at me, and extended his arms. I have great clout with dogs and little children. Also on rare occasions beautiful women.

I picked him up and he chattered happily.

"He seems lively enough now," I said in approval.

His mother beamed, as mothers will, and lifted up her baby daughter who looked unhappy that her big brother was getting special attention.

"Thanks be to God and the Virgin and Doña Teresa. Also to Don Diego who blessed him. They say he works miracles, Padre, is that true?"

Mothers invariably know what I am when I talk to their kids.

"I know him well," I said with full truth. "He is a remarkably holy man."

Even Milord Cronin would testify to that truth.

I blessed both kids—Diego and Catalina.

"My mother," I said, "was called Catalina."

"But is not that little church over there named Catalina!"

"I must go over and pray to her."

"I have great devotion to her, Padre."

I blessed the grinning little brats again and accepted her ebullient gratitude. I asked her to pray for me and she asked that I pray for herself, her husband, and her children, and also for La Doña.

So that was what they called her.

I assured her that I would and promptly fulfilled that promise inside the little white gothic church, where many women and elderly men were praying, most of them up front, where God could see them and hear them.

I knelt at the last pew and began my dialogue with the Deity who, on the record, is always ready to listen.

"To begin with I must thank you for sending that pretty mother and her ingenious children to remind me that I haven't prayed since I landed in this country. A fine coadjutor archbishop with right to succession I am. That reminds me before I go on. I call your attention to your faithful servant Sean Patrick Cronin, for whom my instincts tell me I should be praying. I do not want to lose him. He is one of the delights you have put in my life. I do not want his job, now or ever. Grant him a long and healthy life and protect him and those who love him. This is my personal and high-order priority. I am being selfish by mentioning him first. Consider, however, the needs of your poor, bedraggled church. It has few prelates who have the courage which comes from not really giving a damn. Spare him for us. I propose a deal, though I know that on the record you don't do deals. Keep him alive and with us and I will take over his responsibilities, which as you know I do not want. I will rely on your grace to preserve the Archdiocese from further disaster. Is that not a reasonable deal? I mean, we both live in Chicago and so we both understand about deals, don't we?

"Secondly, I pray for that good woman and her family. You surround our lives with so much grace . . . and then I pray for the two Catherines in my life, my mother and my sister who is Mary Kathleen, as you well know. I assume she speaks to you with the same authority that our mother did and probably a good deal more because she is an MD, not to say a headshrinker. I also pray for my father, to whom I owe so much. He ratified the persona you blessed me with, so I knew it would work. He also gave me a great good example on how to live by speaking softly and not carrying a stick at all. And I pray also for Mary Kate's son and his betrothed who are in the final stages of abandoning the freedom of the single life for what is always unknown—surprises and gifts superabundant and commensurate responsibilities. It would be nice if they named a day while on this trip because I could claim credit for their decision.

"Thirdly, I pray for my colleague in your service, El Moro. Unprepared for it, he was yanked by your hyperactive Holy Spirit from his chair at Salamanca and deposited on the bishop's chair in that gaudy Cathedral. From instructing adolescents he now becomes the de facto leader of the local hierarchy who are doubtless not at all pleased. Grant him the wisdom and courage necessary for his tasks and the sense not to turn his back on who and what he is.

"Fourthly, I pray for all the people up in that moth-eaten palace. Protect them with your grace and your love, particularly Doña Teresa who must be suffering intensely in her widow-hood."

I paused, thought about whom I might have forgotten. Then I remembered.

"And lastly I pray for this useless little priest who solves puz-zles which stand in the way of the grace you want for people. Like the good Peggy Anne. Help me not to mess up their lives.

"Thank you for listening.

"Amen."

4

"I hear you work miracles."

For the first time, Don Moro did not smile at my effort at wit.

"Spaniards are a superstitious people. They crave the wonderful, the marvelous, the spectacular. A man in crimson waves his hand at a sick person and thus does nothing to interfere with a recovery. That person and his family thinks that God has intervened directly . . . Who made this charge against me?"

"A mother up in Macarena who also gave due credit to Santa Catalina and La Doña."

He relaxed.

"They believe that Doña Teresa is being tortured by her family in that back-lot palace up there."

"Not physically anyway . . . Sit down and have a sip of the sherry her family produces before you engage in resting of your eyes."

A splasheen of sherry would not hurt and arguably would contribute to the success of that project.

"What did you think of the *palacio*?"

"Kind of down-at-the-heels . . . uh . . . worn-out. May have ghosts and the occasional demon."

"I like the metaphor. I must remember it."

"With all the money they have, they could improve it, could they not?"

"It is a very lovely place, but the money is restricted by several wills, the late Duke's of course, and that of his revered father, Don Estevan. The 'trustees,' as they call themselves, claim control of all the money, though the courts have ruled that Teresa should have full responsibility. The matter has been before the courts for several years. Don Marco and Don Teodoro contend that the Duke wished to grant them complete power over the entire estate and not just the bodies of the women. They have tried to compromise with Teresa. She dismisses their proposals—always made through lawyers of course—and it drags on. The courts permit Teresa limited access to funds. The 'trustees' struggle constantly to contain that access."

"Is the fix in?"

El Moro grinned.

"I am learning your Chicago slang which I like . . . No, the courts are very careful to avoid all taint on this conflict. The sentiment of the people of course is with Doña Teresa. She will win eventually, but you must understand that the conflict is not only about her body but about her gold. . . . It would have destroyed a lesser woman."

"What kind of man was her husband?"

"A homosexual, though no one dares to say it. He was able to sire the lovely Maria Luisa but no other children. Naturally, he had to pretend that he was a brave and aggressive male, poor man. He took risks which is why he was too close to the ETA bomb. Teresa did not hate him and indeed felt some affection for him, or so I am told. She did not take a lover until after his death."

"And this is a good man?"

"Don Leandro? Oh, yes, a very good man, a widower about her age, very devoted and very gentle. He is her lawyer."

"Very complicated."

"Teresa did not know passion in her marriage. Now she

experiences it for the first time . . . It is, as one would expect, a very intense relationship."

"Might they not marry secretly?" I asked.

"Not under my saintly predecessor. But he is dead and now there is a new Cardinal, isn't there? They both fear scandal, so there is a small apartment above a tapas café in a quiet corner of Santa Cruz where they meet on occasion. Not nearly often enough, in the view of this celibate."

"Do not the trustees suspect?"

"Naturally. Don Marco, though he is married to Doña Inez, claims a right to her, based on an alleged final whisper from the Duke which permitted him a certain amount of adultery. He is angry that she denies his right. I think he is capable of rape, though he grows feeble with the years. Don Teodoro, El Jefe as he calls himself, theoretically the *novio* to Maria Louisa, hungers for Teresa too."

"So you suspect murder? Either of or by Teresa?"

"Alas"—he waved his little hands in frustration—"and there is nothing anyone can do about it till it happens."

He waved his hands again.

"Moreover, both Jefe and Marco need money. It is said that Madrid is investigating the quartermaster transactions in Andalusia. Money has been spent on supplies of grain purchased from local farms. The grain was rotting by the time it reached the Army's bakery. Some of it was perhaps from Don Marco's hacienda."

I had complained just a couple of days ago that there was no adventure left in Seville. Now there was too much altogether.

"Murky business."

"They want Teresa and her money. If not her, then Maria Luisa would suffice. I worry about them as if they were my own children."

"Teresa's lover?"

"Don Leandro? He and I discuss the matter. He has been able

to introduce some of his people into the *palacio*. They provide protection . . . This cannot continue. Either they will kill Teresa or she will kill them."

"Unless Maria Luisa prevents it."

"She is, after all, her mother's daughter. And she has a fearsome temper which her mother never displays. But she is so young . . . You must rest your eyes, Don Negrito. Already they are drooping."

I withdrew to my spare bedroom. Almost at once my eyes went into their resting mode.

My cell phone rang from a great distance, possibly another galaxy. Or, if one were to believe the speculations of some astronomers, another cosmos. In either case they would not speak my language. Mexican—which was now causing headaches much of the day. Yet I was a priest. It might be for someone needing a priest, a generic priest. Even if they were calling from beyond Max Planck's constraint.

"Holy Name Cathedral Rectory. Father Ryan . . ."

"Blackie, where the hell is Tangiers?"

Ah, my sister Mary Kathleen. What was she doing beyond a black hole?

"It is a port on the northern fringe of Morocco, a few miles across the straits from Gibraltar."

"Those aren't real places, are they?"

"On the maps and in mystery stories they purport to be real places."

"What are my kids doing there?"

"Which kids?" I asked, still trying to figure out where I was. Not in Tangiers, I thought.

"Joseph and Peggy?"

"The latter is not the name of one of your children."

"Poor child's mother is still in the funny farm."

"Not a proper term from a past president of the American Psychiatric Society."

"Whatever! Are there Muslims in Morocco?"

"The Crusaders have yet to retake it, as far as I know. However Morocco is a relatively peaceful country whose King takes a dim view of jihadists."

"What are they doing there?"

"I believe they went on an excursion to Cadiz this morning, with the option for a visit to the straits, in the company of a local family."

"You let them go?"

"They do not ask me for permission."

"Well, they called me from Tangiers today to tell me I should keep open the Friday of Thanksgiving weekend."

Ah, we had got to the point of the call. I myself had been hoping for Labor Day weekend.

"So you're rejoicing."

"That's too soon to get ready for the wedding!"

Why had I not expected such a reaction?

"Let it be done and over with," I said with the wisdom of not being a mother and not married to one either.

"There's too much to do. And they won't say that is a definitive day."

"Then there's still hope that you will have more time."

My own hope was that the nuptials would occur before the end of summer, Labor Day if not the Fourth of July. The two lovers belonged in a common bed. They had delayed too long.

"Whatever. You know how unreliable they are . . . Did she land the plane properly?"

"Like she'd been flying over the Sierra Nevada Mountains every day."

"Those are in California!"

"The folks down here in al-Andalus stole the name."

"Whatever . . . Don't tell them I called you."

"Heaven forfend."

My valiant sister is the most sensible of women, save when

her children are involved, especially in preparations for a wedding. Or on the occasion that a mere "child" is planning to fly one of her offspring across the Atlantic in a "tiny" jet—which is not how one usually describes a Gulfstream 650, with its maximum range of 6,700 miles and a speed of Mach .88.

My own mother would not have wanted me to fly in such a plane either.

I had played my fraternal role of listening and had been duly warned to keep an eye on the young couple, though in fact there was no expectation that my supervision would have the slightest effect.

I rolled over in my narrow bed and permitted my eyes to rest again.

At breakfast the next morning, as I was disposing of my cornflakes—two boxes in a bowl intended for only one—and complaining about European breakfasts, Peggy Anne, no longer able to contain herself, announced, "They're taking us to a flamenco tonight, Uncle Blackie, and they want you to come!"

"Who? When? And where?"

My jet lag had not abated. I did not want to go to a crowded tavern, dense with smoke, and listen to barbarian music, created no doubt by the Vandals or the Visigoths.

"Teresa and Leandro invited us and they said they hoped you would come too, but they did not want to cause you any embarrassment."

"They have great respect for the priesthood and especially a Cardinal."

"I am not a Cardinal," I said firmly, "and do not plan on becoming one. I have caused my family enough embarrassment."

"Teresa wants Leandro to meet you, Uncle Blackie. She thinks you're like totally cool."

"Leandro"—my nephew explained his future wife's enthusiasm, which, judging by his broad smile, he enjoyed—"is her lover. Nice man. Smart. Very respectful and protective without being a bore. What a smart man always is."

"Like totally . . . They're very low-key, Uncle Blackie. You'd think they were just good friends and then you are aware of a spark between them that could set the launch on fire . . . They won't go to hell, will they, Uncle Blackie?"

"Our God," I replied, "on the record is a God of mercy and love. He sent Jesus to tell us that."

"They're like married lovers," Joseph added, more outspoken than usual. "They are totally committed to one another but don't make a big deal out of it."

Joseph had learned a lot at the University of Chicago.

"And she is totally deadly in a two-piece swimsuit," Peggy Anne, not to be outdone, informed me. "And they're so good to poor Mary Louise. She totally adores them both."

"And Don Isidoro?"

"Isidoro just drives the boat and smiles," Joseph said.

"Ah . . . Did they have anything to say about their relatives?"

"Mary Louise told me a few things when we were alone. It sounds like an asylum. I don't know why they can get away with it."

"Because her father made some mistakes when he was dying. Leandro says that it won't stand up much longer because the court will reject the whole will and they can throw the creepy crowd out of the palace and Teresa and Mary Louise can move into a casa in Santa Cruz."

"That would surely be an improvement . . . Then, Uncle Blackie, they could marry—see I got it right!—and Isidoro could be Marylou's real *novio!*"

"And they would all live happily ever after!" I said. "Which means only fight a couple of times a week!"

"But at least they would be free to make their own decisions."

"Mary Louise said she would kill everyone in her family to protect her mother."

"I wouldn't doubt it. This is a harsh, cruel place, Peggy. It's been that way a long time. Maybe as Doña Teresa and the Cardinal say, it's getting better, but only a little better. A lot of hatred has been stored up through the centuries. It exploded in the Civil War. Most people here don't want it again. And prosperity can heal a lot of anger. Still, for all the smiles and the laughter, there is a current of rage beneath the surface."

They both were silent and solemn.

"If anyone in that house does harm to either of those beautiful vulnerable women, the other might kill them. That threat hangs in the air."

"You won't come to the flamenco tonight?"

"Of course I will!"

They would pick me up at the *palacio arzobispo* at nine.

We walked back to the Cathedral Plaza, I for my morning conversation with Don Moro and they to explore for gifts in Santa Cruz.

"Cadiz, once called Gaites, was the first city in Europe, three–four thousand years ago, the beginning of civilization in Western Europe, long before Rome. It is an incredibly rich country—gold, silver, and tin mines, some of which are still around. Fertile fields for wheat and olives and grapes and oranges. Superb wines. Skilled craftsmen. The Egyptians, the Phoenicians, and probably some Hebrews were here, long before history started anywhere else. A steady stream of traffic from one end of the Mediterranean to the other. From the Cedars of Lebanon to the Pillars of Hercules—which was their name for Gibraltar. Such prosperity stirred up greed and war long before Father Abraham left behind Ur of the Chaldees. As time went on the Carthaginians, from just down the coast of Africa, set up colonies here. We call the people that were local in those days Celto-Iberian because they were a mix of the original folk about whom we know very little and the Celts who were suddenly all over Europe. Rome became very worried about Spain because the Carthaginians were using it as a route to Italy during the Punic Wars—Hamilcar and Hannibal and that bunch. So the Romans took over and formed colonies like those in France, a little bit of Roman architecture and law and brute force when necessary."

"Lots of opportunity for rage so far," Joseph said.

"And it was just the beginning. Then the barbarians arrived, searching for land and under pressure from even worse barbarians like the Huns and the Avars and eventually the Slavs—all looking for land because their populations were growing. Some of them headed straight for Rome, were beaten off, and went looking for land elsewhere. The Vandals messed up Rome pretty bad and then headed for here, having given a name to rampage on the way. There wasn't much in northern Spain that appealed to their greed. But they loved it down here on the Costa del Sol and settled down to stay. Actually became Christians, though of a heretical kind. They were then followed by the Goths who looked likely to take over here—the West Goths or Visigoths, that is. The East Goths took over northern Italy and part of Switzerland and Austria and were replaced by the Lombards in due course. The Irish monks converted them to Christianity and did a pretty good job of it."

"They were everywhere too, weren't they, Uncle Blackie?"

"And charming and clever and generous. They didn't have to kill anyone. They just founded monasteries and educated people."

"A mistake," Joseph said. "Educated people think for themselves."

"I've noticed that. The Visigoths had Spain to themselves for a couple of hundred years and built up a Catholic civilization and culture here, of a sort. They had the bad habit of setting up local monarchies, which was easy to do in a country that was chopped up by rivers and mountains and different tribes of their predecessors. So by the time Islam arrived at the other side of the Pillars of Hercules, there were fifty separate kingdoms making war on one another. The Muslims thought they might be able to make progress against these contentious folks and swept up to the Pyrenees and across into France where they were defeated at Tours by Charles Martel. They fell back into Spain and produced one of the great civilizations of history. They brought the best of Greek and Arab civilization to Europe—philosophy, poetry, medicine, so much so that a German nun writing in Cologne called al-Andalus 'the gem of Europe.' It was. Thomas Aquinas earned his living by debating the Arab philosophers, who were followers of Aristotle like he was . . . Is this getting too much like a lecture?"

"You're saying all this violence created rage in Spain that lasts till today?" Peggy said. "Go on, it begins to fit together."

"Well, the Arabs were remarkably tolerant people. They took the Prophet seriously when he said that no one should be forced to convert, as long as they paid a tax. They hired Christians and Jews and paid them for the use of their talents. The three religions got along pretty well together, especially in places like Toledo. The Muslims established a Caliphate in Cordoba and built a mosque which was almost as large as the one in Baghdad on top of a Visigoth Cathedral which was on top of a Celtic shrine to the god Lug, as in dancing at Lughnasa. The Caliph was supposed to impose unity on the various Islamic groups who had established kingdoms throughout Spain. Up north the remnants of the Christian kingdoms began to stir and started the Reconquista. They played the same game as the Muslims played before—divide and conquer. It took seven hundred years, more or less, to do it, including such real heroes as El Cid and comic heroes as Don Quixote."

"Both warriors," Peggy murmured. "High on testosterone."

"And both fools," Joseph added.

"The Berbers came over from North Africa and established

new dynasties which were not as tolerant as the Arabs had been. Isbiya was the capital of the local province of the Caliphate of Marrakesh and the largest city in Spain with a large and beautiful mosque, the minaret of La Giralda, the golden tower and the silver tower, and eighty thousand people. But the Castilians kept coming. In 1236 Ferdinand captured Cordoba and twelve years later Isbiya which was now Seville. The Reconquest, between the fall of Toledo to Alfonso VI and the capture of Seville, had taken a little less than two hundred years. Both cities surrendered without battles because by now the armies of Castile were overwhelming and St. Fernando promised to respect Jews and Muslims, which he did, more or less. The Muslims were left with one kingdom, Grenada, which Ferdinand and his followers respected for two hundred years. In Cordoba he left the mosque standing— Catholics would later build a cathedral inside it—and destroyed the one here, though he turned La Giralda into a bell tower. However, with the fall of these two cities the Reconquest was over. Ferdinand of Aragon and Isabella of Castile finished it when they took over Grenada and then sent the Jews and Muslims packing and turned the Inquisition on those who had pretended to convert."

"You think the memories of all these battles are still part of their subconscious, Uncle Blackie?"

"Sometimes not so subconscious, Joseph, especially when the Catholics in Spain fight with one another. Poor against rich, devout Catholics versus anticlericals. 'Liberals' against 'conservatives,' region against region. Barcelona and Madrid have a rivalry based on language and pride and power which makes the New York–Chicago rivalry look like a game of marbles. The Basques consider themselves another country and the Galicians (self-consciously Celtic) are leaning in the same direction. Andalusians just want to be left alone by Madrid. Castilians like the people who live in that *palacio loco* feel that victory has slipped through their fingers."

"And it all blew up in that Civil War they talked about the other night . . . Will it happen again, Uncle Blackie?"

"Thanks be to God and the EU, probably not. My point is that pride, passion, honor, cruelty, and revenge have had a fertile field in which to grow. As well as wonderful art, music, poetry, literature. A beautiful and deadly country. The rage is weaker but it persists. Every time there was a battle, there was murder, torture, pillage, rape. Hundreds of thousands of women have been raped in Spain and their collective anger at men for what they have done is just beginning to emerge . . . Stick a knife into Don Marco's back, a bit of poison into El Jefe's sherry . . . a relatively easy thing to do, especially because they consider themselves to be warriors."

"How terrible!"

"They don't know that they are really followers of your man from la Mancha. Silly old fools."

The sky had turned gray and a slight chill wafted across the plaza. Above us La Giralda reported that it was 11:00.

I summarized my conversation with the next generation after our noon meal and over the usual glass of sherry.

Don Moro sighed, a soft mournful sigh, not at all like my own.

"They are damned by the history of this terrible country!"

"Not true, at least I don't think so. Your position is too fatalistic. Because certain strains appear often in a culture does not mean that any individual person is fated by them."

He regarded me carefully over his sherry glass.

"Spoken like a true disciple of William James . . . And, very well, like a true disciple of Jesus Christ."

"Tonight they take me and my entourage to flamenco."

"Then you will meet Don Leandro . . . a man sent by God.

Their strengths and passions converge nicely . . . They have never asked me. Perhaps they think that the Cardinal would be out of place. Which he would be. But a future Cardinal . . . ?"

"At the slaughterhouse over in the Arenal, the insignificant little coadjutor would be out of place, not in a supper club."

He waved that pious hope away.

"I have heard this afternoon from my colleague in Toledo who likes to convey gossip to me that the situation for those who also live in the *palacio* grows very serious. Justice is weaving her webs around El Jefe and Don Marco. Jefe agreed to buy very large shipments of supplies from Marco's hacienda and those of his neighbors and friends, enough for the whole year, at a cost substantially lower than the market because they believed the market would rise and they both would make money on it. Jefe, however, billed the Defense Ministry for the price the bureaucrats had ordered. He then split the profit with Marco. The wheat market, however, has fallen and the Ministry is demanding some of its money back."

"They went long and were shorted out."

"I do not know the language, but I assume that's what it would be called. The farmers will not give them their money back. And our two friends have invested their dirty money and almost all else they have in plans for a ski resort they are building up in the Sierra Nevada. The most modern ski resort in all of Europe. The director of the national park has forbidden it, perhaps because their bribe was too small."

"Real gombeen men."

"Ah . . . Please have another drop of sherry . . . but the bottle is empty . . . Don Pedro, please if you will, our poor guest needs one more sip before he rests his eyes."

I put my hand over the goblet and removed it only when it became clear that Don Pedro would pour the precious liquid gold on my fingers.

"Yes, gombeen man, how delightful. Of course, as you know, Irish culture was first created here in the land of the Vandals, though long before the Vandals came."

"In the era when the good god Lug was worshipped up above in Cordoba."

"Yes . . . Perhaps . . . Nonetheless the gombeen men have stolen from the farmers, from the Ministry, from their own bank accounts, and from those who made the plans for their infernal resort. They must pay the Ministry at once. It will be a great scandal, two members of the PP and both of them military officers stealing money from a Socialist government. Both parties will demand prosecution and try to improve their positions before the election. Marco and Jefe will be destroyed—unless La Doña gives them the required funds, to which they now are claiming in court they have a right."

"Your colleague in Toledo is well informed."

"But of course. Therefore I do not have to ask Don Pedro to gather information about what is happening. Both of our parties are corrupt, Padrecito Negro, as they have always been. The PP learned, when it lost the last election to the Reds, that it must be absolutely transparent. Some of the bright younger men like Don Leandro know this. Perhaps this time or maybe the next time . . ."

"Teresa will not pick up the tab for them?"

He wrote some words on a pad, the sole item on his vast mahogany desk. "Yes, excellent, pick up the tab . . . But of course Teresa won't do it. The excellent Don Leandro proposes that she, uh, pick up the tab this time . . . yes? . . . if they renounce all the rights they claim from her husband's will and immediately leave her home. Stern matron that she is, she absolutely refuses. My colleague tells me that the PP will reveal the scandal within three days to anticipate the SP's revelation. Time is running out for everyone. You will, of course, sense none of this at the flamenco tonight."

"Sounds like a great time."

"Oh, it will be. She is a wonderful hostess. The tapas and wine at your table will be special. Still, if you have any opportunity to suggest moderation, it would be a great favor for all of us."

His small, lively face became sad.

"I will do so if it seems prudent," I said with the kind of west of Ireland sigh that suggests I may well drive into a brick wall.

"Doña Teresa is the closest we have to a queen here in Seville, indeed in all of Andalusia. She will be of little use if she dies a martyr's death. We have had more than enough women martyrs here south of the Sierra Nevada."

I placed my goblet on its tiny pad, both lovely crystal, but hardly like Irish crystal. Celtic culture created here indeed!

"No promises, Don Moro."

"Of course. . . . Do you have, by the way, a name of someone in the American police who can confirm the estimation of your, uh, forensic abilities as reported by the good Cardinal Cronin?"

"But of course."

After some searching, I pulled out of one of my pockets the little packet of indispensable cards I carry with me.

"Michael Vincent Casey, author of *The Art, Craft, and Science of Detection*, with his e-mail and phone number. Very impressive list of responsibilities."

"I hope I will not have to use it. I will return it to you when I no longer need it."

He placed the card, worn and tattered as all my magic cards, into a small drawer in the middle of his desk with the same reverence that he would assume when returning a pyx to the tabernacle. In this town both pyx and tabernacle were surrounded by substantial amounts of gold, plundered gold.

5

"The flamenco here is very nice, Padrecito," Doña Teresa assured me confidentially as she leaned in my direction. "The performers are excellent. Very professional. If one wants to see real flamenco one would have to go across the river to Triana and into the bars and the bistros and the brothels and even the street corners. However, Triana would frighten the tourists and quite properly so."

I was sitting next to her at a crowded table in the front of a perfectly presentable restaurant. The diners were all respectably dressed. A stage filled the front of the room. We were at a table next to the stage. Nothing but the best for Doña Teresa and her party of seven, three of them Yanks who'd never been to flamenco before. The waiters wore tuxedos.

"One needs to experience it in a reassuring place for the first time," I said in the same bland tone she had used.

She was a disturbing presence to be next to. Her scent—tasteful, expensive, and determined—again absorbed me. Her exquisite breasts pressed against her multicolored gown. Blackie Ryan is a man of the world, is he not? Is it not true that he encounters many disturbing women? He can take care of himself, can he not, even if this is the first Castilian Duchess who has disturbed him? He is protected by the grace of holy orders, no?

OK, OK, OK! Already all right. You can safely relax. You will remember this evening as a pleasant interlude and not a temptation. Well, not exactly a temptation. Nonetheless she is scary. Delightful but scary. Besides, her lover is next to her, a mild, gentle man with twinkling brown eyes behind rimless glasses, amused and surprised by his good fortune. Occasionally her eyes would ask a question of him and he would smile approvingly. As well he might. She would blush slightly and perhaps touch his hand briefly, both of them complacent in a passion that had astonished and overwhelmed them.

Well, good enough for them.

The Duchess was not trying to seduce me, not in the ordinary sense of the word, any more than she had tried to seduce Don Moro. She was a vulnerable, beautiful, frightened woman. Automatically she recruited supporters. Who could blame her? She tried to win to her side the lawyer and won a lot more than she had expected. Again good enough for them. If erotic passion between a man and a woman is an image of God, as the present Pope asserts (in fidelity to Saint Paul), then God was hovering over our table. That thought, however valid, did not lessen her erotic appeal. No way.

"May I call you by the name Don Diego calls you," she asked with a modest blush, "Padrecito Negro?"

"My name is Blackie . . . I'm told that is a Spanish equivalent."

"The wonderful Señorita Peggy Anne calls you Uncle Blackie, does she not?"

"Actually, her *novio* is my nephew."

"Would you believe, Padrecito Negro," she said in ordinary tones, "that I danced flamenco once? Over in Triana! When I was very young, younger even than my dear Maria Luisa?"

"I would not dare to doubt it, Doña Teresa."

"I know you were just totally good," Peggy Anne Nolan burst out.

"Abandon, Peggy, is the essence of flamenco. You and my daughter will not believe but one must be of a certain age to know abandon."

"Why did you stop, Doña Teresa?" my nephew asked.

"My father and my future husband insisted that I give it up. They were right. A Duchess should not do flamenco in public."

She wore a long and free-flowing dress of red and blue, appropriate for a retired flamenco dancer watching a polite performance. Modest as it was, the gown left no doubt about the disciplined strength of her womanly body, perfect, one must assume, for abandon.

"Mama is teaching me how to dance. The music disturbs our tenants and they forbid me to dance, but I laugh at them."

Mary Louise was a handful, probably worse than her mother at that age.

"She is quite gifted," Teresa said. "More talented than I was at her age, but also, how should I say it, more restrained . . . that is probably a good thing too."

"Wait, Mama, till I reach a *certain* age!"

"You don't dance for *anyone* else?" the wide-eyed Peggy Anne demanded.

"Doña Teresa," Leandro said, "promises that someday she will dance for me."

He blushed, as did his beloved.

"Well, Mama, you should dance in your lingerie like we do when we practice."

Her mother and her putative future stepfather were acutely mortified by the suggestion, but not totally displeased either.

"I would not dare tell your mother how to dress for dance, Maria Luisa, or anything else," Don Leandro said, now painfully uncomfortable, but not rejecting the image.

"We must wait to see what happens," Doña Teresa said, tilting her head at a saucy angle which hinted at mystery, wonder, and surprise.

"I'd buy a ticket for the show," the usually proper Isidoro said, as if he had weighed the choices and made a rational decision.

"Isidoro!" Maria Luisa and her mother protested in unison.

The lights dimmed and the flamenco company appeared on the stage.

"My daughter is outrageous, is she not, Padrecito Negro?" she whispered to me, once again enveloping me in the narcotic of her perfume.

Then a tall, elderly man with a big mustache and a guitar began to sing an achingly sad plaint, a protest it seemed against all the pain and the suffering, the agony and heartache, of his life. Teresa seized her lover's hand. Lucky fellow.

Then two more men, one in his middle years and the other a good-looking teen, joined him, both with guitars, in the lamentations. My Mexican Spanish did not permit understanding, especially since they were using a dialect, perhaps Roma.

Then two women appeared in the expected flamenco dress—including sharp heels and castanets. The men were silent, as all men are expected to be in the circumstances. The women began to dance, softly at first, then with an explosion of vehement defiance. Next to me, Doña Teresa's feet tapped lightly on the floor.

This is the blues, I told myself, melancholy replaced by a bold refusal to comply. I did not know what Doña Teresa meant by abandon, but it seemed to me that the dances—which went on for a long time with new groups of dancers, each drowning out complaining males—were indeed orgiastic. The tattoos of defiance rose from womanly sexual pleasure which guaranteed the continuation of the species.

I discovered that I was snapping my fingers in time with the castanets, abandon of a sort for the likes of Blackie Ryan.

"We must provide you with castanets, Padrecito Negro," Doña Teresa said, absorbing me now in her smile, a much more deadly narcotic than her scent. I would dream about her tonight, misty gray eyes, flawless complexion, abandoned body.

"Is your mama better than those dancers, Maria Luisa?" The brave Isidoro continued skating on thin ice.

"Certainly!"

"Isidoro!"

But Doña Teresa was not displeased.

"Flamenco," I said, retreating into my professorial mode, "is not unlike African-American blues. Complaint, lamentation, sadness, which end often, not always, in hope and defiance. I don't know that the defiance is gender-linked, both men and women end with defiance of evil and abandon if not to God then to hope."

"God is involved with the blues?" Leandro asked, still holding his woman's hand.

"I think so. Often the complaints seemed directed at God, who is ever present in African-American culture. Blues and gospel music move back and forth with each other, especially when sung by women."

"And how do you account for the orgiastic element of both kinds of music, Uncle Blackie?"

Joseph was playing the role of a good nephew, feeding me lines.

"I don't want to shock anyone. . . . It's a wild cry of hope, of life, probably something which women experience in full sexual pleasure, a hope that absorbs the world because life goes on."

Silence around the table.

"I think we all understand that, Padrecito Negro," Doña Teresa said as though my insight was self-evident and hardly inappropriate. Indeed it was shocking and hardly self-evident, save to the Deity who had settled in at our table to enjoy the evening.

"Hope," I said, still the professor of theology, "is structured into our brains so that every act of human love contains within it organically an act of hope; even the lovers don't intend the hope or accept it."

"As my sainted mother would say," Joseph continued to be my straight man, "so much worse for them."

"Love is as strong as death," I said, ending our joint sermon.

"I think here in Spain," Doña Teresa said, "we know that deep in our souls, though sometimes we doubt it."

She had released her lover's hand.

"It seems to me," I said, "that given your history, it might be more difficult for you."

"In some twisted way, the bullfight means the same thing," Leandro said. "I don't know why we think that when the matador survives we think humanity survives, but that idea is lurking inside us."

"And it is celebrated tomorrow in the Feria," Isidoro said, "when we celebrate God in a human body."

"Feria" means feast or festival. Tomorrow was the Feast of Corpus Christi, celebrated by a procession outdoors. It begins after the Eucharist in the Cathedral and proceeds to two other churches where "Benediction" was performed and then back to the Cathedral for a third blessing while hymns were sung in Latin and Spanish, especially the great medieval hymn "Pange Lingua" written by Thomas Aquinas. It was stretching the theme a bit to link the Feast of the Body and Blood of Christ as we now called it with human passion, but maybe not.

Then the tapas and the wine came and our serious conversations came to an end. Doña Teresa however remained silent, lost in thought through the two remaining intermissions, her lovely face partially hidden behind the fan that was apparently required equipment for Sevillian women. She did, however, snap her fingers and tap her feet lightly during the remaining performance. And during the final performance she did seize her lover's hand again, as though she would never again release it.

At the end of the concert while the crowd struggled to escape through the narrow door, the Spanish men draped light cloaks over their women's shoulders, though there was no evidence of chill in the air.

"You have many good thoughts, Padrecito Negro," Leandro said. "I do not understand them all, but I like them. I must pray over them."

"Cool," Isidoro agreed. "We need more priests who think like you."

"I doubt it."

"Padrecito Negro, tell Isidoro who has a filthy mind that Mama and I will *not* sell him tickets to our first flamenco."

She giggled and slipped away from her *novio.*

Teresa was the last to take my hand.

"I enjoyed the flamenco very much," I said.

"You are a very wise man, Padrecito Negro," she whispered. "I wish I could talk more with you. You will be leaving Seville soon?"

"Not soon enough."

"Perhaps we could eat some tapas after the Feria tomorrow. . . . You will of course be in the procession?"

I hadn't thought about it. I didn't want to walk through Seville under a hot Andalusian sun.

"Certainly. Where should we meet for lunch?"

"You know Santa Cruz? The Calle Mateos? Number two? Bar Giralda?"

"I can find it."

"Good. Thank you. I fear I am damned."

"I very much doubt it, Doña Teresa."

She started to say something and cut herself short.

"I will wait for you after the final ceremonies. I do not want to lose my soul."

"If you do, God will find it for you."

She turned away and hurried to her lover who was waiting patiently. She snuggled up to him as though her blood had run cold.

Now what had I said that caused that reaction?

As Joseph and Peggy Anne and I walked back toward the Cathedral Plaza on the Paseo Cristobal Colon, Joseph asked, "Does the Cardinal expect you to straighten out that crowd?"

"Both Cardinals."

"I hate to sound like my sainted mother, but that doesn't seem fair."

"No one ever promised 'fair' in the life of a priest, Joseph. Besides, they're interesting people."

"I know that but they all think they're damned."

"Joseph is right, Uncle Blackie, but you can talk them out of it."

6

We were eating breakfast in the kitchen of the *palacio.* Don Diego was pacing around, trying to be an executive as he issued detailed commands to the serene Don Pedro, just as Milord Cronin had to turn super CEO on big feasts at our Cathedral. He had not called in several days. I hoped he was well. . . . My sleep had been serene, untroubled by flamenco rhythms and images of mother and daughter dancing in their underwear.

"Any success last night?" El Moro turned to me in the midst of an order to Don Pedro.

"We will have lunch after the Feria, in Santa Cruz?"

"Bar Giralda?"

"Cierto."

"It's her favorite rendezvous for people she likes. What is her worry now?"

I hesitated.

"It is not the seal of confession, Padrecito Negro. She fears that she and her lover will go to hell. You must use all your ingenuity to persuade her that our God is not like that."

"She's Spanish nobility, she knows better."

"You are right, we must pray for her during the procession. It will take two and a half hours. We no longer go out into the main streets where my sainted predecessor delayed traffic. Rather we proceed out of the Cathedral, march to the Church of the Savior, do the first Benediction there, and then go to the cross at the entrance to Santa Cruz and have Benediction there. Then we walk back to the entrance of the Cathedral where an altar will have been put in place and finish the ceremonies there. Do you have Corpus Christi in Chicago?"

"In some parishes, including the Cathedral where I was pastor before I became coadjutor, a much easier task than being a pastor. But we only processed around the Cathedral plant. Liturgists have been critical of us of course. They call it medieval mummery. But in general they have no sense of the importance of processions and outdoor services."

The good Don Pedro arrived with a stack of purple birettas.

"One of these will surely fit you, Padrecito Negro."

Sure enough the last one did.

"You may wear this alb, which is too big for Don Diego."

"Ha!" The local Cardinal laughed at his aide. "Tomorrow you go up to the ski resorts in Sierra Nevada. Forever . . . but you would love that assignment."

"You may want to wear your unusual pectoral cross and episcopal ring."

The alb did cover my jeans and Bears T-shirt, but not my black sneakers. So what, I was the crazy American, was I not . . . I would report this to Cardinal Cronin tonight.

We walked out of the *palacio* and by the statue of the Virgin of the Queens, so named because the kings staying in the Alcazar Royal could look out their windows in the morning and see her, much good it would do to their religious faith which generally was nonexistent, even the present King. We paused in front of her and said a Hail Mary for all political and religious leaders.

Then we entered the grove of orange trees next to the Cathedral. Several score auxiliary bishops, monsignors, priests, papal knights, and other dignitaries waited for us as well as the

choirs—men's choir, women's choir, and kids' choir. Also recent
first communicants and confirmands. Finally, unspecified participants in various strange clothes, civil officials, I assumed, and leaders of various long-defunct guilds. No Protestant or Jewish or
Orthodox leaders, such as I would have had back home. And no
imams.

The aroma of orange trees filled the air, still pleasantly cool.
The grovelike La Giralda was a remnant of an earlier era. The
Muslims had provided such areas next to their mosque so that the
faithful could remove their shoes and wash their feet. San Fernando saw no reason to destroy such agreeable places, even when
he tore down mosques and replaced them with cathedrals. La Giralda informed us that it was nine o'clock and we fell into line under the brisk direction of Don Pedro and marched into the
Cathedral to cheers of triumph. I wondered how many of the
faithful who packed the gold dense Cathedral had received their
Easter Communion, a question unworthy of me, but I was already sweating. So was everyone else. Fortunately the incense was
already filling the Cathedral, diminishing the smell of human
bodies. No air conditioning in the Middle Ages, worse luck for
them.

The other folk with purple hats followed after the Cardinal
who, it seemed to me, was faltering already. I prayed for him and
for Milord Cronin. Good men, who deserved better lives than the
Church had given them. I on the other hand had a better life
than I could possibly deserve—if I could only survive the sun,
the heat, and the smell.

I do not believe in long ceremonies. When I was responsible
for the Cathedral, I edited the ordeals proposed by the liturgy
committee (*libera nos, Domine*). My argument was that the genius
of the Roman liturgy was that it did not dawdle. It moved along,
did what it was supposed to do, and then was done with it. We
were not Greeks who could not do anything without shaking
censors to fill the air with various suspicious oriental smells. We

were not Ethiopians who had been infected by the pagan African custom of night-long services. We were Americans and the last thing we wanted to do was to bore people. The chairperson of our liturgy committee (one of the *damas* who called me "Jackie") said that we needed to teach the faithful that the worship of God was never boring. To which I replied that we needed worship of God that was never boring.

The liturgy in the Cathedral proceeded with proper pace until it came to the Gloria, which required twenty minutes of choir work, during which I fell asleep twice, because as I explained to the Lord God, I was still on jet lag. I didn't particularly like, I added, Spanish baroque music. The Deity did not deign to respond. The local Cardinal's homily lasted five lively minutes. As best as I could understand him, he assured us that we celebrate today because it is the delight of God to be with the children of humans. There must have been a touch of humor in it, because the congregation smiled through the whole five minutes and rose with a standing ovation, followed by a polyphonic credo. I registered my protest by falling asleep again. A five-minute homily, I informed the reality who is being itself, bracketed by a half hour of polyphony and not good polyphony at that.

I awakened at Sanctus which foreshadowed the Eucharistic prayer. Gregorian chant for a change and sung enthusiastically if not flawlessly by the whole congregation. I looked up to see the truly flawless Don Pedro looming over me.

"Don Diego wonders if you might help with the distribution of the Eucharist, indeed by the third pillar on the right?"

"His wonderment is my command, Don Pedro."

My assignment, it turned out, was where parents with babies and little kids received the sacrament—a grand locale for Blackie Ryan.

Fortunately I had removed my deep purple hat before I collected the ciborium at the main altar and ambled down into the isle, where parents and little kids were assembling. However, the pectoral cross attracted immediate attention because many of them wanted to take it home. I smiled when I said, "Corpus Christi" and deposited the sacrament into waiting hands or, for some of the older folk, on waiting lips. I smiled at every communicant. Most smiled back. I blessed the kids who were too young to receive and grinned at them. I tell priests in Chicago that every sacramental encounter is an evangelical occasion. Don't waste it. A smile, warm and happy, is sufficient. If people return to the pews with a smile, it's been a good day for them. If the priest smiles after the exchanges of grace, it may be the only good experience of the whole week.

I was the last of the Communion ministers to return to the high altar where Don Diego and Don Pedro were patiently waiting.

"Next time I distribute Communion," Don Diego murmured, "I'll do it that way."

"The poor faithful are entitled to the occasional smile. As the woman who is well known in this country once remarked, 'From silly devotion and sour-faced saints, deliver us, O Lord.'"

"From Avila, I believe. I think she would approve of this devotion."

"Teresa was Spanish."

After the final blessing, the program began to take shape. The Cardinal and the purpled ones were led to the orange grove. The latter would bring up the rear of the crowd. The Cardinal would sit on the wagon, with the golden monstrance ahead of him. Sometimes he would rise and, with help from a coterie of his staff, lift the monstrance in blessing and then put it back on the solid table at the front of the wagon. The crowds would cheer as we passed them. Were they cheering, I wondered, for Jesus, or the Cardinal, or their ancient Catholic heritage?

I discovered that many little ones were waving to me. So I began waving back. We sang all the way to San Salvador. People cheered. Bands and orchestras, behind the cross bearer, took turns supporting the hymn singing, the children's choir had the right to intone the "Pange Lingua" as a new cycle of hymns would begin.

Pange, lingua, gloriosi	Sing, my tongue, the Savior's glory,
Corporis mysterium,	of His flesh the mystery sing;
Sanguinisque pretiosi,	of the Blood, all price exceeding,
Quem in mundi pretium	shed by our immortal King,
Fructus ventris generosi	destined, for the world's redemption,
Rex effudit Gentium.	from a noble womb to spring.
Nobis datus, nobis natus	Of a pure and spotless Virgin
Ex intacta Virgine,	born for us on earth below,
Et in mundo conversatus,	He, as Man, with man conversing,
Sparso verbi semine,	stayed, the seeds of truth to sow;
Sui moras incolatus	then He closed in solemn order
Miro clausit ordine.	wondrously His life of woe.
In supremae nocte cenae	On the night of that Last Supper,
Recumbens cum fratribus,	seated with His chosen band,
Observata lege plene	He the Pascal victim eating,
Cibis in legalibus,	first fulfills the Law's command;
Cibum turbae duodenae	then as Food to His Apostles
Se dat suis manibus.	gives Himself with His own hand.
Verbum caro, panem verum	Word-made-Flesh, the bread of nature
Verbo carnem efficit:	by His word to Flesh He turns;
Fitque sanguis Christi merum,	wine into His Blood He changes;
Et si sensus deficit,	what though sense no change discerns?
Ad firmandum cor sincerum	Only be the heart in earnest,
Sola fides sufficit.	faith her lesson quickly learns.
Tantum ergo Sacramentum	Down in adoration falling,
veneremur cernui:	Lo! the sacred Host we hail;
et antiquum documentum	Lo! o'er ancient forms departing,
novo cedat ritui:	newer rites of grace prevail;

praestet fides supplementum	*faith for all defects supplying,*
sensuum defectui.	*where the feeble senses fail.*
Genitori, Genitoque	*To the everlasting Father,*
laus et jubilatio,	*and the Son who reigns on high,*
salus, honor, virtus quoque	*with the Holy Ghost proceeding*
sit et benedictio:	*forth from Each eternally,*
procedenti ab utroque	*be salvation, honor, blessing,*
compar sit laudatio.	*might and endless majesty.*
Amen. Alleluja.	*Amen. Alleluia.*

Note that the Latin version does more with fewer words than does the wordy English translation, The Latin tells the first two verses of the story in five words; the English requires fourteen words.

Moreover in Seville they have another music form— Mozarabic (pre-Arab, Visigothic) which shapes the hymn. The Goths loved to linger on single syllables and modulate around them. It's a tour de force, but to my ears, kind of weird. Nobody speaks Visigothic anymore and in fact there are probably no more than twenty extant documents of the chant. Andalusia was hardly so militant that the locals wanted to learn a new dialect, as the Catalonians up in Barcelona wanted to do. Accustomed to the Gregorian chant music for the hymn, I was not prepared to accept these weird sounds the Visigoths fixed to the hymn. On the other hand, as a pluralist I cannot oppose variety. Didn't your man Jimmy Joyce say, "Catholic means Here Comes Everyone"? I would have to ask El Moro if he would seek permission for an occasional Visigothic Eucharist in this Cathedral. As I remembered there were only four churches up in Toledo that could do it.

We left San Salvador and the parish Church of Santa Cruz to march through the Murillo gardens and back into the Cathedral Plaza. I continued to sing the few hymns I knew, wave at kids, and search for Doña Teresa's face in the crowd. Finally we were at the entrance of the gold-laden Cathedral again where the final Benediction would be performed. I was dragged up on the temporary altar for the third and final Benediction. The ever-present Don Pedro made me responsible for spooning incense into the thurible. Then, to the powerful words of the "Tantum Ergo," the final stanza of the "Pange Lingua" and the final blessing of the crowd, which cheered triumphantly, another Feria was brilliantly executed. Don Pedro loaded the pyx into its golden container and carried it up to the altar where El Moro removed the pyx and carried the Sacred Host to the tabernacle. Then the ceremony petered out and the various clerics scattered to return to the work of the day, masses at their own parishes perhaps.

I had a different kind of priestly work ahead of me.

7

I hurried back to the **palacio** for a shower and a clean shirt. Not proper to eat tapas with a duchess at Bar Giralda without proper grooming, not if one was an American, fixated on the need of deodorant. Did Cristobal Colon, conveniently interred next to the Cathedral, carry any such on his voyages from Seville?

Doña Teresa stood up when I entered the bar, supported by heavy and curling arches from the days when it was a Moorish bath.

"What did you think of our Feria, Don Negro?"

"Powerful and moving, even for an American."

"I saw your Peggy Anne and her *novio* when the procession ended. Even they were impressed. They did not seem at all surprised at the attention you drew from the children."

"If there were puppy dogs around they would swarm to me too."

Doña Teresa seemed washed out or perhaps hungover. She was wearing a gray dress, black mantilla, and dull black shoes. Her face was innocent of makeup. However, she was wearing an impressive scent even if it didn't have the same narcotic effect as her previous aroma. She was still a disturbing presence. That was the way you made her, I told the Deity. Don't blame me.

"The beautiful Peggy Anne, as she calls herself, tells me that you are her spiritual director. Could you also be that for me?"

Peggy and her big and generous Irish mouth!

"I thought Don Diego filled that role in your life?"

"Oh, no," she said with a blush, "he is my adviser. Spiritual directors are supposed to tell you what to do."

"Only if they already know what their charge has already made up her mind to do."

"I will be obedient. You know Santa Teresa on obedience to a director?"

"That was another era."

"Please, Padrecito Negro, I need someone to tell me what to do. My father is dead, my husband is dead. I have no brothers. The relatives who live in my house are evil people. I have no one to whom I might turn."

"Your lover? Your daughter?"

"They are too close to me."

"I will have to go home in a couple of days."

"I know you have e-mail."

I didn't believe in the kind of spiritual director, one who decides other people's lives. However, in the short run something like that might work for this poor fragile woman.

"You won't do what I tell you."

"Perhaps not immediately because I will have to meditate on it, but I will strive to obey you . . . PLEASE, Padrecito Negro . . . you are a good and kind and wise man. I don't know where else to turn."

Tears appeared in her misty gray eyes. I didn't need this responsibility. Well, I told the Lord God, you got me into this mess. So if I blow it, it's your fault.

I knew that argument was worthless.

"All right, where do we start?"

The tapas plates arrived with a bottle of wine.

"I love Leandro so much. I don't want to drag him down to hell with me."

"Ah," I said. Let her talk awhile. Sound strategy, I hoped.

"I was always faithful to my husband while he was alive. It was not easy, as you may imagine. He wanted a son so much, as did I. But he had his problems, as you no doubt know."

I nodded wisely.

"Then when Don Diego urged me to seek a repudiation of the will, he suggested Don Leandro because he was a man of great brilliance and impeccable ethics. My heart beat faster. I had known him when we were at the University. There was an attraction between us but we did not act on it or even try to sustain it because my father would only approve of someone who was noble like we were. He wanted me to be a Duchess. I could not think, not at that age, of disobeying him."

"Indeed."

"I knew Don Leandro had lost his wife whom he loved very much. I rejected the thought that perhaps we could finish what seemed possible, however remote, twenty years ago. I resolved to be stern and aloof. I needed a lawyer far more than I needed a lover."

"Indeed."

"I have always been a fool, Padrecito Negro. I did not dress to appear beautiful. I promised myself that I would be professional at all times. I did not realize what was certainly going to happen. I did not seduce him. He did not seduce me. We fell into each other's arms. Now we are both addicted to each other. He is so kind and gentle and sensitive. I did not realize men could be that way. He is also an enchanting lover. I am mad in my hunger for him. I could not survive without him, nor he without me. I never realized passion could be that powerful."

"What does your daughter think of this relationship?"

"She is happy to see her mother in love. She thinks Leandro

is wonderful. She says frequently that I should not let him get away, not that I wouldn't fight to keep him."

"I'm sure you would."

"Is it not sinful to feel that way?"

"No."

"Every day?"

"Most would consider that a very great blessing."

"I can't help myself, Padrecito Negro. I know that Don Leandro cannot have respect for me."

"He may not know the theology, but then again he might. Yet he understands that you're a sacrament of God's love."

"A woman is a sacrament of God?"

"One of the most ingenious God has ever designed. Lovers don't pay any attention to that truth, even though the last two Popes have written about it."

"I feel so dirty . . ."

"Only afterward and on reflection. A voice tells you that you are a slut. You yourself feel proud and grateful . . . whose voice?"

"Doña Inez, of course . . ."

"Tune her out. . . . After you and Don Leandro commit yourself to one another publicly in the presence of the Church, she will continue to whisper. She speaks for the devil, as you well know. Turn her off before she ruins your love."

"I must think about these matters. I fear that reflection on them will drive me to find Don Leandro and play the whore again." It was suddenly very warm in the Bar Giralda. This conversation was necessary, but it was very difficult. I must divert it a bit.

"Doña Teresa"—I swallowed a large gulp of wine—"you couldn't play the whore no matter how hard you might try."

"What am I playing? Who . . ."

"God."

"Who says so?"

"St. Paul, Papa Benedetto, among others."

"God can't behave that way!"

I sighed.

"You are a very beautiful woman, Doña Teresa, as I'm sure you know though you don't like to acknowledge it, save in the skill of your dress. Your beauty is only part of the glory and wonder and mystery and splendor of the Creation in which God has clothed himself . . ."

"No!"

"Yes! Moreover God sheds his glory when he humbles himself in the incarnation. He empties himself and takes on the form of a slave in order to reveal how great his love is. So when a woman discards her clothing for her lover, she is in effect emptying herself for him to reveal her love just as God empties himself for us. And vice versa. That's all in the last encyclical. . . ."

"I do not want to listen to such blasphemy!"

She buried her head in her arms on the table.

"You are an obdurate and stubborn child, Doña Teresa. . . . And his two daughters hate you for sleeping with their father?"

I had clumsily changed the subject to cool off the heat we were creating.

"They are sweet little girls, eleven and thirteen. They seem to adore me . . . I don't know for certain. The younger one said that they were glad that their father was happy again."

"Ah."

"We are committing mortal sins, we are condemning ourselves to hell for all eternity. We must stop."

"Ah . . . What is the sin you're committing?"

"Fornication! Isn't that a mortal sin?"

"In theory yes, in pastoral practice, it depends on circumstances. Often, however, it is a prelude to marriage, an aching and rewarding pain which moves members of our species to the responsibilities of marriage and parenthood."

"How can you say that!"

She recoiled as if I were Satan.

"Moreover," I plowed on, like I would drive a ski boat on Lake Michigan, ignoring the waves running against me, "you and Don Leandro are good people. No way God will let you end up in the other place. He loves you as much as you love one another, only more so. That ought not to be your spiritual concern. I think your most serious spiritual fault is not to believe strongly enough in God's love."

She lowered her head and gulped.

"What does that mean I should do?"

"It means you have a family, one husband, three daughters, and perhaps a son to arrive someday soon. So you should follow the recommendations of Don Diego and formally in his presence administer the sacrament to one another."

"I can't do that," she muttered through lips that were clamped together.

"Why not?"

"It would not be *honorable*, not until the court rules on the will."

"Your husband, for whatever reason, had no right to bind you under such rules. It is required that you stamp your feet and click your castanets and defy the whole lot of them. Have the police remove them from your house, or at least find another place to live with your family until you are legally free to insist on your defiance. But you must let your lawyer direct how this is to be done."

She frowned.

"I will not obey you."

"I said you wouldn't."

I rose from the chair.

"Sit down, Don Juan Negrito. Have another glass of wine and this tasty cheese tapas."

Nothing to lose. So I sat down.

"I so much want to do what you demand," she said, her eyes focused on the tapas plate. "It would make me happy . . ."

"And you do not want to be happy?"

"I am afraid to be happy. I don't deserve to be happy."

"Who says that?"

"Doña Inez. She has been my duenna all my life . . ."

"And if both Don Diego and El Padre Negro, as it pleases you to call him, say she is wrong?"

She sighed, her elegant and disconcerting breasts pressing against the thin gray fabric of her dress. That's a dirty trick you play on us men, I protested to the Deity. Also a great gift.

"Then she must be wrong."

She did not lift her eyes from the tapas.

"I must think about all these things," she said with another sigh, more disconcerting than the last one.

"Naturally," I said, indicating my impatience.

"You don't want me to think?"

"So long as it is Doña Teresa thinking, not the voice of Doña Inez out of your past."

"I must leave now or I will sob and disgrace my honor."

"Tears of sadness or of joy?"

She sat up straight, her back pressed against the wooden chair, her teeth clenched.

"Joy."

She rose from the chair and turned to flee.

"Doña Teresa," I said, as one who gives orders to vulnerable women all the time. "Come back here!"

She returned to the table, head bowed.

"When you appear before God's high judgment seat, he will ask you who sent you and say we don't want anybody up here who nobody sent."

"And I should say?" She smiled a bit at my depiction of God.

"You should say El Padre Negrito and add that it is all your fault because you sent him to me when I needed joy. And God will smile at you with great affection because you are one of the most beautiful creatures he ever imagined and he's very pleased with you and he will say nothing but just wave his hand at heaven's gate."

She turned again and ran out of the Bar Giralda. Beware, Don Leandro, God is coming after you.

Trembling from the surge of emotions which had enveloped me even more powerfully than her scent, I tried to focus on the superb cheese tapas. Well, I remarked to the Deity, you didn't let me down that time. I said all the right things which I would never have thought of myself. Thanks for the help. Now she's in your court.

As usual there was no answer. Someday there will be and I'll be scared silly.

Then it was my turn to tremble. The day had been too much. The body of Christ, the body of Teresa, both sacraments to be respected and treasured. I laughed. A very clever God to think of sacraments. As for Teresa, before siesta was over she would make love to Leandro to see what it was like to be a passionate God for your lover. Poor Leandro wouldn't know what hit him.

8

"*Don Diego is already resting his* eyes," Don Pedro said as I entered the Cardinal's office. "He said that I should suggest the
same thing to you. . . . He left a carafe of sherry for you in your
room."

"It was an exhausting morning for him," I said.

"For everyone," Don Pedro agreed. "Don Diego is a healthy
man, though not very strong. He must pretend to the people that
he is very strong because that is what they expect of a leader."

"He must act like a warrior. This after all is al-Andalus."

"Yet already the people love him and he does not act like a
warrior."

"Perhaps al-Andalus is changing," I said.

"Or perhaps all of Spain."

"As we say in America, from your lips to God's ears!"

I ambled up to my bedroom and collapsed into my bed,
drinking half of the carafe of sherry before my eyes began to
rest themselves. I hoped there were no dreams about Doña
Teresa.

If I had dreams about her I had repressed all memory of
them by the time I awakened from a very heavy session of eye
resting. I experienced a deep sensation of guilt. I had failed in an

obligation. Which one was it? I was to call someone in America, but whom? . . . My eyes, resisting the affront required to stay open, closed again. Chicago was so far away . . .

Sean Cronin! I hadn't called him for two days!

I reached for my mobile phone and could not find it. Not in my jeans, not in my Bears jacket, not in my briefcase, not on the dresser. Did I have it during the Corpus Christi ceremony? I didn't think so! Where could it be? I reached for my shoes. I would have to explore the *palacio* in search of it. Aha, inside my left shoe, precisely where I had left it!

I pushed the magic buttons which should produce the Cardinal's private phone. It didn't work. I reached for my glasses and tried again. A long ring.

"Cronin."

"Blackie."

"I was following your good example and resting my eyes."

He sounded very tired.

"We did Corpus Christi here this morning. Exuberant."

"Father Coyne's efforts here were more in keeping with the liturgical and rubrical rules than in prior years. Fortunately the people wanted the previous largely uncanonical version and George, being more flexible than you are, returned to the Blackie rite."

"Admirable."

"Did you meet that woman Jimmy wants you to save from some crooks?"

"I ate lunch with her after the ceremonies. We have made some progress. The issue is still in doubt."

"Straighten her out, Blackie. She's apparently very important."

"I quite agree. She's caught between the late Middle Ages and the post-modern world."

"Yeah, well see to it, Blackwood. I'm going back to sleep."

I ignored the lure of the half carafe of Jerez. The situation called for clear thinking. Who to call next?

Nora Cronin, the Cardinal's foster sister, sister-in-law, and sometime lover, briefly and a long time ago. The two of us had become allies in a struggle to keep him alive. We were for a long time the only people in the world about whom he gave a damn. No one in Rome, neither Pope nor curialist, had any effect on him at all. As they would say in Ireland, at all, at all. Hence he was a remarkably effective leader, respected in Chicago and feared in Rome. Somehow he had arranged that I be his successor, something that the Vatican rarely permits. There was, I told myself, every chance that they would cancel that out and send me to a new diocese, say, in Yuma, Arizona. The danger was, as Milord Cronin put it with characteristic pungency, that they would send some pompous asshole to clean up the Cronin mess.

I did not want to be Archbishop of Chicago, but better me than said pompous asshole.

"Nora Cronin," said the warm and gracious voice at the other end of the line.

"Blackie. In Spain but only because your very good friend sent me here."

"So I understand. Have you solved the problem?"

"Partially. How is our mutual friend keeping?"

"Irritable, more so than usual. Had an unusually contentious meeting with the Priests Council."

"Idiots."

"So I understand. . . . Have you talked to him? . . . Of course you have. Otherwise you wouldn't be calling me. What did you think?"

"My guess is that he should go into the hospital for observation and tests. You should keep an eye on him while he's there and bring Father Coyne's sister-in-law."

"Nuala Anne, the beautiful witch? Good idea. Sean is more afraid of her than he is of me."

"He may not want to do it with me over here in Seville. Tell him to appoint Father Coyne acting Vicar General or some such. He should have done it in the first place."

"Good idea. Turn your sister loose on him. He's afraid of her too."

The virtuous Mary Kathleen was several years younger than the Cardinal, but she called him by his first name and kept him in his place.

"Dr. Ryan," she said as she picked up. "Is that you, Blackie? What are you doing now? Any progress with our reluctant lovers?"

"I am to sup with them tonight."

"When do you think the wedding will be?"

"I have no hard data. If I had to guess I would say the Friday of the Labor Day weekend. Friday because there is a Domer game on Saturday."

"You're kidding!"

"No, just guessing."

"There isn't time to get ready!" she shouted.

"They could always elope to Grand Beach."

"That would save a lot of money," she said thoughtfully. "But it wouldn't be much fun."

"Consider, sister, that you would have it over long before you had to start holiday preparations."

"There's that. The sooner the better, I've been saying since she came home from New Orleans."

Ah, that was useful information to pass on to a potentially nervous couple who did not want a "BIG" wedding. Most young people solemnly proclaim that desire, but they don't really mean it.

"I have another issue . . ."

"Two!"

"It would be appropriate for Sean Cronin to undergo tests,

observation, and relaxation at Northwestern University Medical Center."

"Why?"

"Because Father Coyne, Nora Cronin, and your brother worry about him."

"Good reasons. You want me to make sure that proper care is taken at NUMC, shape up admissions, nurses, chew out idiots, that sort of thing?"

"Father Coyne will coordinate all of this with you."

"Sure . . . Will that beautiful witch be there?"

"Arguably."

"That's good. Sean is scared of her. So am I. . . . Are you, Punk?"

"If she is anything, she is a good Witch of the West. I am no more afraid of Nuala Anne than I would be of a local seraph."

"OK. You keep me informed and I'll keep you informed. Understand?"

"Arguably."

She never liked my use of that word.

I called George Coyne again and summarized the plans.

"Your virtuous sister-in-law will be available?"

"Couldn't keep her away. She'll see seraphim moving around the hospital room."

"You think this is the end?" I asked.

"Boss, I'm scared that it might be."

My chest tightened at the thought.

I then turned on my portable computer and plugged it into the local phone line. After some considerable reluctance, AOL appeared and asked me what I wanted. I demanded my mail which it produced even more reluctantly. In addition to spam, hate mail, demands for answers, and the usual drivel from the office of the National Conference, there were two important pleas for help and a letter from Tessa at seville.edu.hsp.

I did my best with the pleas and then turned to Tessa.

Don Padrecito Negro,

I must begin by thanking you for taking me on as your spiritual child. I fear that I will be a heavy burden to you. I also want to say that the way you treated children during the Feria was profoundly moving. I noticed that Don Diego has started to imitate you. That is all to the good.

On the way to my siesta, I encountered Don Jose and Señorita Peggy Anne. She asked me quite bluntly whether I had asked you to be my spiritual director. I said that I had. I love her joy and her bluntness. I wish I were like her, but I am not an American.

Yes, I said. He is a very holy man. He talks about God and makes me afraid, but not of God. She told me that sometimes you say things that sound crazy, but that you are always right.

I am beginning to think that is true.

Muchas gracias for your help. I will continue to need it.

Respectfully,

Teresa Maria

I thought about a reply and decided tentatively against it. The woman, vulnerable to begin with, had made herself more vulnerable. She had revealed more secrets of her intimate life than she had intended. I must walk very carefully among the closets of her soul. I wondered what had transpired between her and Don Leandro during siesta. That was none of my business unless she chose to talk about it. I did not need and did not want any more secrets. I must not seem to pry. A short, professional reply was appropriate.

Doña Teresa Maria,

Thank you for your note.

I'm always available to help.

God bless you and protect you.
El Padrecito Negro

I dressed and wandered down to Don Diego's office. He was sitting at his desk, smiling contentedly as he consumed a small dish of chocolate ice cream.

"It was a wonderful *representation collectif,* was it not?"

He was using a term that the French philosopher Emile Durkheim had applied to public rituals in which people became conscious of their group cohesion and then equated the effervescence of that moment with God.

"Maybe the most ingenious such ritual that humankind has ever constructed."

"Perhaps you would like to share some of my ice cream? I will ask Don Pedro to bring more?"

"I must eat dead fish tonight with my nephew and his *prometida.*"

"They will marry soon?"

"I hope by the end of summer."

"That is good. There are events which must not be delayed, eh?"

"There is a proper time for everything, as the Wise Man says."

"I have heard much praise for your ability to make little children smile. And their somber parents too."

"Any day a priest can do that is a good day for him."

"His reward will come great in heaven."

"I don't understand it. Perhaps the children see another childish person. Little dogs like me too, which is odd."

I did not add that sometimes beautiful women in distress also liked me.

"It is simple. They like you because you like them. . . . You had tapas with Doña Teresa Maria, I understand."

"Don Pedro is very efficient."

"He entered the Bar Giralda to purchase a plate of tapas for our lunch. Naturally we free the staff for the Feria. With pay. When he saw the two of you and Doña Teresa weeping, he discreetly withdrew."

"I was about to report on our conversation, as best I can within the limitations of my new role as her spiritual director. . . . The ebullient Señorita Peggy Anne, for whom I play a similar role, had urged her to seek my help."

Don Diego's grin became merry, no longer the regal fool, but the canny leprechaun.

"Ah, Padrecito Negro, you attract not only little children and dogs, but beautiful women."

"Perhaps because I do not threaten any of them. . . . You may be confident that I urged upon her the same solution that you have urged."

"That she and her *caballero andante* exchange vows privately in my presence and then live in peace and fidelity with one another?"

"Something of that sort . . . She promised she would think seriously about it."

"The woman has had a difficult life. Her mother died from an overdose of pain medicine when Teresa was three. Her father began a long series of affairs but did not remarry. He gave his cousin—the stern Doña Inez Mercedes, already married to that fool Don Marco—care of his daughter and went off to fight with the Generalissimo. She sent the little girl to a convent school which would have pleased the most rigid of nineteenth-century Catholics. From the very beginning Doña Inez Mercedes became a stern duenna."

"Yet she attended the University?"

"The father insisted. When he learned from the duenna that she was dancing, as he said, with gypsies over in Triana, he betrothed her to Don Marco Antonio, though he had reason to think that his friend might be a homosexual. However, by definition, no fellow officer in Franco's army could be gay. She has never been free of the nuns or her duenna. She conceived Señorita Maria Luisa early in the marriage and had no other children."

He waved his hands and rolled his eyes.

"All of this happened before I came to Seville of course. You can imagine what her life was like, a beautiful and fiery young woman, condemned to a life of celibacy which she had not chosen. She turned to works of charity, hospitals, orphanages, schools for the poor, missions, leper colonies. She was generous and efficient, a flawless administrator. There were many possibilities for infidelity but she was either very faithful or very discreet—those who thought they knew could not make up their minds. I personally believe she was loyal to her marriage vows."

"An annulment would have been possible?"

"Certainly, but my predecessor did not believe in them. . . . Then her husband died. In his final years he did not live in their *palacio.* Everyone knew that he kept a lover in his apartment at Madrid, a series of lovers. Don Marco and Doña Inez tried to control her life more rigidly than her husband would have. She fought them off firmly. When they attempted to betroth Señorita Maria Luisa to that popinjay Don Teodoro Guzman, Teresa intervened and forbade the betrothal contract. They would not ruin her daughter's life like they had ruined her own. Don Marco, who is a fool, and is alleged to have tried to rape Teresa several times in recent years, went to court to enforce the will. Some of her allies in her work suggested that she fight him in court and cause the will to be invalidated. It was about the time I arrived here."

"So she came to consult you as God's representative in Seville."

"I told her that she could always appeal to the church court here and to the Vatican. Both would undoubtedly support her plea. She thought it better to work through civil law before turning to canon law. She begged me to recommend a civil *abrogado*. I asked some confidential questions and was told that Don Leandro Santiago y Diaz was brilliant and above reproach. *Un Parfait Gentilhomme.* I spoke to him about the case and asked him if he would consider assuming responsibility. He said that he had always thought that the arrangement at the *palacio* was strange. He thought a moment and observed that there should be a number of grounds on which the first will could be invalidated, but the process might take time."

"So a *caballero andante*."

"Indeed, a man with rimless glasses, firm shoulders, and compassionate blue eyes. He would fight strongly for justice, of that I was certain. I did not know that he had lost his wife recently and that he and Teresa had attended the University at the same time. If I had known that . . ." He hesitated for a moment.

"Being a romantic, you would not have changed your mind."

"Not for a moment. The court was very sympathetic. Doña Teresa is very popular in Seville. The judge restrained Don Marco and Doña Inez from interfering in the lives of the plaintiffs until it made a final ruling. I am told that there is no doubt that Doña Teresa will win. . . . Then I hear that perhaps our perfect knight is spending siestas with his client in a small apartment over a bar on a narrow street in Santa Cruz. I secretly rejoice. The story will have a happy ending, unusual for a Sevillian romance."

"Then she appears in this very room to confess her guilt?"

"And beg my forgiveness. Perhaps I am too harsh. I tell her that there is nothing to prevent a marriage between herself and Don Leandro if they love one another and promise to be faithful to one another for the rest of their lives. She is shocked that God's representative would propose an ongoing liaison, against Spanish law."

"When was the last time such a law was enforced?"

"I told her that. She tells me she will think about it. I insist that she must break with Doña Inez who has no authority over her and never did. She is horrified and leaves this office in tears. The case drags on, the lovers continue to share their siesta, much to the delight of the people of Seville for whom the persecuted Doña Teresa and the outspoken and colorful Señorita Maria Luisa are popular heroes. I meet Doña Teresa at the dedication of a new school and urge her and Maria Luisa to move out of their *palacio* and into a suite at the new hospital which they have prepared especially for her. I tell her that anger is certain to increase among her enemies and her allies and she might be in danger. She refuses to believe me, even if I am a successor to the apostle St. James whose name I shared."

"What more can you do?"

"You call Milord Cronin for advice and he sends a most unpromising expert of murder."

"One, El Padrecito Negro, who has some magic appeal to puppy dogs, little children, and beautiful women."

"She is very lovely indeed, Don Diego, and an extremely disconcerting presence."

"You have found her to be such also?"

"Indeed."

"In our heritage such women are immediately thought by clergy to represent the devil."

"While we now understand that they also can represent God. And thus delight in their beauty—up to a certain point."

"We must both pray for her and her *caballero andante*, Padrecito Negro."

"Patently."

Whereupon I departed to walk over to the Alfonso XIII to meet my nephew and his promised spouse at the Egana Oriza, next to the walls of the gardens of the Alcazares Reales. Since the evening was cool and the air soft, Joseph had chosen an outdoor table. Peggy Anne was bursting with curiosity about my new spiritual child.

"Is she more difficult than I am, Uncle Blackie?"

"I try to avoid such judgments."

"And more beautiful?"

"Perhaps—if you find Spanish martyrs like St. Fausta to be beautiful. If your tastes run to the Irish, as my nephew's tastes seem to, then the comparison is absurd."

"Don't you think Don Leandro is cute?"

"The point is that patently Doña Teresa does."

"You're no fun, Uncle Blackie."

"You know he's not going to reveal any secrets about her," Joseph said, "any more than he would reveal them about you."

"I don't want any secrets, I just want to know what Uncle Blackie thinks will happen."

"All endings are not happy, Peggy Anne. Not in this life anyway."

"I guess we have to pray for them both."

"We have told the waiter that we want some kind of Basque food."

"Turbot in green sauce."

I wished that it would come quickly. Still on my Chicago schedule, I was perishing with the hunger. I should have borrowed some of Don Diego's chocolate ice cream.

"Mary Louise says the whole city is on their side."

"I don't doubt that."

"I tell her she ought to move out of that terrible house."

"Solid advice. Persist in it."

"And that she ought to let the Cardinal marry them privately."

"Equally sound."

"Don Leandro wants her to move into a house in Santa Cruz."

"That would be convenient."

"Don Leandro should drag her out of that creepy place," Joseph said.

"I can't disagree."

"Uncle Blackie, do you think we should marry at Thanksgiving or Christmas?"

As often happened, Peggy Nolan had changed the subject without warning.

Now we were talking about the real reason for this dinner.

"Labor Day."

"That's more than a year away," she protested.

"No, Peggy Anne, it is only three months away."

"This coming Labor Day!" Joseph said, I thought with a gulp. "Why so soon?"

"Do it and get it over with. Friday of the Labor Day weekend, because doubtless the hapless Domers will have an opening day game. We have to keep the whole weekend free."

"At Grand Beach?" Joseph asked.

"Or Christ the King?" I asked.

"CK would be better. It's a real parish . . . Joseph?"

"I think so too."

"You'd preside, Uncle Blackie?"

"You'd have to rally the Chicago Police Department to stop me."

"Won't there be other weddings that weekend?"

"We're talking Friday afternoon, Peggy."

"Oh!"

"I took the liberty of checking before we left Chicago," I said. "CK is wide open. So in effect is The Club. I spoke to the pastor and he has penciled in a wedding for five on Friday afternoon."

"You were planning on this conversation all along, weren't you, Uncle Blackie?" Joseph shook his head as if in surprise.

"Neither of you thought I would be unprepared, did you?

Besides, your family will be at Forest Beach, Margaret Anne, so your beloved grandparents will be able to come, as well as such other family members who so desire."

"That settles it all," Joseph said. "Hey, bride, kiss me!"

"It is time, Joseph darling. I'm sorry, dear bridegroom, that I stalled it for so long."

"Both our faults. We both tend to be procrastinators when the matter is something that's certain to happen."

So they kissed with a certain amount of restraint though not too much, given the presence of an Archbishop.

The waiter thereupon produced turbot in green sauce.

"You have good sparkling wine?" I asked him.

"The best, señor."

"Then a bottle of it if you please. This young couple has just set a date for their wedding."

The owner appeared with a sparkling wine of which I had never heard in honor of the settled date for a marriage. He refused to accept payment for it. I would take care of that when they brought the check.

"As I have often said, marriage is both a gift and a challenge. You must savor the gift, no matter how complex the challenge, and the challenge should recall the utter gratuitousness of the gift."

"Peter Murphy will be your groomsman?"

"Who else?"

"You won't mind if I sign up Cindasue to be my woman in waiting?"

"I would take that for granted. It will be simple that way."

"You can always tell your children that you had a surenuf hardshell Southern Baptist Catholic in your wedding party."

So we laughed and chatted through the dinner. I insisted on the tab.

"The nice thing," Señorita Margarita said while we walked down the street to the Alfonso XIII, "is that we'll be back from our honeymoon in time for the first quarter at the University. You can graduate in June and if I get pregnant right away I won't have to sweat all summer."

One responsibility deftly managed. Some of the others might not be that easy.

9

Back at the store, I turned my attention to Chicago, Archdiocese of.

"Holy Name Cathedral Rectory! Megan speaking!"

"Hi Megan!"

"Father Blackie! Where are you?"

"Spain, I think."

"Hey, you sound like you're upstairs in your study!"

"Remarkable."

"When are you coming back?"

"The sooner the better. Another couple of days."

"You want to talk to the Cardinal."

"Don't want to bother him. Father Coyne will do nicely."

"Right away. Hurry back."

"Coyne."

"The poet?"

"No such luck. I don't have a beautiful wife, not even any wife."

"How's the boss?"

"Cranky. He sees no reason to go to the hospital. He can work on the documents the Conference sent out just as well here as there. Waste of time in either place."

"The man can be very stubborn."

"And, Blackie, when he gets that way, it's a good sign that he needs to be over at the medical center, as you know."

"Indeed."

"Our team. He won't listen to my sister-in-law the witch. He won't listen to your sister the shrink. He won't listen to his sister-in-law Nora. He certainly won't listen to me. The only one we haven't trotted out is yourself."

"I was afraid of that."

"Blackie, he doesn't care whether he lives or dies. He even tells Nora that. She weeps, but he won't pay any attention. He says dumb things like, 'I've been a burden to you all your life.' "

That comment was at least true. What he missed, however, is that all love is a burden on the beloved. No, the burden is part of love. They are inseparable.

"Thanks, George. I'll give it a try."

"Let me know. . . . That blonde from Channel 3 wants to know when you're coming back."

"Tell her that Archbishop Ryan likes it so much in the Costa del Sol that he might not ever come back."

"That's not true is it?"

"I yearn every night for the sound of the State Street subway."

I thought about the best strategy.

Life had done no favors to Sean Patrick Cronin. His father Michael James Cronin was a rich Chicago gambler, which is to say he was a commodity broker back in the days when the exchanges were not subject to the supervision that exists today. Like his bitter enemy and rival Joseph P. Kennedy he was a short seller, he made his money betting that the market would fall. Most "investors" don't like the short seller, the man who is betting against progress, against faith in America, against mother and apple pie. However, all investors are gamblers. The question is not whether going long or going short is more virtuous, but who has made the better bet. Michael James Cronin made the better bet in 1920s America, just as Joseph Kennedy had.

He bought a big house in River Forest, a summer "cottage" in Lake Geneva, and a "getaway" in Hobe Sound in Florida. He married a beautiful young woman who was pious and passive-aggressive. After she had given him two sons, he ignored her. Paul, the older, would be President of the United States. Sean, the youngest, would be Pope. In Michael James Cronin's mind, these were not thoughts nor hopes nor dreams. They were fact. Like everything else in his life, they were certainties. He devoted himself to local politics, something he had ignored when most of his time was spent on the trading floor. He bought not favors but people. He could not have cared less about the mechanics of politics. The patient indirection with which the Irish played the game was a waste of time. You give money to people, you inundate them with your charm, and then you give them more money and more gifts. You treat them with respect and you expect compliance and respect in turn. He did not have a political agenda. He was instinctively a conservative Republican and he hated FDR. Issues, however, were unimportant. Power was what counted. You got power by spending money so people owed you favors. You own them. No one seemed to mind because he rarely picked up his markers.

He took his pleasure by seducing wives of rich North Shore businessmen. Some men hunted animals. He hunted women, preferably proud women, bored women, women who would find his Irish charm amusing and his ruthless masculinity interesting. He would shower them with gifts and affection, tease them, torment them, and then take them to bed. He was proud of his conquests but did not brag about them except to his closest friends from his adolescent years on the west side.

"She might not be a knockout," he said about one woman, "but you don't care what she's like when you have her spread out on a bed and she's terrified of you and desperately wants you.

I own her and there's nothing she can do about it. Yeah, it doesn't last long. After a while they bore me. I drop them. Nothing they can do about it. But they know they've belonged to a real man. I could have any of them back whenever I want."

It was not necessary that others know of his conquests, though many of the women in that social set did know. It was only necessary that he know.

He also bought the outfit. They didn't need money, but he gave it to them anyway. They were wary of rich and generous Irish, but discovered he was a man after their own heart. Whether he had ever sought any favors from them remains uncertain. However, one or two of his business rivals met tragic sudden deaths.

He also bought the Church. He hated Cardinal Mundelein, mostly because he was German. But he poured money into the Cardinal's projects and they became close golf partners at Hobe Sound. He needed to have friends in the Church to advance Sean's career, though he would never permit him to be one of Mundelein's crowd of handsome young priests. He cultivated the powerful men in the local church and eventually in Rome. He was generous in his contributions to the Church and churchmen. None of them seemed to wonder why this man was so generous. That was just the way he was. He was in fact gathering markers for Sean's career. He was devoted to the Little Flower, the recently canonized St. Teresa of Lisieux, in part, it was said, because he wanted favors from God and Teresa seemed to have an inside track to God. Mundelein made him a knight of St. Gregory, which pleased him, though that was a common enough prize, and then a Knight of Malta which was rare (and expensive).

When his long-suffering wife was dying of cancer (still in her mid-forties) he went through a religious conversion, attended Mass every morning, bought novenas for her, invoked the help of the cloistered Carmelites (Teresa's order) around the world. None of his prayers or his gifts worked. God, it turned out, couldn't be bought. Michael James was disappointed. He really could not understand it. He had been raised to believe that God heard and answered prayers, if you prayed hard enough and long enough. Well, if God couldn't be bought the Church could be.

He sobbed through the funeral Mass which those in attendance thought strange because he had not been close to her for a long time and in fact couldn't stand her. He gave Mundelein money for a new Catholic high school which would bear her name, interred her remains in a huge mausoleum at Mount Carmel Cemetery, and seemed to forget about her. However, he carried her rosary in his pocket for the rest of his life.

Soon he returned to his pursuit of high-society women, the more dangerous a hunt, the more exquisitely haughty the prize, the more he liked it.

Then another woman entered his life, Nora Sweeny, the baby daughter of one of his most trusted errand boys. Her parents were killed in the crash of a Ford Trimotor while they were flying to Florida with some documents for "Mr. Cronin." Somehow the baby was thrown clear of the wreckage and landed in soft mud. Michael James Cronin sobbed at the funeral. When he learned that the baby's grandparents would send her to an orphanage (they had not "approved" of the marriage), he arranged to adopt her, hired women to take care of her and raise her, and sent her to the Convent of the Sacred Heart where the Madames (as they were called) allegedly turned young women into ladies. The Cronin sons had a little sister, who annoyed them, then charmed them, then became an appealing woman with whom they both fell in love. Michael James decreed that she would marry Paul because Sean would be a priest.

"Nora," Michael James would brag to his friends, "is smarter than the two boys put together."

She was smart enough to fall in love with Sean who was often kind and sweet with her. Such a marriage was, however, out of the question. Paul was much like his father, crude, insensitive, ruthless. However, he was not as shrewd as the old man and not as careful. So when Paul graduated from Notre Dame and entered flight training for the Marines (at his father's instance—a man destined for the presidency had to have a military record), he and Nora, a recent graduate of the Convent of the Sacred Heart, became engaged. They were married in 1952 after he finished flight training at Pensacola. Sean, recently ordained on the fast track in Rome, presided at the marriage. It was a bittersweet experience for Sean and Nora, but to disagree with Michael James was simply not possible. Even to think about disagreement was out of the question. Neither would know until much later that Paul had washed out at Pensacola. He was not a very good pilot and he was a very poor Marine. His father had picked up some important markers. Paul returned to flight training and managed to graduate.

Cardinal Mundelein was dead when Sean was old enough to go to the seminary, but Michael James did not trust the place. "They want to turn out dolts that can't think for themselves." So he dispatched Sean to St. Ignatius College Prep where he did learn to think and to express himself—not necessarily an asset for an upwardly bound cleric, but in the end very useful. Sean captained the football team, led the class academically, in his senior year his classmates voted him the "outstanding senior award," almost unanimously. He avoided romantic entanglements—after all, he would be a priest. Sometimes he even thought that he wanted to be a priest, but the decision was Michael James's to make, not his. For his part Michael James began to have second thoughts about his elder son. He flunked out at St. Ignatius and it took a lot of Michael James's clout to get him back in. He drank too much and fooled around with young women too much. Perhaps Sean ought to be directed toward the White House. However, one of Michael James's prime principles was that he never changed his mind. His instincts were infallible.

The Navy assigned Paul for carrier training to the USS

Constellation off San Diego. He did not kill himself or even seriously damage any of the Corsairs (F4U) the Marines were using for close ground support in those days. They were ungainly, clumsy aircraft, difficult to fly and dangerous to the pilot. Paul was approved for combat flights, as he knew he would be regardless of his performance. He was not sure he wanted to fly in combat support missions. You could get hurt doing such things. But he had never worried before. His father would get him out of this silly business soon. He missed his wife, whom he truly loved, though his love had not prevented various dalliances during his Marine training. He discovered on his first flight that he rather enjoyed killing little brown people on the ground. The 50-caliber guns on his wings tore them apart.

His third flight was his last. He had knocked out several Korean trucks and killed the troops fleeing from them. It was like the shooting gallery at Riverview. Then as he was pulling up for the return flight to the *Connie,* a jet appeared behind him and tore his fragile aircraft apart with cannon fire. As he bailed out he wondered wryly whether his father had any clout with anyone behind the iron curtain.

Sean, after his ordination in Rome by Archbishop Montini, returned to Chicago for a parish assignment. It was necessary, the Chicago Chancery assured him, that the young priest have pastoral experience before he returned to Rome for education in papal diplomacy in the College of Noble Ecclesiastics. Sean's heart sank when Nora drove him into a very old neighborhood of abandoned two flats with broken windows, decrepit bungalows, deserted cars up on blocks, and a woebegone rectory with a crumbling doorstop. The old man had not been able to buy a decent place for him. Then the door of the school next door to the rectory opened and black kids in school uniforms paraded in dutiful ranks out of the school. I think I'll like this place, Sean said. Nora helped him carry things into the house and promised to come back the next day and clean the place up.

"I was made for that kind of ministry," he would often confide in me. "I loved the people and they loved me. All I had to do was be myself. I should have stayed there."

The appointment to the College of Noble Ecclesiastics finally appeared and it was back to Rome for Sean Cronin. Paul Cronin came back from a Korean prison, thin, haggard, and not quite broken, a war hero with a medal of honor (for exactly what heroism it was never quite clear—perhaps for getting in the sights of a Russian-made MIG 19). Nora embraced him at the airport and presided over his recuperation, funded by the best medical treatments that Michael James's money could buy. He also bought a seat in the House of Representatives for him and four years later a seat in the United States Senate, both supported with the best political staff money could buy.

He continued his misbehavior with even more vigor than before. Women, parties, liquor, drugs, horses, sailboats—he owned a forty-two-footer on Lake Michigan and a smaller (but not much smaller) one in Chesapeake Bay. He did not work too hard at being a United States Senator, but his (still) youthful good looks and his quick wit created an image of a smart young man with a great future. In a chamber in which there were a lot of shenanigans, his reputation was safe if he didn't make any serious mistakes or encounter some bad luck.

After several successful assignments in which his brilliance and grace won him much praise, Sean was called back to Rome for the last session of the Vatican Council. "We beat those sons of bitches in the Curia," Sean would later tell me. "Then they stole it back." His brother and sister-in-law visited him in Rome as Paul was traveling on a "fact-finding" junket to Cairo and Tel Aviv. Paul VI had ordained Sean a bishop upon his arrival in Rome. He doubted that his father had bought Montini. It didn't matter. He had bought Sean many friends in Rome and his success in the curial bureaucracy earned more friends. Sean's job was to clean up the archives of the Council so that the record would be clear for history. The Curia was not enthused by the project, but they cooperated because of papal orders.

Two things about his foster sister were evident. She was unhappy and she was more beautiful than ever. Her two sons gave meaning and purpose to her life but she was nothing more than a decoration for her husband. Their father was slipping but not so badly yet that he couldn't bail Paul out of the trouble to which he seemed addicted—links to the mob, gambling debts, corruption charges, love affairs, bribery. Why did he need to seek illicit funds? Because it was fun, like shooting up little brown men with 50-caliber machine guns in Korea. Or converting your yacht temporarily into a high-class bordello—paid for by high-class lobbyists. He's a sociopath, she said, to Sean. Just like his father. Not nearly as smart.

It was during that visit to Rome, during a weekend trip to Portofino, that the affair began, an intense, passionate relationship which would remain with both of them for the rest of their lives. As best I can tell it never recurred. But the memory and the possibility would always be there.

Then Michael James had a severe heart attack. A Carmelite who was part of the St. Therese devotional team ministered to him. Sean flew back from Rome and Paul from DC, once Nora was able to reach him on his sailboat. She had been in Chicago for several months, taking care of Michael James's final moments. None of the three shed tears at the wake. The wizened old man in the casket did not look like the giant who had shaped their lives, for weal or woe, and whom they had always loved and hated.

Sean presided over the funeral at the Cathedral, despite the current Cardinal's claim that he had the right as the local ordinary.

"He was my *father*, Eminence."

That settled that.

Sean returned to Rome. The Pope asked him what was happening in Chicago. Sean was blunt. "Holiness, he is a sociopath."

113

Montini looked shocked but nodded his head slowly and said he had feared that.

A sociopathic father, a sociopathic brother, and a sociopathic Cardinal, Sean thought. For this I gave up Nora. He and Nora rarely saw each other and never alone. Neither of us quite recovered from the guilt, he once said to me. They did not correspond.

The Pope summoned him to his office one morning and told him that it was time to correct the mistake he had made in Chicago. He was sending him as auxiliary bishop to take care of the priests and the laity and to protect them as best he could. The Cardinal will not want you. You must tell him I insisted and he will have to talk to me. He will not do so. Sean argued that his position would be impossible in such circumstances. The Pope replied that he knew that Sean would obey the assignment.

I think that it was about then that Sean Patrick Cronin stopped giving a damn about the Vatican, the Curia, and the institutional Church. On occasion he may have lost the faith. But only temporarily.

I don't want you, I don't need you, Father, the Cardinal had said. Go back to Rome and tell him that. He anticipated you would say that, Eminence. He said it was an order. You might well complain to the Pope about my appointment. I don't suppose you want to do any work in the Archdiocese. Any work you assign me, I will do. You have a reputation for not being a total failure in working with the Negro, Father. If you say so, Eminence. Good, I will assign you to a parish where there are thousands of them and a school they can't pay for. I've never known why we should educate non-Catholics. Their former pastor just married a widow with three children. They tell me she is a retired whore. It will be interesting to see how well you do. Thank you, Cardinal. He sent you here to spy on me. I am not a spy, Eminence. However, I will respond honestly to the best of my ability to any questions His Holiness may ask me.

So he returned to Chicago, to a Cardinal who hated and feared him, to a priesthood that wasn't sure about him and resented him as an outsider, to a brother who seemed always to skate on thin ice and be dangerously close to the Outfit, to media that was suspicious of him, and to a lover who haunted him. However, his magic with African-Americans was better than ever. He won over the parish, and then most of his priestly colleagues, and then the media. The Cardinal simply ignored him. The Pope gave him assignments to check up on charges of large-scale malfeasance by the Cardinal. He replied that many people believed it, including prosecuting attorneys, but hard evidence was difficult to obtain. Criticism of his brother in the media became more serious. One Chicago paper editorialized, "Even though he is a decorated war hero, Senator Cronin increasingly appears to be the Senator from the Outfit. His image locally is of a man who despite his good looks and charm is somewhat shady. If the various prosecutors who are investigating his life and career have enough evidence to indict the Senator, it is time to act now, to grant him his day in court in which he can defend himself." Paul dismissed the editorial as media foolishness.

Sean had similar problems with grand jury investigations of the Cardinal. Someone in the chancery had been delivering documents to the United States Attorney which, naturally, were leaked to the media. The Pope called Sean again. Will there be a trial? If he lives long enough, Sean replied, there might be. The judge who impaneled the grand jury has delayed their meeting with the hope that the Cardinal will die first. Will your brother go to trial? I am afraid so.

Sean was as close to losing his faith then, he would later tell me, as he had ever been. Then it all fell in on him. The Cardinal died in the hospital. Sean appeared at the Cathedral for the funeral Mass and was asked not to appear on the altar because it would cause scandal among the people. The Cardinal never liked you. The priests don't like you. The people don't like you. Sean

115

Andrew M. Greeley

ignored him. A funny-looking little priest with thick glasses appeared next to him to assist him in donning his robes.

"Patently the consultors will elect you administrator," the young man remarked. "All other alternatives are unacceptable. You would do well to remember that the Vicar General loses his role upon the death of the Cardinal. The Chancellor, Father Ragowski, however remains in office. He has the keys to the house up by Lincoln Park and the office at the chancery. He will be loyal to anyone the consultors elect. I have secreted the key to the suite upstairs which the Cardinal never used. It is pointless for you to drive in from St. Cecilia every day. Patently your good friend over in the Vatican will appoint you as successor. No alternatives."

"What do you do?"

"Teach Latin at Quigley."

"Graduate school?"

"Ph.D. from Northwestern. Methodist school. Cardinal did not approve of that."

"You're a priest?"

"I believe so, but with the late Cardinal, one might have some doubts about the validity of my ordination. On the other hand that issue was settled at the time of one Donatus by redoubtable Augustine."

He peered at me suspiciously as he finished vesting.

"What's your name, Father?"

"Ryan."

"First name?"

"Call me Blackie. My middle name is Blackwood."

Thus did Sean Cronin encounter his future factotum.

"You took a big risk that day in the Cathedral sacristy, Blackwood," he said to me years later.

"I was not very good as a teacher of Latin."

The Diocesan consulters elected Sean as administrator, much to the dismay of the Vicar General who thought that the post belonged to him. Sean looked around the faces at the board. They were all older than he. Many seemed hostile. Why me, he asked. The only available choice who is not tainted. You can clean up some of the mess before the new man arrives. Most priests like you.

Sean was dazed. There would be a lot of mess to clean up, including the Cardinal's cousin in residence at the house. It was all pointless. The Church was sick unto death. Time to get out. Finally. He encountered the virtually invisible little priest as he prepared to leave the Cathedral. TV cameras were waiting outside.

"Arguably you will say to those vultures that you will do your best to be honest and fair to everyone during the interregnum. They will ask you whether you expect to be the new Archbishop. You will laugh as you say not a chance. What about the charges against your brother? Like everyone else you will say that he is innocent until proven guilty. Then you will leave and enter the car I have provided for you at the entrance to the rectory. You have a funeral to attend at Queen of Heaven where your father and mother, God be good to both of them, were buried. It would be wise to permit the former Vicar General, as we now must call him, to preside over the obsequies. I assume you will want to pray at your family graveside."

"See to it, Blackwood."

And the rest, as one might say, was history. It was not a history that I was seeking in those days, however. During the next two years, he presided over many arguments at the Cathedral dinner table, testing the wit and intelligence of the priests in the rectory. I kept my own counsel because I was not in the race. He would ask me occasionally what I thought. I generally pleaded that I knew very little save Latin grammar. Then one day he informed me that I would be the new pastor (once called the rector) of the Cathedral. I told him that I did not want to be rector of the Cathedral.

"You've taught Latin too long," he informed me. "This place

117

needs spiffing up, physically and intellectually. See to it, Black-wood."

And thus it started.

Senator Paul Cronin was indicted the following week in the federal district court in Washington. He flew immediately to Chicago, drove to New Buffalo, boarded his yacht *Nora Jane*, and sailed immediately into one of the worst late-spring storms in memory. Both the boat and the Senator disappeared.

"He knew what he was doing, Blackwood. He always listened to the weather forecasts. He was making a bet, a long-shot bet. If he made it to Chicago through the storm, God wanted him to live."

The headlines, now on the front page of the *New York Times*, proclaimed, "Indicted Senator Missing in Lake Michigan Storm." The assumption was that he had devised an ingenious method for escaping from the United States Attorney for the Northern District of Illinois. The hunt for Paul Cronin promised to be good copy for days, weeks, even years to come. However, his bloated body washed up on the sands of Beverly Shores within the week.

The funeral took place at the Cathedral in the District as we used to call it before it became the Beltway. I was deputed to be the spear carrier, invisible to all, save for the widow who noticed everyone. She actually smiled at me. For Nora Jane Sweeny Cronin I was never the little man who wasn't there again today. I noted the restrained tenderness between the two of them at the wake and funeral at Arlington National Cemetery where he was buried with full honors as was fitting for a Medal of Honor hero. Patently the virtuous Nora was protecting her brother-in-law from questions by the Chicago media whether he would resign as administrator. His response, which I had suggested, was that he would serve until a new Archbishop would come to Chicago. Asked if he would be that person, he laughed and said you gotta be kidding.

Nora Cronin, I concluded, was a beautiful woman with

grace, courage, and enormous intelligence. She would have made a better senator than her husband and a better bishop than her brother-in-law—though in these times that would not be possible.

The details of the rest of the interregnum are irrelevant and its most intimate dimensions are only my surmise. Sean Cronin may have lost temporarily all his faith. He may have suggested to Nora that he would resign from the priesthood when the new man arrived and they would marry. He never had a vocation anyway. It was his father's from day one. Nora's response was that the Governor of Illinois intended to appoint her to fill out her husband's term in the Senate and that she would accept the appointment. He would doubtless be named Archbishop of Chicago and he should accept that appointment. It was far too late for any other option.

They would, she may have said or he may have said, always love one another.

Soap opera stuff? Perhaps. Sorry about that.

She served with distinction for two terms, her husband's unfinished term, and one which she won on her own. The media tried not to like her, especially some of the more feline of the news hens. They gave it up because everyone loved Nora. She married a famous East Coast sportswriter noted for his kindness to players and his wit. He helped her through the adolescence of her sons who grew up to be fine young men. "Not much Cronin in either of them, thanks be to God," their Uncle Sean said.

When her second term ended, and her sons were happily married (to young women from Chicago) and her husband dead, Nora returned to the shores of Lake Michigan to be with her children and grandchildren and administer the vast resources of the Cronin Family Foundation. She and Sean encountered one another often, usually in my presence. The magic was still there but damped down to wait for whatever joys Judgment Day might bring.

10

Senator Nora Cronin was one of those women who believed that men were quite incapable of taking care of themselves.

"Keep an eye on him for me, Blackie," she said once with a knowing wink. "He drives himself too hard. You and I may have to form an alliance someday to slow him down."

"I have essayed that task," I remarked, "with little success. I agree that it must be a team effort. There are a number of problems . . . He works too hard, he sleeps poorly, he loses his temper frequently, he drinks too much coffee, and too much of the creature, he doesn't take time off, and he won't listen to any-one else's advice. He smokes too many cigars. Otherwise he is a normal American celibate male."

"Patently," she said, mocking my favorite word.

Milord Cronin had turned the Archdiocese around, restored the morale of priests (insofar as our self-pitying group is capable of good collective morale), and won their support and even affec-tion, brought lay folks into administration, put competent women in positions of power, opened new schools, raised money for a foundation to support Catholic schools, defended the rights of minorities, including Blacks, Hispanics, and gays ("The Church believes that no one chooses a sexual orientation willingly"), acted quickly in the sexual abuse crisis, and suffered no fools gladly (save for this correspondent). He became adept at fending off the media with charm and wit. He hassled the Vatican and the American bishops constantly, firing off astringent memos every time they did something with which he disagreed or of which he disapproved. Your boss, Blackie, one of his colleagues said to me, is one mean, nasty son of a bitch.

Only, I protested, when you get to know him.

However, the problem arose dramatically when under the Roman midday sun (when according to legend only mad dogs and Englishmen go out) Cardinal Sean Cronin collapsed in the center of the Piazza San Pietro. Nora and I confronted him in his room in the Gemelli Clinic where Popes tend to die.

"Sean Patrick Cronin, Blackie and I have decided we don't want you to die just yet. So you must reform your life beginning yesterday. Is that not our position, Blackie?"

"Blatantly."

"One cup of coffee in the morning, one small tumbler of whiskey every night, no more cigars, regular exercise every day, a day off once a week when you see no staff members except Blackie and take no phone calls. No sudden trips to Rome without our permission. A vacation every summer and every winter, better temper control. Let me get mad for you. Isn't that right, Blackie?"

"Yes, ma'am."

"We will tolerate no exceptions, isn't that right, Blackie?"

"Inarguably."

"Why?" he asked glumly.

"Because we want you to live out your appointed days."

"Why?"

"Because the world would be a poorer place without you. Do you agree with our program?"

"Do I have a choice?" He smiled faintly.

"No."

"No way."

"Will you move into the Cathedral rectory to check up on me?"

"For the present, I'll trust Blackie to keep an eye on you."

A touch of tease there, I thought.

"OK."

He kept our rules and his health and disposition improved enormously.

He announced the rules in detail to the media at a press conference. "If any of you see me violating any of them, you should report me to Blackie or my sister."

I noticed—and I was not the only one—that Nora was around him more often than before. She made common cause with the Megan so he could not escape without her knowing about it.

If anyone whispered about the relationship, they kept it to themselves.

Knowing about the past I was mildly uneasy. They were both handsome vigorous people, capable, I daresay, of sexual arousal and its consequences.

"Don't worry, Blackie," he said once. "If I had courted her when I was at Ignatius or at the Dome, I could have, would have, married her. Paul was no competition. I didn't have a vocation then, but Dad was insistent that I go to Rome and be a priest . . . But I do have a vocation now."

That was that.

I pondered the various human loves over which I was currently presiding—Nora and Sean Cronin; Joseph John Ryan and Margaret Anne Nolan; Doña Teresa and Don Leandro. Love was a painful, difficult, discouraging affair. Sometimes, many times, the payoff hardly seemed worth the effort. Why then did the Deity, in his infinite wisdom, choose this messy relationship as the prime metaphor for Himself? Why did St. Paul and St. John and John Paul II and Benedict XV ratify and proclaim this choice?

Why did not any of them insist at great length about the anguish of its messiness? Why did Augustine, the only father of the Church to be exercised on the subject (and knew of it personally from his marriage career in which he played the role of a heel), end up in effect denying the metaphor or trying to sanitize it?

And why did he not throw in all the qualifications that we use today to hedge the intensity of passion?

What good was it doing for the Cronins who had so much bad history with it?

How dare you challenge the Lord your God? How dare you say that the love today between Sean and Nora was not a God-given grace that had made him one of the greats of the contemporary hierarchy? How dare you doubt that grace has kept him alive? Already, all right, enough!

I punched in his private number.

"Cronin."

"Blackie."

"I suppose you're part of the conspiracy."

"I organized it."

Silence.

"What the hell did you do that for? Those witches circle around me muttering their incantations. They won't let a man die peacefully."

"I believe Father Coyne may be involved."

"Sure, but that lineup of powerful, dominating women is enough to send a man to his grave even if he isn't exhausted!"

"They are at least not attractive women."

"Nags, hags, bags."

"If you make those charges it will only increase their fury."

"I don't know which is worse, that young witch who knows what's going to happen if I don't move over to Northwestern and looks like she's ready to burst into tears. Or your smart-ass sister who analyzes unfavorably my resistance to their wisdom; or Nora . . ."

"Your constant lover."

"I suppose so . . . OK, Blackie, what's your argument?"

"Same as theirs. I don't want you to die just yet."

"Why the hell not? You'll become the Archbishop of Chicago, and very shortly the Cardinal Archbishop? What more do you want?"

"I was around when you took over. I whispered wise strategies from the very beginning."

"I can't deny that."

"Very well, I want you around whispering in my ear when I take over."

"Nuala can arrange a channel from heaven on which we can communicate."

"I am serious."

"You want me to resign now so I can be your éminence gris?"

"Gray is not the color I'm thinking of."

"Why me?"

"My biological father died too young; I still needed his advice. It is unacceptable that you do the same thing."

"Oh."

"We all need you, Sean Patrick Cronin, myself included. We all love you, please don't leave us."

"Oh . . ."

Silence.

"I can't live forever, Blackwood."

"You can live some years longer."

Renewed silence.

"All right. . . . What should I do?"

"Call my sister and have her set up the situation at Northwestern. Call Father Coyne and tell him. Also make him administrator pro tem till I come back."

"Damn you, Blackwood . . . OK. You win. *This time.*"

I sighed. My hands were wet, my fingers trembling. I knew

the man well. My risky strategy—appealing to him as the father figure I needed—had worked.

Thank you, I whispered to himself. Now it's up to the cardiologists. And to you.

I waited ten minutes and then pushed my sister's code.

"Dr. Ryan."

Both authoritative and sympathetic.

"Blackie."

"What the hell did you tell him?"

"Someday I'll tell you."

"We've got it all set up. I don't think there's any immediate danger, but we'll have a cardiologist there when he arrives."

"Good."

"We're all crying, Nora, Nuala Anne, and myself."

"Good on you, as herself would say."

"Nora isn't crying anymore."

They really were lovers, weren't they? Someday I'd ask my sister about her opinions on celibacy. My own suspicion about Nora and Sean Cronin was that a marriage between them would have never lasted. But what did I know?

The next morning my nephew and his promised one and I ventured up from Seville to Cordoba, the site of the Caliphate of Muslim Spain until the Moors tore apart their country with internal conflicts—and the Christians began to get their act together. Cordoba was a center of Islamic culture, architecture, poetry, philosophy, and what was still the second-largest mosque in the world. When San Fernando occupied Cordoba (the local prince took one look at the size of the Castilian army and decided to deal) he promised religious freedom to Muslims and that he wouldn't destroy the mosque (as he did later on when he captured Seville). However, hundreds of years later, his descendent Don Carlos (Charles I in Spain, Charles V in the Holy Roman

Empire) approved and later regretted a plan to build a Catholic Cathedral inside the mosque, a truly weird idea. I had always been interested in how it worked out. I would not have ventured to Spain to view it but now that I was here I figured I might as well take a look.

We were a sleepy-eyed threesome when we entered the gleaming new train stations in Seville and boarded the gleaming new fast train. Despite La Giralda and the Cathedral and the remnants of reverence for the Generalissimo in Spain, everything seemed brand-new. The lovely Teresa and her problems were a remnant of a rapidly fading past.

The young people were tired because they had stayed up for the *paseo* last night without a siesta in the afternoon.

"Why should we take a nap when we're in such a fascinating place?" Peggy Anne demanded. "We can sleep anytime back home."

"Because the locals have organized their lives around the nap. They don't wake up in the morning feeling goofy."

"I don't feel goofy! I'm raring to go! I love riding trains, though I don't do it very much!"

Why do it when you own your own Cessna 310 Bravo and have available your own Gulfstream 560?

However, when the train had barely slipped out of the station and into the morning fog, as quietly and as stealthily as a burglar escaping the scene of a crime, Peggy Anne rested her head on her young man's shoulder and redeployed to the Land of Nod. He put his arm around her shoulders and cradled her with an amused and affectionate smile.

I on the other hand was sleepy because I had spent a restless night haunted by dreams of the colorful characters I had agonized about before my inspired call to Milord Cronin, for which inspiration I once again thanked the Deity. There had been no need for my unconscious to conflate Nora, Teresa, and Peggy Anne. However, since it has a will of its own, it nonetheless conflated them. I'm not responsible for all three, I informed the Deity, who paid no attention to me at all. Joseph will take care of her, I insisted. You are her spiritual director came the reply.

However, the smooth, hypnotic movement of the train eased me into my eye-resting mode. Almost instantly, it seemed, an awed young female voice across the aisle exclaimed, "Oh, Uncle Blackie, it's so beautiful!"

I pried open my resistant eyes and, sure enough, it was beautiful—orange groves, wheat fields, vineyards, all in orderly rows under a clear blue sky and bright sun, a land still flourishing despite all the invading armies that had swept back and forth through the millennia, a rich gift to the rocky Iberian peninsula. No wonder they had come from rocky Phoenicia and desert Egypt to marvel at its fertile beauty. And to seek gold and silver in its mines.

"Take a train west from Chicago to Omaha," I grumbled, "and you will see the same beauty."

"The farmhouses aren't as beautiful as those white haciendas."

"Which were built by slaves and serfs and now farm workers who not so long ago were anarchists shooting priests and nuns."

"This is one strange country," Joseph said as he released his promised bride from his protective arm. "Maybe they'd think we're strange."

"Yes, but, Uncle Blackie, they are *really* strange!"

"How so?"

"Well take Teresa . . ."

"Ah!"

"She seems as modern as any American mom, loves her daughter but doesn't spoil her, wears the most fashionable clothes, exercises every day, runs that foundation like my dad runs Avel, sleeps with a man she hasn't married."

"Yet."

"Whatever."

"Looks great in a two-piece swimsuit," Joseph added.

"Yet she still is, like totally, part of the Middle Ages."

"Ah."

"I mean she's superstitious, believes in bad luck, wears medals, prays to the patron saint of women who want babies that she will have a son with Leandro, though their love is a great sin, is terrified of hell and still believes she must respect her aunt and uncle who are like total assholes, and blesses herself with holy water before she leaves her house and after she comes home when she's made love with Leandro."

I sighed inwardly.

"Does her daughter offer any explanation for this puzzling behavior?"

"She just shrugs and says that's the way she is and that's why she loves her so much."

"Umm."

"I'm not being critical. I love her too. I think she's a great mom, but I can't figure it out."

"I don't suppose anyone has told you," Joseph intervened, "that we went to court with the two of them yesterday. As far as I could tell the judge said that he had grave doubts about the legality of her father's will and would rule on that definitively soon. However for the moment he forbade Marco and Inez from interfering in the lives of either Teresa or Mary Louise, 'under pain of severe penalties,' whatever that means."

"Leandro and his assistant were like totally pleased," Peggy Anne said, continuing the story. "Isidoro said it was a twenty-point lead with a half minute to go. But poor Teresa was depressed. It would go on forever. They would never leave the house. She would have to respect them because they were the only family she had. It would go on forever."

"We had dinner with them later on," Joseph said. "A celebration. Teresa tried to celebrate because everyone else was happy. But you could tell that she felt their big victory was a defeat. I don't get it."

"We went on the *paseo* which is kind of fun, but I could get bored with it pretty quickly. Teresa and Leandro excused themselves because they both had lots of work in the morning. Mary Louise told us that they weren't going back to the house. It would be bad luck to make love there. They had a room above a bar in Santa Cruz. They didn't make love *every* night. Some nights they just slept in each other's arms which is a lot of fun too . . . I suppose it is."

"So I have been told."

"Am I being silly, Uncle Blackie?"

"Not at all, Peggy Anne. Doña Teresa lives in two worlds—the Spain of her namesake and John of the Cross. And the world you live in. They are very different. She has built a combination of them which fits her situation and holds it together fiercely, though doubtless with considerable strain. Mind you some of her values and behavior are precious and ought not to be lost. It is good to pray to the saints, good to remind yourself of your baptism when you go out. It is good to wear medals which are a sign of faith. It is good to be modest in your love relationships, good to respect your family."

Margaret had frowned during this recitation.

"Still . . ."

"Teresa Maria is caught in a transition which has affected much of the world, especially the Catholic world. Many of us, most of us in some places, go to university. We are taught by our teachers to think for ourselves. Our parents expect it up to a point too. But the old habits of doing what we're told persist. With any good fortune we are able to combine the old and the new with some ease. Catholicism has permeable boundaries, room for everyone. Maria Luisa's mother is maybe a generation behind Maria Luisa and maybe two generations behind you. She never had a chance when growing up to figure things out. Then she went to the University, did flamenco in Triana, and fell in love from a distance with Don Leandro. Then her father and her aunt ended that life for her. She was pulled back into the nineteenth if not the seventeenth century."

"She's got to get out of that house and marry Leandro properly!"

"Advice which the Cardinal has given her and I too in my own clumsy way. This is a crucial time for her. We must pray for her that she will be able to absorb the grace which is inundating her."

"Will she, Uncle Blackie?"

"Please God."

Then the train sneaked into the brand-new gleaming station in Cordoba. What, I wondered, would Abdul Rahman II and his son Abdul Rahman III think of both the train and the station, to say nothing of what the infidels had done to his lovely mosque.

"It doesn't look all that big," Peggy Ann murmured as we stood in the orange grove outside the mosque. "Is it still a mosque?"

"Do you mean can Muslims still pray in it? Their religion would say sure. But if they took off their shoes and washed their feet in the courtyard, the police would probably keep them out. If they prostrated themselves in front of the Mihrab—the prayer niche—they would be quietly asked to move. Recently an Iman at an interreligious meeting did so without any objections. Then a local Muslim leader asked if they could pray there at least several times a year. The local bishop said he was afraid it would cause confusion among the simple people. That's what bishops always say when they don't want to do something . . ."

"Not Cardinal Sean!"

"Certainly not. They can of course pray in here anytime they want, just so long as they don't look like they're praying."

"Gross!"

"I would not be surprised in years to come if the Church suffers another burst of amnesia and says why not, with the help of God."

I added the Muslim aspiration to Allah, just so the Deity would know that I was politically correct in such matters.

Inside the place was a beautiful mess. It might have made more sense if San Fernando had simply consecrated the building as a church, thus keeping his promise not to tear it down and making it impossible for his descendants to try a shotgun marriage between two faiths that weren't ready for it and are not ready for it now. Yet some of the breathtaking multicolored marble arches were made from the ruins of the Roman-Visigoth cathedral beneath it, just as elements in that building were surely remnants of the shrine of Lug, the Irish fertility god. Both must have been beautiful because in this part of the world with its lasting cultural traditions they didn't build anything that wasn't beautiful.

Except for cathedrals inside of mosques!

Maybe someday there would be no more problem between Catholics and Muslims than those we have today with the Lutherans and the Southern Baptists.

"They can't have statues or saints or angels or stained glass or the Madonna, can they, Joseph?"

Since he was almost a theologian, certified by the University of Chicago, he was the one to whom the question should properly be addressed. Clever young woman.

"The Prophet picked up from the Jewish refugees with whom he lived an absolute opposition to idols. And stained glass is an idol. But they have angels and saints and shrines and great devotion to the Blessed Mother, though without any statues to her. In fact there are more lines in the Holy Koran about her than in the New Testament."

"Well, Uncle Blackie, it looks like I'll be getting lessons in theology for the rest of my life!"

"It's what they call value-added."

We walked through the Cathedral which was not much like the one in Seville, not to say Chartres or Cologne, to give full vent to my prejudices. We knelt in front of the Blessed Sacrament following Peggy Anne's good example and prayed as long as she wanted to pray, which was usually pretty long. I prayed for them, well-balanced and well-matched young people with great hopes and dreams for the future. They would be astonished by the problems of the intimate life as the years went by, on occasion almost overwhelmed. Yet their love would flower and grow. Take good care of them for me, I instructed the Lord God. But he would do that anyway.

We ate some tapas and wandered around Cordoba, a beautiful place, but I had seen enough Moorish ruins and read enough lamentations about the destruction of the Caliphate in the guidebooks to last me a lifetime. None of the books, written mostly by the Brits, bother to weep for the losses of Visigoths, Hispano-Roman or Celtic culture.

They insisted on taking me to supper at their Moorish hotel for roast beef, Andalusian style. It was quite tasty but I preferred it American style. They wondered when I wanted to return to Chicago. Soon, I said, very soon. We all pined for the sight of Lake Michigan. There would, however, be some delays.

II

A knock on the door.

"May I come in?"

Don Diego. I was kneeling on the prie-dieu that they had thoughtfully provided for me.

I had been nodding over my morning prayers, not yet fully aware of where I was.

"Cierto."

He entered, dressed in a black cassock with crimson buttons, and promptly sank into my chair.

"There have been three attempts on the life of Doña Teresa Maria. I was called to John XXIII Hospital several hours ago. She has been seriously injured, but the doctors expect her to recover. It remains uncertain. Maria Luisa, the doctors say, saved her life."

"Who?"

"We do not know. She is still mostly unconscious. Maria Luisa blames the three guests. But there is no evidence. Also the killer or killers entered her bedroom even though the door was locked and only she and Maria Luisa had keys. The police are there guarding her and waiting till she is fully awake. Also two senior doctors, two residents, and five nurses." He grinned wryly. "It is her hospital. They all worship her."

"Three attempts?"

"She was poisoned. Strong barbiturates in her final glass of sherry at the end of the day. A knife stuck into her belly. A gunshot that creased her head . . . whoever it was really wanted to kill her."

"The relatives should be suspected!"

"They apparently have alibis. The police are interested in Don Leandro. Maria Luisa insists that he does not have a key. She argues that he and her mother meet every night in a small apartment above a café in the Santa Cruz."

"One would expect her to be discreet."

"She asked for me as soon as she was brought in. The knife was still in her. Maria Luisa, who desires to be a doctor, would not let the ambulance attendants remove it, lest it cause a catastrophic hemorrhage. She held her mother's hand while the doctors removed it from her intestines and I heard her confession. Before they gave her a sedative, she asked me to send you over. I take care of her sins, you take care of her soul. My task is much easier." He grinned. "Please wear a cassock and something purple . . . I told them you are an Archbishop."

I produced my cassock with the purple buttons that I had kept secret.

"A descendant of Isabella the Catholic is entitled to purple buttons."

He laughed.

"She is a brave and wonderful woman, Padrecito Negro. And her daughter is a fearsome and admirable child."

I dressed in my lightweight cassock and pried out my biretta with the purple pompom.

My cell phone rang. At this hour of the morning?

"Padre Ryan. *Buenos dias.*"

" 'Tis yourself."

Nuala Anne.

"How you keeping?"

"Never better."

"And the woman you're taking care of?"

No point in asking her how she knew. She wouldn't be able to answer the question.

"Someone tried to kill her last night. She's surviving."

"Sure, her daughter is a fearsome young woman, isn't she now?"

" 'Tis true."

"What's her name?"

"Mother or daughter?"

"Don't I want to know both?"

"Teresa Maria is the mother. Maria Luisa the fearsome child."

"Didn't she save her mother's life?"

"She did."

I was shivering. Even for Nuala Anne this was over the wall and round the bend.

"My future niece calls them Teresa and Mary Louise."

"That one would, wouldn't she now?"

"How's Cardinal Sean keeping?"

"Och, don't worry about that one. Won't he be outliving the lot of us. Still it was good you made him go to hospital."

Why should I bother making calls to Chicago?

"Take care of them, Blackie. They'll need your help. They're not out of danger yet. Stay there till after the wedding."

"I will. . . . Did you give her any message?"

"Wouldn't I have been a terrible eejit altogether if I didn't. I told her to do what you tell her to do because Father Blackie is always right."

"That was helpful."

"Sure, she knew it anyway. . . . Och, why don't you tell her that she'll have a fine healthy son."

"I don't think she's pregnant."

"I never said she was, did I?"

"Showing off again, Nuala Anne!"

She chuckled because she had a reputation of knowing a child's gender before the baby was conceived.

"Are you over here now."

"Sure, am I not in my own bed with me lovin' husband. Why would I be after going to Spain?"

She hung up.

And herself having a grand time altogether.

These experiences were not always happy for her. This one was for some reason great fun.

The Cardinal's limo, a small Lexus driven by the always efficient Don Pedro, awaited me. He drove me to the new hospital of Blessed John XXIII where the cops at the door—in their gray fatigues and baseball caps—greeted me with some reservation, purple buttons and purple pompom notwithstanding.

"Tell Señorita Maria Luisa that El Padrecito Negro is here."

The cop called his buddies upstairs and told them, without much confidence. In a moment Mary Louise herself appeared and embraced me.

"Padrecito!"

She led me through the door and I bowed to the cops.

"*Muchas gracias,* señores!"

"*De nada.*" They grinned as they bowed back.

"Mama is badly hurt, but she will survive," Maria Luisa babbled as we entered the elevator. She clung to my arm as we rode up to the top floor.

"The door was locked to our apartment. I used my key to try to open it. But there was another key jammed inside it. Mama had locked it. I pounded the door, I screamed. She did not answer. I screamed again. Candida, the maid who is a security guard, came. We both tried to force the door open. Then we summoned Enrico and Nicalu, the other two guards, and we finally pushed the door open. Mama was lying naked on the bed, her gown torn away and this big knife was sticking out of her stomach and her head was bleeding. I ordered the guards not to touch the knife because I knew that would cause a torrent of blood. Then I called an ambulance and gave them the same order. They looked at me like I was loco. I told them I was in medical school—which is not yet true—but they believed me. We brought her here and the doctors removed the knife and stitched her up. They told me that I had saved her life. I was not modest, Padrecito Negro. I said that I knew *that*."

"Naturally."

Her tears turned to laughter as we left the elevator.

"I will never let Mama forget it as long as she lives."

"And that will be a long time!"

"*Sí,* Padre, *SÍ!*"

"There are only two keys to the apartment, one for you and one for your mother?"

"*Sí* . . . the police say that Don Leandro must have one. But he does NOT. Mama would not make love in that ugly old place. They have a room above the Bar Giralda for love, though sometimes they are perfectly happy just to be in each other's arms . . . that is possible, Padrecito?"

"That's what people tell me."

We entered an anteroom filled with police in their gray uniforms and medical personnel, the latter watching a bank of monitors. Like the rest of the hospital, it was bright, clean, and new. The monitors beeped reassuringly. Maria Luisa glanced at them and nodded.

"She continues to do well."

A young MD, dazzled by this gorgeous and authoritative young woman, nodded. "Yes, Señorita Maria Luisa. She is resilient."

"It runs in the family."

She caught my eye and shrugged.

"Sometimes," she whispered.

The hospital room itself was more like a parlor in an expensive apartment or a luxury hotel, a broad window overlooking the Guadalquivir, with La Giralda in the far corner so we would know where we were; excellent Moorish carpets and matching drapes; and an array of inviting chairs and sofas; and even a seventy-two-inch, wall-mounted television.

A hospital room, nonetheless, was a hospital room.

"Mama designed this room for herself. She thought perhaps she would die in it. She wanted the mourners to be comfortable."

She introduced me to the two doctors and two nurses who circled the bed at a respectful distance.

I was Monsignor Reeyan, Archbishop of Chicago, and Mama's spiritual director.

The medicos were duly impressed. Two of them approached to kiss my ring and I pulled it back with my number one smile, which I have designed to relieve embarrassment in such situations.

"Padrecito Negro, you have come at last . . . I know I am going to die."

She was talking softly. I knelt at the side of the bed so I could hear her.

"Doña Teresa, you are not going to die. I forbid you to think that way."

"*Sí,* Padre."

A touch of her sunny smile.

"The mother of Jesus came to see me, I think when they were sewing me up. She told me that I would not die, that I should do whatever you told me to do, and that I would give birth to a healthy son."

So now Nuala Anne was the mother of Jesus and herself not looking Jewish either.

"Congratulations!"

"I am not pregnant, Padrecito," she said dolefully. "The Virgin said she knew about such matters before they happen."

Now Nuala Anne was a virgin, news to her husband Dermot Michael Coyne and her four children. Yet in Teresa Maria's world who else comes to a dying woman in her dreams? The real Mother of Jesus would not mind. Quite the contrary, she would be amused.

"I'm sure she does."

She was silent for a few moments and shut her eyes. Then with great effort opened them again.

"Are you there, Padrecito Negro?"

"Where else would I be, Doña Maria Teresa?"

"I have one horrible sin to confess."

"Don Diego absolved you of all your sins."

"I don't think I told him this one . . . I had a terrible argument with Leandro in the Bar Giralda. He wanted me to sign the papers for the arrangement with my relatives. We would provide money . . . they need to stay out of jail . . ." She paused, struggling to reach her thoughts. ". . . and they would leave the house and renounce their claim on us. I told him I wouldn't sign it. He insisted. I lost my temper and hit him and kicked him and called him many names and stormed out of the bar. I told him that he was not my husband and never would be and that he had no rights over me. He could not tell me what to do."

"Ah . . ."

"I signed the papers before I left, of course."

"Naturalmente."

"He was wrong, wasn't he?"

"You know better than that . . ."

She closed her eyes for a moment.

"He is my lover, not my husband, he has no authority . . ."

"Does not authority come with love at least to make strong suggestions? Does not love give you authority over him?"

She nodded.

"*Sí*, Padre. I order him around often, like he is a servant."

"You signed the agreement?"

"Yes, I went back and signed it. Then I slapped his face and told him I did not want to see him ever again."

"Which you did not mean?"

"No, Padrecito, *por supesto no.* But I have lost him forever. He will never forgive me."

"*Absurdo,* Teresa. Certainly he will forgive you. You must, however, apologize to him as soon as he comes to visit."

"He will not visit me. I know that. I humiliated him in public."

"Go back to sleep," I said.

"*Sí,* Padre."

I stood up and approached the white-haired doctor who was apparently in charge.

"Is the sleep the result of a sedative you gave her?"

"No, Monsignor. Apparently someone put powerful barbiturates into her sherry. We were able to remove the knife and insert the sutures without administering any more sedatives. In fact, it would have been dangerous to do so. She felt no pain."

"It is a wonder that the poison did not kill her. And the trauma."

The doctor lifted his shoulders.

"Monsigneur, Doña Teresa is a woman with enormous resilience. She will recover from this. It is interesting"—he glanced at the monitors above the bed—"now that you have talked to her, she rests more easily."

"Priests are occasionally useful."

"I am an anticlerical and even I know that."

I adjourned to a couch by the window. Santa Cruz and the Cathedral Plaza were just beneath us. I couldn't quite find Bar Giralda. It must have been quite a fight. I hope it didn't make the papers. The Seville papers had always been respectful of Doña Teresa. A murder story could change that.

As I watched, a crowd of cops and TV cameras surrounded a man who wanted to get into the hospital. Don Leandro. A good thing, I thought, that she had signed the papers.

I walked over to the daughter who was sitting at her mother's bed, keeping cool towels on her forehead.

"Señora Doctora, the police are preventing Don Leandro from entering."

"Bastards," she snapped as she strode over to the sergeant who seemed to be in charge and snapped her orders. He nodded his obedience and picked up his radio.

La Doctora looked at me and grinned. She was having a good time. It wouldn't last but that would be all right because her mother would be recovering.

Don Leandro was escorted into the room by two cops, one holding each arm. He looked a little worn, like a man on a perhaps terminal hangover. His tie was missing, his suit rumpled, his shirt soiled with wine stains, his face unshaven, his eyes bloodshot. Tears poured down his cheeks as Maria Luisa embraced him.

"Mamacita is recovering, she will be fine. She is resting well after talking to El Padrecito Negro. Don Diego heard her confession earlier and administered the Sacrament of the sick . . ."

"Where were you last night?" the sergeant demanded briskly.

"I was in the Bar Giralda all night, *Sargento*. La Doña and I had a terrible fight, about which you have heard no doubt. She left and I began to sleep. The owner woke me up and I drank more. I left only a half hour ago. You might ask the owner. He will tell you."

The sergeant made a phone call, to higher officials no doubt, closed his mobile, and slipped away. Good police work. Check the alibis immediately. Leandro continued to cling to her. The cops backed away. Maria Luisa poured out her story. For the first time since he had entered the suite, Don Leandro smiled.

"Don Leandro, you are a very handsome man. I was happy that Mamacita fell in love with you. I will always be a respectful stepdaughter to you. But I have to say that now you look terrible.

She acts up sometimes, not often. Just laugh at her and she'll come crawling back."

She led him over to the bed. I slipped in behind him, just to remind her of the spiritual director's instruction.

"Teresa," he said gently, kneeling at the side of the bed.

She stirred but did not open her eyes.

"Mama," the daughter said briskly, "Don Leandro is here."

Teresa looked up, blinked, and then reached her hand to touch his face.

"Leandro, what did they do to you?"

"I have a hangover, beloved. First time since I was at the University."

"He drank all night at Bar Giralda because you fought with him."

The daughter was a stern angel.

Teresa closed her eyes, took her breath, and began to talk.

"El Padrecito Negro says I must apologize to you. Of course you have rights over me because of our love and I over you because of the same love. You did nothing wrong by insisting I sign the document I had agreed to. Maria Luisa will tell you that sometimes I am intolerable. Pay no attention to me, please I beg you. I knew when I walked away the second time that I would have to fall on my knees this morning . . ." Her voice faded. "I would have too, if this hadn't happened . . ."

Leandro reached his hand toward her face and touched her lips with his fingers, gently, playfully, tenderly as if her face were a delicate musical instrument. She smiled compliantly and dozed off again, his hand still held in hers.

The sergeant entered the room and with a wave of his hands and a broad smile signaled that Don Leandro was clean.

"Leandro, Mama designed this suite so that people could relax at her deathbed. I have a room and a shower and I'll get a clean shirt for you while you sleep."

I intervened before they left.

"Don Leandro, did you ever have a key to her apartment?"

"*Cierto non!* I did not ask for it and she did not offer it to me. Once it became clear to me that it was not . . . a single event, I rented the tiny apartment in Santa Cruz. I've never been inside the *palacio.*"

"I thought as much."

Blackie Ryan had done his work for the day. Now it was time for him to ride over the mountains and into the sunset.

12

"We have received this interesting e-mail from Superintendent Miguel Casey. I believed you're acquainted with him, Padre?" Manuelo Lopez, the Investigating Judge (a combination of State's Attorney and grand jury), said.

"He is a cousin," I said.

"You are aware that he is one of the best authorities on police work in all the world?"

The second question came from Pepe Garcia, the chief detective of the SPS, Seville police force.

"I think I had heard that once or twice."

"His Reliable Security Company is universally respected. Interpol works with them frequently as do many police agencies in Europe which do not want to be caught up in the bureaucracy of your FBI."

Both men were young, darkly handsome with thin mustaches, Italian suits, regimental ties, and spotless white shirts. They were able professionals rising in the ranks of the new Spanish criminal justice system, thin, sleek, polished. One of them, I was told, was a member of the PP and the other of the PS. I could not figure out as I worked with them which was left and which right (both I thought were resolute anticlericals). It didn't much matter because there could be no hint of corruption or favoritism in an investigation of a vicious attempt to murder such an important national celebrity as Doña Teresa Maria Romero y Avila. Did not the papers say that she was a national resource? A national resource about whom no one much cared until she was almost dead!

"Don Diego told us that we might write him about your skills in these matters," the judge said shyly.

"We received this e-mail today in response," the Juiz said softly.

> *I'm delighted to tell the truth about Archbishop John Blackwood Ryan, with whom I have worked for many years. He is a good priest and a holy man. He has no taste for investigative routine, though he is quite capable of seeing something that the investigators themselves might miss. However, he has the best pure detective intuition that it has ever been my good fortune to observe at work. He sees solutions in a single quick insight in which everything we know fits into place. I have never known him to be wrong. I repeat, never.*
>
> *At times he may be a nuisance. He wanders around as though he is in a deep puzzle (which he is) and makes strange paradoxical remarks which seem irrelevant. But he is also funny and gentle and sympathetic. He presided over the romance between me and my wife for which we will always love him.*
>
> *You will enjoy working with him and he will solve your mystery for you.*
>
> *MPV Casey.*

"MPV," I said, "stands for Michael Patrick Vincent."

"Is it true what he says?"

"I am sometimes ill-tempered."

"NO! About never being wrong?"

"Oh, that . . . Well, not so far . . . No guarantees."

"How will you work with us?" Manuelo the Juiz wondered.

"Tag along."

"Pardon?"

"Come with you on your rides. Sit here in this excellent headquarters . . ."

"Newest in the world."

"Patently. When you are doing interviews, I usually wear my invisibility cloak at such times so no one sees me."

"Invisibility cloak?" Pedro, the Chief of Police, asked uneasily.

"I am blessed with the ability to be inconspicuous. People simply don't notice and then forget I'm around. I'm very good at that, as you will see. The little man who wasn't there again today."

I doubted that they understood the reference. I must now stop befuddling them.

"You will represent Don Diego?" Pepe asked.

"No. Don Diego asked me to participate but I represent only myself and the desire to help solve the crime. . . . I'll keep out of the way."

"Do you have any questions?" Manuelo was the senior in rank and eager to get to work.

"Only one. Why do the media, even the television stations in Madrid, scream that Doña Teresa Maria is a national treasure . . . I'm from out of town and I don't quite understand what that means here."

They both were uneasy. Manuel slicked down his mustache and Pepe brushed back his thick black hair, indications if I were not mistaken that they were uneasy.

Good.

"Well," said the judge, "she is a very beautiful woman."

"I've noticed that," I admitted.

"Occasionally we see in the summer a picture of her in a swimsuit down at the Costa del Sol. Modest of course, but compelling."

"I understand."

"She gives away a lot of money, her family was very rich, so was the Duke's. Her gifts are intelligence and she sees that there is rigor in the spending of the money."

"And the whole country knows her sad story? Including the gay husband?"

"*Cierto.* No one talks about it, however."

"And the relationship with Don Leandro is well known?"

"We know about it here," Manuel said. "But most of Seville does not."

"However," Pepe added, "she would be admired for that too. Lifelong widowhood is admired in our culture, but only with limitations."

"She also writes articles for the media, Madrid but here too. Maybe once a year. Always measured, balanced."

"There is only one Doña Teresa Maria Romero y Avila."

"Have you met her Padre?"

"Oh, yes."

They had no right to know I was her spiritual adviser.

Why had Don Diego not told me that she was a national celebrity? He probably figured that everyone knew about her.

A police officer announced that Don Leandro Santiago y Diaz was waiting.

"Punctual as always," said El Juiz. "He apparently has a perfect alibi."

"He is a fortunate man," Pepe observed with a sigh.

"In many ways."

Leandro was dressed like the other two men, three responsible professionals. They embraced him, one of their own. Except he slept with a national resource.

"I trust Doña Teresa is recovering?" Manuel asked.

"More quickly than we might have expected. She still suffers some discomfort but she is out of the hospital bed and working on her papers. She is easily tired."

"Poor woman. We must interview her, as you know, but only when she is ready. We do not want to hurry her."

"On the contrary, she is eager for the interview. Unfortunately she remembers nothing."

"The sedative in her sherry. Our technicians report it was powerful enough to kill her. Fortunately she realized it was dangerous and spilled it on her table."

"Most fortunate," Leandro sighed.

"May we ask some questions, Leandro?"

"Of course, Manuelo. I assumed you would."

"How long"—he hesitated over the words—"have you and Doña Teresa, ah, been together?"

"One year, seven months, and four days." He blushed slightly. "It is my first love affair and I assume it will be my last."

A young woman, an immigrant from South America judging by her complexion, entered with a teapot, cups, and a plate of scones. Since I was wearing my invisibility cloak, she didn't notice me.

She filled cups for the three yuppies and gave them plates on which to place their scones and clotted cream. A very polished performance.

She didn't see me. Sometimes the invisibility cloak causes problems.

"You have been in the *palacio* often then?"

"Only a few times, Pepe, and then only in her office on the ground floor. She does not invite me to her apartment."

"Do you know why not?"

"I believe she considers it a private retreat for herself and Maria Luisa."

"Who opposes the relationship?"

"Oh, no! She is outspoken like her mother but more direct."

"You and Doña Teresa plan to marry?"

"*Cierto,* as soon as is convenient. We spend our evenings together in our room above the Bar Giralda, which you have searched."

"And you find that a satisfactory setting for an affair of the heart?"

"When Teresa is with me there, I hardly notice the setting."

A deft answer.

"*Naturalmente,* Leandro."

"We are powerfully in love, Manuel. There is no reason to try to hide that."

"Will you live in the casa after you are married?"

"We have not discussed that. She would like to be close to her daughter, though there is strong trust between them."

"We know about the suit against her relatives."

"It is in all the papers again."

"Indeed . . . You have no key to her apartment?"

"It is enough that I have her . . . No, I don't have a key. As I understand it, and as you doubtless know from your investigators and from her security people, there are only two. She has one and Maria Luisa has the other."

"Thus she is isolated completely from the other residents, Don Marco, Doña Inez, and El Jefe, as he is pleased to call himself."

"She is a very modest woman, Manuelo, and values her privacy. Also she does not trust her relatives and Don Teodoro who claims to be betrothed to Maria Luisa."

"Has he made, uh, advances . . ."

"Remote."

"And the young woman . . ."

"Rebuffs him of course."

"How?"

"She says that if he so much as touches her, she will kill him. I believe that my beloved has made the same threat. I need hardly tell you gentlemen that they both mean it."

"So the suit has moved forward recently?"

"Very slowly. On the day before the attacks the court ruled that Don Marco and Doña Inez could not interfere in their lives until a final court decision."

"And that means you and Doña Teresa would be free to marry? Don Diego would certainly approve?"

"El Cardinal is a very good friend of Doña Teresa."

"Do you plan to do so?"

"We haven't had time to talk about it, Manuelo. Both Maria Luisa and I believe we should immediately. Teresa hesitates out of respect for her family. I feel this is foolish. They haven't earned respect and they don't deserve it."

"You will persuade her?"

"You know, Pepe—as does everyone in Seville—about the argument we had in the Bar Giralda the night before last. I'm not at all sure I am quite brave enough to try to persuade her of anything . . . But Maria Luisa will insist and she may very well win."

"But your discussion at the Bar Giralda was not about that case."

"No, I know little about women, Manuelo, but I had intended to discuss our changing situation gradually. It was the more recent case. As you know charges are pending against Don Marco and El Jefe in Madrid. They demanded that she give them the money because of family loyalty. Naturally, she refused. There would be a scandal but it would not hurt her. However, I proposed a compromise: she would advance enough money to keep Madrid happy and they would renounce the will and move out of the house."

"She approved the plan?"

"Reluctantly, I would say. She hates them and doesn't like to save them, but she wants to be rid of them. I contacted a lawyer who represents Don Marco. We worked out an agreement. Teresa's check would go directly to Madrid. We did not trust Don Marco not to spend it some other way—on his resort in the Sierra Nevada for example. They would sign a document renouncing all further claims and leave the *palacio* within two weeks. I read the agreement on the phone to Teresa. She did not like it, but reluctantly agreed. That is where I made my mistake. I learned that one ought not to push her on some matters. You— and indeed all Seville—knows the result."

"She hit you and kicked you and cursed you and slapped you again. She threw a glass of wine at you and stalked away. Then she came back and signed the document and said she never wanted to see you again. You were surprised?"

"She had told me several times that she had a terrible temper and that when she lost it she was 'disgusting.' She also said that when it happened I should simply ignore her. The bella Maria Luisa also advised me to duck."

"Yet you feared you had lost her forever. So fortunately you drank two bottles of wine and fell asleep and awoke the next morning only when the proprietor brought you the morning paper?

"And then hangover and all, you rushed over to the John XXIII to make peace?"

"She apologized before I could and gave me instructions on how to deal with her should she ever do it again. . . . I think I need not detail those instructions."

They all laughed nervously.

"And the document will be executed today?"

"She insists. I do not know how this attempted murder will affect it."

"Let us understand again what happened in the apartment after your, uh, contretemps."

"It seems a simple matter but obviously it is not. Maria Luisa returned from walking the *paseo* with her *novio* Don Isidoro de

Colon. She went up to the first-floor entrance to their apartment. Don Isidoro naturally accompanied her. She tried to open the door but found that another key had been jammed in from the other side. She told Isidoro, a very nice young man, incidentally, to get the security guards. They shoved the door open and found Teresa spread out on her bed, a knife in her stomach—intestines actually, a shot wound in her scalp, and a broken sherry glass on the bedstand. Maria Luisa forbade them to touch the knife, called the hospital and an ambulance to take her to the hospital. Maria Luisa took charge and let no one touch the knife till the surgeons were ready to remove it. She saved her mother's life and immediately proclaimed her vocation to be a doctor of medicine. If you go over there this morning you will find that Maria Luisa is still in charge."

"Do you have any idea, Leandro, how these things could have transpired?"

"I'm sure your investigators are trying to determine who might have a third key."

"We continue to search."

"So."

He rose from his chair and picked up the morning paper with a front page color picture of Doña Teresa in her two-piece blue swimsuit on the Costa del Sol.

"You have seen this?" he said.

"As does everyone in Seville."

"Does it offend you, Don Leandro?"

"Doña Teresa merely sniffs and says that it was the only modest swimsuit on the beach that day. If she does not find her privacy violated, why should I."

He shook hands with his friends and left the office, still baffled by his *amante.* He had better get used to it.

I emerged from my invisibility cloak and asked if I might have a cup of tea.

"What did you think, Monsignor? The man is besotted, understandably so."

155

Shortly thereafter a police Mercedes of a certain age, painted red and gold, was summoned and we were driven the five minutes required to arrive at the John XXIII Hospital. Several TV cameras were waiting for us along with a couple of cops and some detectives and the usual crowd of curiosity seekers. I slipped back into my invisibility suit.

"Are you near an arrest, Don Manuelo?"

"How did the killer get into the room?"

"Is Don Leandro under suspicion?"

"Will you interrogate Doña Teresa?"

My colleagues waved them off.

We rode up in the elevator. Maria Luisa waited for us at the door, clad in tight black jeans and a Seville T-shirt with a bull on it. Leisure clothes no doubt.

"My mother will be happy to talk with you," she said with a smile worthy of her mother.

In the main room of the suite, the bed was tightly made and the monitors were off. Doña Maria Teresa in a luxurious white robe was sitting behind a huge oak desk with a computer and a stack of papers.

"Thank you, Maria Luisa," she said, not rising from the desk. "You don't have to remain with us."

"I want to."

"Very well . . . Gentlemen, do come in and sit down," she said, gesturing at a coffee table and chairs. "I was just catching up on some of my work. The medical staff insists that I take at least two siestas every day. I am glad you came now."

She rose slowly from the desk chair and, leaning on Maria Luisa's arm, walked slowly to the most comfortable of the chairs. She was wearing makeup (and that intolerable scent), and her hair was brushed carefully and hung to her shoulders. She was obviously (to me anyway) still in pain. Despite that she had reassumed her role as the self-possessed national treasure. I noticed that, as we left the desk behind, the Costa del Sol picture was opened and folded.

"Maria Luisa, would you be so kind to bring a pot of tea and some *pastels*?"

I'd better get some this time. Back in the police station, the scones had disappeared before I got to them.

"Yes, Mama . . . And don't start the questions until I return!"

As the young woman left the room, she winked at me. You can't hide from me, Padrecito.

"My daughter saved my life, you know, gentlemen. Now she believes that she may order me around as I usually order her around. It is indeed an interesting experience. I rest more easily when I know a clone is in charge."

They laughed politely.

"We are happy that you are recovering so quickly, Doña Teresa."

"Thank you, Don Manuelo."

Recovering quickly! Nonsense! She was putting on an act because that's what you do if you have the blood of Isabella the Catholic in your veins. Maria Luisa brought me an extra plate of pastry.

"We understand that you may not be able to answer all our questions."

"As many as you ask that I have answers to. I have no clear memories of what happened in my room. Only a sense of humiliation and horror and terrible pain. Then nothing at all until I woke up in that bed with a team of doctors and nurses hovering over me and heard my daughter giving them orders. The doctors say that memories may come back in time. I confess that I don't want them. They also say that I may be able to recover them with hypnotism. I will attempt that when I am a little stronger if it is necessary."

Her daughter frowned.

"Our investigators found no fingerprints on the knife. You have seen it, no?"

"Absolutely not," the daughter intervened. "Maybe later.

There are many knives in our *palacio,* some of them left perhaps by the Moors. Our family is a warrior family which means these days we steal from the Army. I didn't recognize the knife. You may search the whole creepy place if you want to."

"You don't seem to like the house, Señorita Maria Luisa?"

"Hate it! Hate it! Hate it!"

"Where would you like to live, señorita?"

"Perhaps a second-floor apartment in the Santa Cruz?"

Her mother blushed crimson.

But she took Maria Luisa's hand in hers and they clung tightly to one another.

Were these high-level, professional cops able to cope with such outbursts? Perhaps in Spain they had to.

"My mamacita says that I am out of control. I say that I will be until she finds a papacito for me."

"Like Don Leandro?"

"He would be all right if Mama doesn't kick him again with the whole of Seville watching."

This sounds like harsh talk. In fact it was a deeply affectionate dialogue between two women that loved each other dearly.

"Do you think," Manuelo returned to the subject matter, "the other residents might have been involved in the attempts on your life?"

"They are ugly, vicious, greedy people. But murder of a member of a family . . . they would have to have been in deep trouble. But I had already signed the document which would have protected them from Madrid."

"Would they have known that?"

"Their *abrogado* and mine had agreed on it earlier in the afternoon. I presume he called them promptly. Since they hoped to get money from me, why kill me?"

"Perhaps they would kill you after they got your money because they hated you so much."

"My relatives are vicious and greedy, but they are smart enough to know that my death would stop the flow of funds."

"The money has gone to Madrid already?"

"Despite everything that happened, Don Leandro, poor dear man, wired it to the proper authorities yesterday. . . . You have to understand that neither the government nor the opposition want a major scandal. The government would face another corruption case and the opposition would have to admit that the corruption was on both sides. My relatives are not in fact part of the Popular. They are Falange."

"And they are hoping it comes back," her daughter added, "then they can steal money without any fear."

"Might we be so bold, señora, to ask about your estate?"

"When all the charities are seen to, Maria Luisa here, with Don Diego and Don Leandro as trustees."

"It will be a substantial amount."

"If the economy of this country continues to improve."

"Do you have any idea—and this will be our last question—about the problem of the keys?'

"I know of only two, mine and Maria Luisa's. I believe she turned both of them over to your investigators. . . . You must understand how they work. They lock both from the inside and the outside. From the inside, you merely press a knob. So we can stay in our apartment and play music . . ."

"And no one can bother us unless they use the house phone. We don't need a key to lock from the inside, but if you do lock it from the inside with a key, the lock holds the key and you can't unlock it from the outside. I don't think we ever do that. I am sure I didn't do it the night before last."

"Someone could have turned the key from the inside and then left the room deliberately so no one could get it, perhaps to help you?"

She frowned for a moment.

"I think so . . . One could turn the lock from the inside, leave the key in, and shut the door."

"And the maids?"

"If they are not finished when I leave, I take my key with me and they close the door and lock it from the inside."

"And your sherry in the evening . . ."

"From our own vineyards . . . I keep a bottle of it in my liquor cabinet. The maid fills a small carafe and leaves it on my bedside table in the morning. If I drink it before my siesta, she replaces it when she remakes the bed, if the door is still open. I didn't take a siesta the day before yesterday because I was so upset about buying off my persecutors. The carafe must have been the one left in the morning."

"Thank you very much," Manuelo said. "We appreciate your cooperation."

They both stood up and I did too.

"One more question, Doña Teresa," Pepe interjected. "Did your guests harass or threaten you?"

"They would storm down, late in the evening usually, and make absurd statements. I should construct a statue of the Generalissimo in our courtyard. Or make a contribution to the local Falange. Or to Opus Dei. I should prevent my daughter from seeing Don Isidoro because she was already promised to El Jefe. Especially that I should stop living in sin with a known socialist. I would listen patiently and tell them I would see them in the morning during my office hours . . . They never did that. They always came when we were preparing for bed."

"And I would make my usual threat about El Jefe. If he so much as touched me, I would cut off his balls. I carried a small knife around in my purse, just in case."

As we descended in the elevator, I murmured a suggestion. They didn't hear perhaps because the invisibility cape was still functioning.

"You might have some of your staff check the apartment for

that sherry bottle. You will find that it is still there and still deadly."

I whispered quickly to Mary Louise in the lobby.

"Any signs of sexual molestation?"

"I don't know. God forbid. I'll find out and call you."

13

"Padre Ryan," I said to the phone, figuring it was a Chicago call.

"Maria Luisa. My mother was not sexually molested according to the doctors. However, when I entered the room, her gown had been torn away and the knife was in her stomach."

"Small intestines."

"And her arms were stretched out in the form of a cross."

"Ghoulish!" I exclaimed.

"After I called the ambulance and the hospital, I tried to cover her up. I didn't tell the police but I will."

"Was she pregnant, Mary Louise?"

"I don't think so. She would have been happy and I wanted my little brother."

"I have two more questions. First, how did you and Mamacita carry your keys?"

"On chains around our necks, like our miraculous medals. She was afraid that fool El Jefe would try to steal it."

Some people still wear them, I thought. Good, they are signs of faith.

"Did you and Mamacita drink sherry together some nights?"

"When we were both there at bedtime," she said with a giggle, "which hasn't been often, we would put on our nightgowns and meet in her bedroom to toast one another."

"She would lock the door after you sipped the sherry."

"No, Padre, whoever was the last one in would close it with the lock on."

"Thank you, Maria Luisa. Take good care of your mamacita."

"Is she in danger, Padrecito Negro?"

I pondered that for a moment.

"I don't think so, but tell the doctors and the police that I said they should double their guard because I fear there might be another attempt. Also tell Leandro that I think he should be around all the time."

"OK, Padre. Pray for us all."

"One last thing: ask the head doctor if she was pregnant."

"Yes, Padre."

I felt like a damp, dark cloud was entering the study at the Cardinal's residence. There was evil out there. I fell on my knees and prayed. Then I went to Don Diego's office to report. He was reading a document from Rome.

"Sorry to interrupt . . ."

"Not at all . . . Do you get these documents from Rome?"

"Sometimes when they think the coadjutors, such as they may be, need to be educated. I glance at the subject matter and then toss them."

"I need to be a little more cautious . . . Yet I am offended that a Cardinal Prince of the Holy Roman Church should be lectured by some barely literate but ambitious young monsignor in the curial bureaucracy."

"You sound like my boss . . . I have come to report on the matter of La Doña."

Which I thereupon did.

"It is all very strange. Clearly the other people in the palace are involved."

"In some way. We must untangle the puzzle of the keys. Then

perhaps we will discover who else in the house is involved in the attempts to kill her and what was the nature of the involvement."

"She must get out of there. Or expel them."

"She also must legitimize her relationship with Don Leandro."

"That should not be a problem anymore, Padrecito Negro."

"It would add a sense of stability to a love relationship for which nothing in her life experience has prepared her. I doubt that anyone has ever loved her implacably and permanently before. As the relationship with Don Leandro becomes more intense, she becomes more uncertain that she can cope with it."

"He is more demanding?"

"No more than any passionate lover."

"So. I will go tomorrow and schedule a date for the wedding. It will then all arrange itself . . . Will she resist my suggestion?"

"At first perhaps."

"Then I will desist . . . You saw the picture this morning?"

"Indeed . . . the paper was folded on the desk where Maria Luisa presides . . . Patently she is ordering the plastic surgeons that her mother must be able to appear at Costa del Sol this summer in similar garb."

"Why deprive readers of such an image . . . Don Leandro is with her most of the time."

"Sometimes, I believe. He will be there more often because I have directed the daughter to insist on it."

"She still is in danger?"

"I would not exclude the possibility of another attempt on her life. There is madness in this attack. One can never tell how dangerous it is."

"You're going to visit her?"

"Perhaps. I must first visit the *palacio* to see how it arranges itself. The problem of the keys."

"Patently!" he said, stealing one of my favorite lines. But, poor man, he was not in a laughing mood.

He offered a ride from Don Pedro, but I elected to walk. I would fortify myself with some tapas on the way. At the Bar Giralda, where else?

The proprietor seated me with great ceremony and instantly placed a plate with what he had decided were my favorite selections. And a small carafe from La Doña's vineyards down among the "white towns," the very path I had urged on my nephew and his promised one for their drive down to the Costa del Sol "for beach action."

I missed them—her exuberance and his whimsical patience. Well, I would see plenty of them back home in Chicago.

"La Doña is recovering, not as rapidly as she wants, so she taxes herself. Señorita Maria Luisa is in charge of everything. Don Leandro is often present."

"He has been forgiven?"

"No, he has forgiven her."

"*Bueno* . . . She is very gracious but sometimes . . . volatile."

"I thought that was expected of all Spanish women."

He laughed.

"From La Doña it is always a surprise. Her outburst here in my bar was shocking. The poor woman realized she was making a fool out of herself. It was good that she asked forgiveness. It shows her great dignity."

"Indeed."

"She is most blessed to have won such a wonderful *amante*."

"*Cierto.*"

Fair play to you, Don Mateo. Most would have thought it was Don Leandro who had done the capturing.

"I was worried," he said casually, "about the man who followed her when she left. He seemed . . . How to say it? . . . Sinister?"

"Don Teodoro?"

"No, no. I know that pig. . . . This one looked like a thief from Triana."

"May I tell the police?"

"*Cierto,* Padre! We cannot lose La Doña. She is a national treasure."

Was there an American woman of whom everyone would agree, perhaps only after the obits, that she was a national treasure?

I strolled over to the castle, arriving ten minutes late, well aware that my Spanish friends would be at least fifteen minutes late and arrive briskly as if they were on time. They would also arrive with sleep still in their eyes and in their brains. How can you accomplish anything in this part of the world? They would have had a drink of sherry or perhaps white wine before the siesta, during which they would be distracted by the attractions of their spouse, then fall into a deep sleep. They would experience upon awaking the second wake-up trauma of the day, not quite sure who they were or what they were supposed to do next. They would kiss their spouse, dress quickly, and swallow as we say in the Old Country another jar of the creature. It wasn't dark at this hour of a spring day, so it was not as bad as in winter. Yet to emerge in the dark after such an afternoon had to be enervating. Admittedly I did on occasion (whenever possible) indulge in resting my eyes. But I do not obtain half my hours of sleep after lunch.

At first the two cops had trouble focusing on my account of the conversation with the proprietor of Bar Giralda. Then they got it.

"This is very serious," said Pepe Garcia.

"You must have your men interview him at once," Manuelo Lopez ordered. "Who would want to follow La Doña?"

"Someone who might want to kill her in the apartment where she lived with her *amante,*" I observed. "It was fortunate that she did not go there."

"A hired killer?" Pepe asked. "Who would hire a killer?"

"Don Marco perhaps or Don Teodoro?"

"You suspect them, Padre?"

"Who else is there to suspect?"

The gates were open to the courtyard of the palace. A porter considered our credentials and summoned Candida Vlad—a Romanian name. She was probably not a relative of Prince Dracula. She was, they told me, one of the security agents who worked in the *palacio.*

A solid blond woman with a wedding ring on her finger, she bowed politely to us and ushered us to the central wing of the courtyard, opened the door for us, and then led us to the second floor which Europeans—for some odd reason—are pleased to call the first floor. Here we entered a very old elevator which struggled to take us to the top floor of the building. The door opened on an ornate corridor with an uncompromising dark wood wall that ran the length of the building. The place reminded me of the convents we'd built in the U.S. in the late nineteenth century. Solemn, gloomy, and dead. In the middle of the corridor an equally heavy double door seemed to forbid entrance. A yellow police tape reinforced the warning. Ms. Vlad pushed the door open and bowed us into a large room, a parlor perhaps. I felt we were intruding on a wake in a nineteenth-century Hapsburg house, a wake in a declining family. In fact, the decor was Bourbon—the people who never forgot anything and never learned anything.

The walls were covered with dull blue fabric ornamented with dingy gold-colored tassels. Pictures of various weak-looking monarchs or generals, mostly with beards and dire expressions hung on the wall. There was, however, a large screen television and a modern end table with fashion magazines in several different languages and stacks of books on another table.

"This is the parlor," Candida informed us. "This is where I enter in the morning at seven. I knock lightly on the door." She illustrated by lifting the large knocker in the shape of an eagle. It thudded against the door like a clap of thunder. "La Doña is normally awake and in her dressing gown and working in her office which I shall show you soon. She admits me with a bright good morning. Sometimes she does not hear the knock and I ring this bell," she explained and walked into the corridor and pushed something. A loud buzz sounded in one of the interior rooms. It would wake up any spare corpses they might have in the apartment.

"Then she always comes and apologizes for keeping me waiting . . ."

"Do you lock the door when you close it?" I asked.

"La Doña usually keeps the lock on; she presses a lever on a very modern system. That way when I leave the door locks itself . . . La Doña is always safe inside. No one can take her papers or hurt her. When she leaves she closes the door and it locks automatically."

She had a hard time with the last word, but her smile said that she found it funny too.

"But you leave the door ajar when you are cleaning?"

"La Doña says to do that. She is a wonderful woman to work with. Such a hard life and yet so kind and sensitive. I love her like everyone else does. Except the others."

"The daughter?"

"That one is a little loco but she is young. She is very like her mother. I love her too . . . The door is ajar so I can bring in the cleaning materials and remove the laundry and garbage. La Doña is also very neat. She makes the daughter be neat too, though it is difficult with that one. La Doña is not worried that the door is open when I'm working because she knows I am really a security guard and would kill anyone who tried to hurt her. . . . Please come after me."

We crossed through an open archway into another corridor.

"The day she was attacked?" Pepe Garcia said, taking over the conversation.

"It was normal. She opened the door, but the lock was on and

169

let me come in. She was fully dressed. She has this wonderful *amante* and he makes her very happy. She does not frown as much and she laughs more and walks with a light step. He never comes here. They have a small apartment down in Santa Cruz where they spend the nights. Sometimes she returns here in early morning to sleep. Sometimes she appears just as I ring the bell, her clothes in disarray, her eyes shining, and her face very beautiful. She blushes and apologizes. And I say, the love was good and she blushes again and sighs.

" 'Very good, Candida,' she says or something like that. 'He takes my mind away.'

"And I say that's what men are for. And we both laugh . . . now the other rooms here are two bedrooms and two bathrooms both with showers. The large one here in the middle is for La Doña and the smaller one next door is where the daughter throws her clothes on the floor before her mother makes her pick them up. They are very close and they love each other very much."

In La Doña's room the decor of the house changed completely. It moved into the twenty-first century and could have leaped out of the pages of the fashion magazines in the parlor. The floor-to-ceiling windows looked out on the courtyard where automobiles were parked on one side and on the other behind a partition a very modern swimming pool.

"La Doña swims often?"

"She and Maria Luisa swim almost every day, even in winter. The *others* object to their swimming costumes. You have seen the picture in the papers."

We nodded.

"I think it is very modest, the one that the daughter wears perhaps not so much, but then she is young. The men over there look out the windows and lust for them.

"Here is the bed where Maria Luisa found her, naked, unconscious, and slowly bleeding to death. With the smell of gunfire filling the room." She sniffed and then tried to control her emotions. "It was terrible . . . Maria Luisa became her mother. She called the ambulance and the hospital and the police. She would not let anyone remove the knife. She saved her mother's life, they say . . . La Doña will return?"

"Oh, yes, Candida, she is recovering quickly."

"I am so happy to hear it."

"Let me ask another question," I said. "The other guests live across the way, do they have access to these apartments?"

"They have no keys. There are only two and Doña Teresa and Doña Maria wear them around their necks like holy medals. However, they can walk the corridors. They have to ride down to the first floor and then come up here in our elevator. So they can wander around the corridors on our side at will. . . . The woman never does except when they come to complain formally about something in the building or the servants that watch them so closely or Maria Luisa's swimming costume. La Doña is always very polite and also very firm. That pig Teodoro—the fat one who wears a uniform that is two sizes too small—claims that Maria Luisa is betrothed to him and he has the right of access to her. Once she took a knife out of her purse and told him if he so much as touches her, she would cut off his cojones. I think she meant it. They are terrible people. I spit on them."

"Do the men appear often in the corridors?" I asked.

"Sometimes . . . perhaps many times . . . They want to ogle two beautiful women . . . Their eyes are hungry and hard. When I am in the corridor, I lean against the wall and wait till they leave. They know that I'm security and they are afraid of me. They don't know whether I have a gun."

"Which of course you do?"

"Naturally. I am authorized."

"We understand."

"The fat one is often outside the door when I leave, perhaps wanting to see the women in their dishabille. He grins foolishly when I catch him. . . . Now these two rooms used to be bedrooms. The first is a dining room. They tell me in the morning whether they will eat here and I take their orders. Then I or one of the others bring up the meal and serve it here."

A very modern Scandinavian wood dining set organized for four people and looking out on the courtyard, an ideal place for two busy professional women to grab a bite to eat during a busy day. In a refrigerator were the usual collection of magic concoctions—juices and such things—which facilitated good health, especially when one also lived on tapas.

Next to the dining room was La Doña's office spread halfway along one side of the building, looking out on the Santa Cruz, Arenal, the Cathedral, La Giralda, the Paseo Cristobal Colon, and the Guadalquivir—purple gold in the light of the setting sun—and beyond Triana where a very young Teresa Maria had danced with the gypsies before her father and her promised groom made her stop.

Had she ever in all her life been loved, save for that young law student at the University who had admired her from a distance long ago?

A long functional desk—more of a table—lined up next to the windows enabled the worker to drink in Seville all day long. She was after all the Archduchess of Seville, was she not? Two computers were arrayed on the table, a Dell and a Toyota, several printers, and two large monitors. Files were laid out neatly on the desk, and immediate work was lined up and held in place with statues of Spanish saints—John of the Cross, Teresa of Avila, Leander, Isidore Agricola, Fernando, Justa, and Rufina. On the walls behind the work station were contemporary Catholic art, including two Georges Rouault, one of them his famous clowns, rich in watercolor blue and deep crimson. Next to the Dell, which was by far the larger of the two machines, an air mouse was waiting for long and delicate fingers.

One would have to assume that whoever worked in this room was a person of deep culture, superb taste, and advanced technological skills. Behind the computers a set of framed photographs lined the wall—a tiny baby girl changing slowly to a defiantly grinning young woman in a skimpy bikini who looked like she was about to break into flamenco. Maria Luisa.

Also two black and white pictures—a fragile girl with a winsome smile and a shy young man of college age. Her own mother and her *amante*.

Beneath one could just barely see Bar Giralda, a hint for her of new beginnings, new possibilities.

"This one"—I pointed out silently—"deserves a break."

"Here," Candida continues, "is the library. Also the liquor cabinet with the sherry and wine that her vineyards produce. All they drink is sherry and wine, no spirits. It is a bottle just like this one which was poisoned."

The label said *Santa Clara Dry Sherry*. It was sealed.

"Every day when I was finished cleaning the apartment, I would fill a carafe with enough for two glasses and put the carafe and the glasses on La Doña's bed table. Often she and Maria Luisa would sit on her bed in their nightclothes and talk about their days. That doesn't happen anymore because La Doña is at the apartment in Santa Cruz. But I put the two glasses there anyway. Sometimes she drinks one of them while she is working. She always tells me not to waste good vintage, so I do not."

"The bottle you filled the day of the attacks on La Doña contained how much sherry?" Pepe asked.

"It was about half filled. I poured one glass, which does not take much out of the bottle."

"You had protected the glass from the previous night from waste?"

"I had to obey La Doña's wishes. She was very proud of their sherry."

Andrew M. Greeley

"And you did not collapse."

"So there was no barbiturates in that glass, but there were in the one you had poured for the coming evening?" I asked.

"I don't think so. La Doña says you can tell good sherry if the sun shines through it like a cloudless day. I always raise the carafe to the sun. It was clear."

"So the bottle would have been poisoned later in the day?"

"*Cierto.*"

"Interesting."

"And only La Doña and the Maria Luisa had keys to the apartment?"

"Yes, Juiz, only they, but why would La Doña poison herself and possibly her daughter?"

"A locked-room mystery?" Manuelo said skeptically. "They make good mystery stories, but they can't happen in real judicial work."

They do, I thought to myself, and I think I know how this one worked, though I don't understand what happened.

"Either," said Pepe, "it was a suicide pact, which is most unlikely, or someone else had a key."

"I wonder if he could have been our friend Don Leandro. He might have borrowed a key from her . . ."

"Why would he or the other people want to kill her? The others will lose their power over her. They will be thrown out of this palace. He will be the husband of one of the richest women in Spain."

They were talking nonsense. I let them talk. Patently Don Marco, "El Jefe," and Doña Inez were the prime suspects. The question was whether this was an elaborate plot they had devised, even though Teresa had signed an agreement to bail them out. Or was it blind folly in which they were very fortunate that they failed. In either event they were quite mad. Which many criminals are. Whatever, they had stumbled on blind luck and blind unluck at the same time.

174

Candida caught my eye and shrugged. Romanians knew how dumb even intelligent and honest bureaucrats could be. The babblers finally agreed that on the following morning they would interview at the Municipal building Don Marco, Don Teodoro, and Doña Inez.

Candida relaxed.

Would I be good enough to present myself at nine?

Of course.

"Have you solved the locked-room riddle?"

"Oh, yes, this is a rather easy one. The hard questions are why it was done and who did it."

They ignored my claim of a solution and turned to what they seemed to find an unpleasant subject matter.

"We had better interview Don Teodoro and Don Marco tomorrow morning," Manuelo repeated their intent. He slicked back his hair, evidence that he did not like the process.

"And Doña Inez too," Pepe added, smoothing his mustache. "These Flangists were even more difficult to interview than when they thought they were in power."

"They answer questions with ominous warnings that it might be 1936 and the Army is ready to rise again when the king gives the signal."

"I don't belong to your party, Pepe, but I think that hope is delusional."

"As is their hope that they will escape their scandal because they will be saved by another civil war."

"With a million dead!"

"And their salvation will come from La Doña whom they have tormented all her life."

"Why then should they take her life?"

"How did her mother die?" I asked.

They both were quiet and then admitted they didn't know.

"Some kind of heart attack during a pregnancy," Pepe said. "I will find out, Padre."

"You might also investigate the possibility that it might not have been inconsistent with barbiturate poisoning."

They stared at me as if they thought the little old priest had gone loco.

I promised them that I would be at the Municipal building at 9:00 A.M.

"They will be late, on that you may rely. They act like the Generalissimo is still alive."

I wandered around Macarena for some time, thinking about my hypothesis. Poison is usually a woman's murder weapon. I decided. I looked up and wondered where I was and how to get back to the Cathedral Plaza. I found that I was standing in front of the Juan XXIII Hospital, *Beato* Juan XXIII Hospital, as we must now call it. The day would come when it would be the San Juan Il Magno Hospital.

14

I ambled over to the hospital entrance still wearing my invisibility cloak and startled the police guards. The sleepy photographers and TV camera did not notice my arrival either, not that they had any reason to be alert for someone like me.

"May I talk to Maria Luisa," I said to the hospital guard.

"*Sí,* Padrecito Negro," he said with a broad smile. He was some kind of South American, probably Brazilian.

"Maria Luisa." A brisk womanly voice warned me that I had better not be some itinerant purveyor of bullshit.

"Blackie, uh, Padrecito Negro. I hope it is not too late."

"The night is still early here in al-Andalus, Padrecito. *Por favor* come up and talk to us. We are all bored."

I gave the phone back to the guard, he listened, nodded, and said, "*Cierto,* Señorita Maria Luisa! Pronto!"

The hospital was dark and quiet. Two medical types sat at the inactive monitors. Maria Luisa embraced me.

"Welcome, Padrecito. Are the promised ones back from the beach yet?"

"I doubt it. I hope they stay overnight. It is a dangerous road."

"Not for Don Jose. He is *muy hombre.*"

A line his sainted mother would savor.

It was a family evening at home, two couples on couches, watching American television, the *Sopranos* in fact. Maria Luisa was holding hands with her *novio,* the ever-grinning Isidoro and the two *amantes* were holding hands also, electricity sparking forth between them.

Maria Luisa was wearing white jeans and a green T-shirt, both tight-fitting. La Doña was clad in pale blue pajamas and a matching blue coat. Her spirits and her appearance had improved in the last twenty-four hours. Her eyes had recovered some of their sparkle and her smile was happier and more frequent.

"It is good to see you restored to grace, Don Leandro."

"I haven't been slapped today, thus far."

Everyone laughed. La Doña blushed.

"She is afraid that he will fight back the next time!" Maria Luisa said.

"Men his age are gentlemen," Isidoro said. "They would never strike a woman, no matter what their provocation. My generation, Maria Luisa, would have no hesitation."

He waved his hand vigorously as if slapping an obnoxious lover back into her proper place.

"Not twice," Maria Luisa said. "I would go to work with my knife."

Again they all laughed, a happy family evening. Hypothetically the younger daughters would be in bed.

I was assigned a vast easy chair—between the two couches—which swallowed me up. Maria Luisa brought the obligatory carafe of sherry and a plate of cheeses. The *Sopranos* continued in silence.

La Doña cuddled close to her lover, her hand clutching his arm.

"I toured your apartment today," I said.

"Doña Candida told me. She said you were more intelligent than the whole Civil Guard."

"No great achievement," Maria Luisa said.

"Did you like my apartment?"

"Oh, yes, very elegant, a nice mix of the eighteenth and the twenty-first centuries."

"The whole place could be fixed up once we get rid of our horrid tenants," Maria Luisa said. "My mama has excellent taste."

"Did you solve the locked-room mystery, which the police ridicule?"

"Oh, yes, easily. They believe there must be another key."

"That is absurd. After the keys and locks were made, the molds were destroyed. I was told that if we lost one, we would need a completely new lock and new keys and they would only make them if I signed some kind of solemn oath."

"We may soon need new keys," Maria Luisa said with a suggestive giggle.

"We could always put other people in the Santa Cruz where we could keep them at a proper distance," La Doña said, kissing her lover. Or should I say "promised groom."

A lot of processes were going on in the room, shy and not so shy sexual communications.

"So, Padrecito Negro, you have solved the crime?"

The sexual innuendos ceased.

"I think I know how it was done, but I'm not sure yet why or by whom."

"You will discover that soon?"

"I hope so."

"I would be frightened to return there unless the criminals were in jail. My headache will never go away, my gut will always hurt, I will always be a little dizzy, and I'll always have these terrible dreams at night."

"You will feel better tomorrow, *querida*," Leandro assured her. "And even better the day after tomorrow."

"You're just tired," Maria Luisa said. "You need to sleep."

179

"I am afraid to sleep. . . . May I talk to my spiritual director for a few moments?"

She stood up, wavered, and began to move toward the window.

Maria Luisa rushed to her assistance.

Teresa Maria, leaning on her daughter's arm, walked carefully to a table and chairs at the end of the window overlooking the river.

"Gracias, cara," her mother said firmly.

"I will bring the sherry and the cheese for El Padricito Negro."

"Nothing for me. I have no appetite."

"Sí, Mamacita."

"So," I said.

"So Don Diego comes here tomorrow morning."

"Indeed."

The last trace of sunlight was slipping into the marshes between the sea and Seville and the moon was asserting its rights over al-Andalus.

"You know what he will talk about?"

"Not explicitly."

"He will insist that I should marry Don Leandro almost immediately now that there's no obstacle to it."

"Not that there ever was."

"So Don Diego will say. He will argue that my image as a national treasure is at stake. I am free of the control of evil people and I am promptly entering an excellent marriage. The disgrace of Don Marco will be quickly forgotten. With any good fortune I will produce a son who will be the new Duke for which all of al-Andalus hopes. There will be a happy ending to the whole tragic story of my father who like my husband died in a terrorist explosion and my grandfather who died at the Ebro Valley during the war. Franco's hold on the country ended twenty-five years ago. Now there is a different line of nobility here, one that is still true to the old blood but open to new ideas. I will be the symbol of this change. He will argue of course that I am entitled to a happy family life at long last and indeed to love."

"Is that a true story?" I asked.

"To some extent. Spain still takes its nobles seriously. Yet we are rather thin symbols. I am hardly the national treasure that I'm called these days. Yet perhaps I have some marginal importance as a philanthropist and a celebrity. Don Diego, good priest that he is, wants me to be happy. That is impossible, as the events a couple of nights ago make clear. I am not fated to be happy."

"You might become an important figure in the Madrid government."

"Bah! For that I would not leave Seville."

"I noticed a picture of your mother on the desk . . . winsome child."

"She was eighteen when that picture was taken. Two years later she died while carrying a son, a little brother whom I would have hated and a new Duke. I would have been unimportant then."

"Of what did she die?"

"Bad blood I was told by everyone—as though there was something wrong with her family that killed not only her but my brother. I don't know the truth. My father obviously loved her very much. He did not marry again and served in the various Spanish colonies until his death in the Canary Islands."

"You have searched for the records about the death of your mother?"

"That was during the Generalissimo's time. The private lives of loyal Falangists were always carefully protected. There are no records."

"Who profited from their deaths?"

"Don Marco of course. I don't think he and his cronies wanted a male heir. That's why they gave me to a homosexual. My father simply didn't care anymore."

"So you have never been loved in your whole life."

"My mother loved me. I know that. The servants told me how much she loved me. No one else, not really until my bossy daughter came on the scene."

She paused in her narration and smiled proudly.

"My life has not been wasted. I am very proud of her. No one will do to her what they did to me."

"I also noticed next to Maria Luisa a picture of a young man of college age."

"You notice him," she said. "But I am not ready for marriage to him or anyone else. I never will be."

"Yet your renewed *aventura amarosa* seems to have been, how shall I say it, rewarding?"

"You are learning our euphemisms quickly, Padrecito Negro."

I said nothing as I awaited an explanation.

"I did not know such passion was possible. Neither did he. The reactions were like a firestorm. He swept me away and I did the same to him. But I've told you all of this before. Marriage is different. It requires more than passion and pleasure to sustain it. . . ."

"And you are afraid that you could not cope with such an *amante* in your apartment at the palace."

"His demands would be too much for me. He wants a wife. I only wanted a lover. It would be too much for me."

"You can escape from him?"

She frowned.

"I don't know. I hope so. But then, Padrecito Negro, I hope not. I want to escape from him. Yet I tingle with anticipation at the prospect that he will carry me off, one way or another . . . I have never been loved by a man, not ever. They are strange creatures. I will do everything I can to resist him. Yet I may surrender . . .

"And then I will have lost my freedom myself. I will be imprisoned again . . . Anyway, my poor violated body is not ready for lovemaking."

Don Diego would have his work cut out for him. He would come with all the plans for the wedding outlined. He would have to find a place for them to live after the wedding which would be private and comfortable and provide time for La Doña to recover sufficiently to revive sexual activity, before they embarked on a wedding trip somewhere. Those were the simple elements. Maria Luisa of course would be on his side. But they were both dealing with a love-starved and badly frightened woman. Still it would be a good work to reassure her.

"It takes time to organize a wedding," she continued her ruminations for her spiritual adviser. "One must arrange for a bridal party, choose a church, plan a dinner, make an invitation list, buy gowns for a wedding party . . . I won't be able to do that at least for weeks."

All true. But they were irrelevant. If La Doña could fend off a wedding for two weeks, she would be relatively safe from the desires of her *amante*. Don Diego would have his work cut out for him.

"What does my spiritual adviser say about these arguments?"

"They are matters of such ambiguity about which spiritual director sayeth not. However, he will venture a prediction."

"Which is?"

"That you will indeed marry Don Leandro. It will be a long and happy marriage because, granted that you have never been properly loved, you are nonetheless—and as much as you doubt—very easy to love. And you will come to Chicago to celebrate with us and conceive the new Duke on the shores of Lake Michigan."

"Are your predictions on such matters of the heart ever wrong, Padrecito Negro?"

"Just as my solutions to locked-room mysteries, not so far."

I helped her out of her chair and, absorbed by the light of the pale gold moon, led her back to her family.

"You will share this conversation with Don Diego?"

"I do not violate confidences, Doña Teresa. I may remark that he has his work cut out for him, as we say in my country. But he knows that."

She laughed, a woman who understood that the playing field was tipping toward happiness.

I reported to Don Diego in his study where he was reciting the Psalms.

"You have solved the locked-room mystery?" he asked.

"*Cierto.* I know how it was done, but not who did it or why."

"*Les flics* accept your solution."

"They rarely do. However, we interview the Falange cell in the building tomorrow morning. That should be interesting. I have reason to suspect that La Doña's mother was murdered the same way, while pregnant with what turned out to be the new Duke still in her womb. Do not quote me because I need evidence."

"La Doña is inclined to marry her lover?"

"I cannot violate my confidences in that area. I can say—and I told her I would say it to you—that you have your work cut out for you, as we say in America. But you knew that."

He nodded. "Would you violate her confidences if you summed her up in a sentence or two?"

"I told her that she was a woman who had never been loved in all her life and yet who is very easy to love. But you know that."

"*Cierto.* Don Leandro will be a good husband?"

"She's not ever likely to find another so good."

15

I drifted away from his study and into my own room, my home away from home. The late May sunset on the Guadalquivir was lovely, but nothing like sunset on Lake Michigan. I yearned to be home.

So I called Milord Cronin on his cell phone.

"Cronin."

"Blackie."

"Where are you?"

"At the Cardinal's palace in Seville, in my own little bedroom which is too small altogether."

"As fancy as my palace up on North State?"

"Far fancier . . . I still have some work to do on the project you assigned me."

"This gorgeous woman whom they call a 'national treasure.' Is she?"

"Arguably."

"You didn't prevent them from trying to kill her."

"Indeed. But we will get those who tried."

"She's in the *New York Times* newspaper this morning. Small piece on page three with a picture. Does she really look like that?"

"Oh, yes."

"Well, get rid of the bad guys, Blackwood. See to it."

That was his sign-off line.

"Hold on! How you keeping?"

"Ticker is a little irregular. They're keeping an eye on me. The wicked witches are hovering around, determined to keep me alive . . . I keep telling them that I won't mind dying. My life has been a failure. I won't mind signing off."

"You are, Sean Patrick Cronin, full of shit!"

He laughed at that and hung up.

A very difficult man, Milord Cronin.

Since I had heard no bad news or complaints from the coterie of strong women who had surrounded him, I decided not to call them.

I settled in for my night prayers in which I thanked himself for enlightening me about how the locked-room caper had gone down and asked Him to continue to help me toward a solution. I thanked him for my conversation with La Doña. She thinks she's never been loved, as you doubtless know, since you know everything anyway. That reaction is understandable given the multiple conspiracies which have buffeted her. However, she has been loved by that argumentative and adoring daughter and by yourself who doubtless sent Maria Luisa to keep her mother alive. She is one of your better efforts—the mother I mean. You must assure me that you will take good care of her and not permit her to escape from that fine man who much hungers for her and will take such good care of her. I trust all this is clear to your divine omniscience.

I then mentioned my other intentions, including Milord Cronin. Also my nephew and his promised bride.

My cell phone rang before I could complete my orisons.

"Hi, Uncle Blackie, we're back!"

"I rejoice."

"No problem, we're both careful drivers. Costa del Sol is OK, but it is not as nice as Grand Beach."

"How could it be? Nothing is as nice as Grand Beach. Everyone knows that."

"Fersure. . . . We talked to my sainted mother today and told her we planned to be married on Fourth of July weekend. She went postal."

"You changed your mind? It's still Labor Day weekend?"

"So we settled on that as a compromise. Then she was delighted we'd set a date. Cool, huh?"

"Arguably."

"Now everyone is happy."

"Except Uncle Blackie who will be blamed for the July Fourth decision."

"Yeah, there's that. But you get blamed anyway."

"Then we called Spike and Annie Nolan. They were totally happy. They want to see their Margaret Anne married to a nice young man and it's all right if he is a theologian."

"Indeed."

"We told Mom to pass it on to Peter and Cindasue. She and Peggy really bond."

"What could be more natural than a creature from the hollers of West Virginia down to stinkin' Crik bonding with a young woman who owns her very own Cessna 310 Bravo and flies her own Grumman Gulfstream 560, right?"

Joseph's sense of irony is often silent, but not always.

"Only in America, right, Uncle Blackie . . . How's Teresa?"

"Recovering."

"Great. . . . When you going home?"

"Soon. You?"

"Whenever you want. Herself is doing a lot of good work with her magic screen. We have folks coming in from LOT and Aeroflot tomorrow . . . Hey, you want to come have a drink with us? I think they have Bailey's here at Alfonso XIII."

"Another night. It's midnight which is not as late here as in Chicago, but I have a mystery or two to solve tomorrow."

"Yeah, hey, Peggy said to say 'hi,' she crashed in her bedroom ten minutes ago."

Good for her.

The next morning I had a suggestion for my good friends Manuelo and Pepe.

"You might try to locate a death certificate recording the death of Anna Rosa Robbles y Alverno, the mother of La Doña. She died during the end of the Franco regime and the record may be lost or hidden. Should you locate it you might find that she died of an overdose of barbiturates, in circumstances perhaps which would make her death appear to be suicide. She was pregnant at that time with the young Duke."

They both were startled, as well they might be.

"If, after unsatisfactory interviews this morning, you should decide to search their quarters carefully, I predict you will find a bottle of such barbiturates in the room of Doña Inez Mercedes."

"You are saying that she murdered La Doña's mother twenty years ago and tried to murder La Doña two days ago," Manuelo gasped. "I would have to possess incontrovertible evidence to bring such a case to trial."

"I don't know that there can possibly be such evidence for the first death. But I believe that we must be persuaded that my scenario is possible."

"If she has barbiturates in her possession there is legitimate grounds for suspicion."

"Pepe, see if you can find a death certificate. Look in the secret files first."

"Immediately!"

He left the office at high speed. Outside the sky was gray for a change. It might rain, Don Pedro said at breakfast, the river is thirsty for water. The river did indeed look flat and sullen.

Manuelo slouched at his desk.

"This would be a great scandal, a terrible scandal. The trial would be like a circus."

"You have insanity pleas over here?"

"*Cierto* . . . the court can make that judgment even before the trial begins."

"If I'm right, there should not be much doubt about the madness."

"Why would they kill an unborn Duke and his mother?"

"I would speculate that the target was a possible duke, because I'm sure they didn't do scans in Spain in those days. Anna Rosa was a harmless child, but if her son were the Duke, she would have power over the whole estate. Don Marco would be out of work. It was Franco's time, they could get away with it. Everyone knew the young woman was depressed during her pregnancy."

"No doctor would prescribe something that strong."

"I'm sure that question would not arise in those days."

"It is all very speculative, Padre. The nobles used to dispose of unwanted women and children without hesitation. That was in the old days. Even in the time of the Falange, that would not have been tolerated . . . However, a man of Don Marco's influence could perhaps have thought that he still had the right . . ."

I knew I was missing something.

"When your people are searching their apartment later today they should look for knives like the one that wounded La Doña. I assume that it was made in Toledo and that it is part of a set of matched knives that are on someone's wall. If they are as crazy as I think they are, they have not removed the rest of them."

El Juiz made a note on the sheet of paper in front of him.

"And while you are searching, you might ascertain whether Don Teodoro's fingerprints happen to be on the container of barbiturates."

Don Pepe returned with a document in hand. His brown eyes were filled with tears.

"This is a copy," he said. "I have returned the original to the secret files and asked my assistant to put another copy in the open files."

"Take some of your people over there and search that apartment everywhere. Here is my authorization."

He signed a document that he had removed from a file. It looked like a form . . . That easy to get a search warrant in Spain . . . excuse me the Spanish state.

"*Sí*, Señor Juiz!"

Pepe left the room briskly. He knew he was on the track of a vicious killer.

A scenario was outlining itself in my mind. It was not necessary to have three killers. One would do. Two accessories perhaps.

"Don Marco Antonio and Doña Inez are here to see you, sir. They are very angry. Don Teodoro Guzman refuses to come. It would be necessary to arrest him to bring him in."

"If necessary, we will do that. Show the others in."

Two very angry-looking grandees strode into the room. Don Marco wore his full military uniform with a towering hat which accentuated his long, lean shape. A vast array of medals adorned his thin chest. Doña Inez wore a funereal black gown, silver jewelry, a black mantilla, and carried a black fan. She was still a striking woman, except when her face was contorted with rage.

We were playing in the big leagues. Younger staff people drifted by the window that provided transparency to the office of El Juiz. They wanted to observe this view into the past.

"I protest this indignity," Don Marco Antonio Navaro y Gomes announced in his squeaky voice. "I am a decorated general officer of the Spanish state. I deserve superior treatment."

"And I protest your sword, Don Marco Antonio. It violates the civil laws of the Spanish State to bring such a weapon into this building. If you do not remove it and give it to Don Pepe, I will order your arrest."

The grandee hesitated. In the old days he would have drawn

the sword and defied arrest. But now he tried to pull it dramatically from its sheath. The recalcitrant weapon failed to budge. He had to tug it loose and give it to Pepe, handle first, in a gesture of contempt which failed when the blade slipped out of his hand. Pepe picked it up and placed it on his desk.

I know who you are, fella. You're Don Quixote de la Mancha. And as outmoded as he was.

"Please sit down." Manuelo gestured to comfortable chairs across from his desk. Upon their entrance I had hastily donned my invisibility cloak. No tea and cookies for me during these interviews.

The suspects, for such they were in my book, sat down as solemnly as they could.

"*First,* I want to thank you for your kindness in joining us for this visit. We are, as you know, investigating the mysterious attacks on Doña Teresa Maria over whom you've had some control, though we understand now that such control has been relinquished."

"She is a bitch, a whore, a slut, a disgrace to Spain. I spit on her. She should have died . . . You've seen that picture in the papers . . . She belongs in a brothel. When Spain was still a truly Catholic country she would be publicly horsewhipped."

"Yet I am told that nobles dressed in nothing at all down in the Costa del Sol before it was so crowded and before there were cameras, even before the Civil War."

No news to me, but it was nice to know that human nature had not changed all that much.

"Lies! Lies! Lies!"

"You know of course, because you look at the papers, that the first attempt on Doña Teresa Maria's life was from an overdose of barbiturates which had been introduced to a glass of sherry from her own vineyards. Did you not find it interesting that a similar overdose killed her mother and her unborn brother several years ago?"

191

"She was a silly little twit who could not accept the difficulties of pregnancy. A shallow, whiny little fool. We did not miss her in the slightest. We would not miss her slut of a daughter either."

"And the unborn Duke?"

"Small loss. A duke with that kind of blood would be worse than no Duke. She had bad blood from the beginning. You can see that from her behavior. Bad blood."

Don Marco had been twisting in his chair as the hatred poured out of his wife's mouth.

"That is too harsh, Inez. Much too harsh. Anna Rosa was a lovely frightened child. A young Duke would have not tolerated his sister's public behavior. We would be much better off if he were alive. He would have understood what Spain stands for and not permitted a woman to disgrace us the way Teresa does. She has been trouble for us all our lives."

"Do you happen to have any barbiturates in your house at the present time?"

"Certainly not," Marco Antonio sputtered. "We do not keep drugs in our home. Ever. If the Army stands for anything it stands for self-control."

"This is the knife with which La Doña was stabbed," El Juiz said as he displayed an evidence bag. "Have you ever seen it in your house?"

Don Marco considered the evidence very carefully.

"I cannot say I recognize it. We have many weapons in our apartment. We are a military family with a long tradition. The weapons remind us how often we have been called on to offer our lives in the service of Spain. I came across from Cueta in 1936. Most of my colleagues died in those early days. We did free Sevilla from the Reds who had swept in from the fields, cruel anarchist farmers. We killed them all!"

Except the *palacio* did not belong to his family. It belonged rather to the family of his wife, Inez, and her niece, Teresa Maria.

I wondered what inheritance laws were in this country. Would the lands and the money revert to Inez if La Doña died? Or was there some shirttail cousin, as we say, who would become the Duke and owner of everything?

"Is the Army waiting for a signal and a leader as it was in 1936?" Manuelo asked.

"Some believe that to be true, even my good friend Jefe Teodoro Guzman. I doubt that very much. It is not the same army, not the same Spain. Prosperity has taken away our iron will."

"I firmly believe that Rosa was the illegitimate daughter of one of those fiends," Inez continued her rant. "Where else would the bad blood come from, except from apelike anarchists pouring in from the fields."

"She was a sweet little thing," Don Marco said. "It was not her fault that she was having a difficult pregnancy. Bad blood was causing it. She had no depression during the first pregnancy."

"You are an idiot, Marco. You were always sweet on that little fool. Just as you have been on Teresa, too sweet for my taste. She is a fool too but a dangerous fool. Bad blood! Bad blood!"

"If I may say so, Señor Juiz, Teresa is very important to us just now. As you may know, Don Teodoro and I have had some financial problems recently. Some accounting mistakes, some misunderstanding about the use of funds. The Madrid media have published many innuendos but no proof. The army, perhaps rightly, demands that we return some money. We had not anticipated such a demand and hence did not have the liquid capital to repay them. Teresa provided the money for us on a generous loan. We had every reason to want to keep her alive."

"Did not that money clear the Army Accounting Office before the attempts on her life?"

"It may have, but we did not know that."

The old man was persuasive. Quixote could not have carried it off so well.

"Besides," he continued, "if La Doña had died, there would be many questions about her loan and Madrid might have frozen it. The young accountants in the Army are far too careful with senior officers."

"And she has driven us out of our home as part of the loan. We must leave within a month. Why can't she fornicate with her pretty boy in that apartment in Santa Cruz?"

There was an important hint in that comment which the reader will have not missed, but I did.

"It is really her house. It always was all along. She probably wants to remodel it and make it one of her museums."

"Bad blood! And you, you old fool, always lusted after her!"

That was a dangerous admission for all of us.

Doña Inez was perhaps sixty-five years old, and a strikingly attractive, well-corseted woman, perhaps what La Doña would be like in twenty-five years. Yet when she opened her mouth, her face twisted with rage and one forgot about the rest of her beauty.

God protect my spiritual child from such rage.

"That's not true, *querida*. You've always been jealous of her, but I never lusted after her. I love only you."

Perhaps what was an admiring look with a touch of desire to one was lust to the other.

Don Marco struggled from his chair, Don Quixote betrayed by his Dulcinea.

"I think, Señor Juiz, that it is time to end this interview. It has served no purpose. I cannot see why we were summoned."

"We are trying to solve a mystery of attempted murder in a house in which you reside."

"I deny all knowledge of it except what I hear on television."

"Bad blood, she has bad blood and it is all her fault, like it was her mother's fault."

Don Marco winced. Poor guy. He knew more than he was telling.

"I warn you, Don Marco, that while we were talking this

morning, the police have been searching your apartment. We reserve the right to recall you. If you refuse to appear then we have no choice but to arrest you."

"On what grounds, sir!"

"Refusing to cooperate in a murder investigation."

Don Marco snorted at the argument and, riding on an imaginary Rosinante, rode out of the office, hat back on his head with his Dulcinea trailing behind him.

"Poor bastard . . . What do you think, Padrecito?"

"He's protecting her, but we'll never pry a word out of him. He would kill himself first."

"It will be interesting to see what Pepe finds."

My cell phone rang.

"Diego. I thought I would tell you that all went well. We will have a wedding *pasado mañana.*"

"Bueno!"

At some time in the future, La Doña could demand a decree of nullity on the grounds she was forced into marriage. I doubted that would happen.

"Pepe will find the pills in wherever Inez Mercedes keeps them in case she wants to eliminate someone else with an overdose of barbiturates. Her own private medicine cabinet, presumably."

"She killed Anna Rosa?"

"Do you have any doubts?" I asked.

"No," he said, "none. But it will be distasteful. Perhaps her *abrogado* will want to plead insanity . . . Did she try to kill La Doña?"

"Not with the barbiturates . . . we will probably find when the inestimable Pepe returns that the container of the pills will have her fingerprints on them, but over them will be those of Teodoro Guzman, the so-called Don Jefe."

It was almost time for lunch and the close of everything in town when Pepe returned.

"I found the pills"—he held up a container—"half filled with barbiturate pills. It had been recently opened. The killer must have put half in the bottle of La Doña's sherry."

"And the fingerprints?"

"Older prints from Inez Mercedes and new ones from Teodoro Guzman."

It was time for me to exit right . . . quietly. If there was still an outpost of the Holy Office of the Inquisition down here, they would have considered burning me at the stake.

16

"*You were correct, Padrecito Negro, as* you always are—a dangerous and suspicious trait. I must report this to the Vatican. What can the Church do about an Archbishop who is always right."

I had just given him a brief rundown about what we had learned at the Municipal.

"Pretend that he does not exist."

"A wise strategy."

"And I assume you were correct in your strategy in dealing with La Doña."

We were in the dining room, eating lunch, yet another variety of irresistible tapas.

"She is a very complicated woman, as you know. I thought at the beginning I would perhaps lose. I argued for an almost immediate marriage, to put closure to this romance, a fine romance, but we must protect it and the romantic lovers from too much of the public eye, no?"

"Yes. And too much possibility that La Doña might revert to her self-hatred."

"I proposed a *pasado mañana* wedding—the day after tomorrow—in the Church of Santa Catalina, a brief meal thereafter at the Bar Giralda which I would provide, and then the departure of the two principals to a small, excellent sanitarium of which I know where there will be both absolute privacy and constant medical care of the best kind. I have already spoken to the *doctora* in charge and she understands that she must maintain total security and privacy until they are ready to leave on their *luna de miel.*"

"Is La Doña strong enough for a wedding?"

"Her doctors say she is a very strong woman. Yes, she can survive it but she will be worn out afterward. I argued that this was the best procedure to combine a wedding with an opportunity for her to recover completely before they leave on their wedding trip to, I believe, Chicago. An interesting notion, no? Incidentally, how does my brother Sean do?"

"Better. He accepted the wisdom of being in hospital, but he shows little desire to live longer."

"That is unfortunate . . . When do you return?"

"The day after the wedding."

"That is excellent because you are scheduled to preach at the wedding, which I think is a very positive idea. . . . Will you need time to prepare?"

"No, I have an all-purpose homily. It's about why God made *las fresas.*"

"A wedding homily about strawberries?"

"*Sí. Cierto.*"

"I'd like to hear it."

"But you will. . . . You will be saying the nuptial Mass."

"That is true."

There was an annoying little scruple in my mind. Something important I had forgotten. It was important and dangerous, but what was it?

"Your nephew and his promised bride will of course be present? La Doña wants the small party to include the servants, the guards and the police who protected her, her secretarial staff. This is a happy solution because society will understand her usual generosity. They will also know that Santa Catalina is a very small old church."

"I have prayed in it!"

"Really? That is impressive. But why? There are so many little churches in our city."

"My late mother, God be good to her, and my oldest sister are both Kathleen."

"How nice! . . . I had a very difficult time this morning. La Doña, poor woman, is frightened, as I suppose she has been all her life. Everyone else argued for my plan, Don Leandro of course, Maria Luisa, her *novio,* the doctors, the nurses, all to no avail. She wanted marriage, oh, yes. She wanted a husband, oh, yes. Who else but Don Leandro, oh, yes. But not now, later. When later? She could not say. Then Don Leandro's children, tears in their eyes, begged her. They wanted her for a mother. She would be a wonderful mother for them just as she had been for Señorita Maria Luisa! Please, please, PLEASE! Many tears to which, needless to say, La Doña succumbed and with great happiness. Maria Luisa will live with them while the married couple are away. More tears of happiness. Voilà!"

I applauded and he bowed. He would have made a great parish priest.

Now details, please, about what happened at the Municipal today.

I rehearsed my account, dictated into my portable dictator on the way back to the Cathedral Plaza.

"It is incredible! Those old nobles are always a little mad. They lived through too much—as for generations they have attempted to rule this country. You understand the need of removing the married couple from the city before all this is revealed?"

"Oh, yes."

"The happy couple will appear on television at the hospital entrance tonight and announce their plans. On the news after siesta."

We rose from the table, our eyes heavy after our tension-filled morning. He was bound for his siesta and I to make some arrangements.

I brought my computer down to Don Pedro's office and attached it to his printer. With some complications, we managed to print out the English and French texts of my strawberry story.

I detached my computer from his printer cable.

"Don Diego has decreed that I preach at the wedding *pasado mañana*. Would you ever be able to translate it into presentable Spanish?"

"How very interesting. Il Padrecito Negro brings his wedding homily with him wherever he goes."

"One must be prepared, Don Pedro."

"*Sí,* Padre, I understand! It will be an honor to translate it. I will learn much."

His grin, I thought, was that of a benign leprechaun who loved little jokes, especially on his boss. I waved a finger at him.

"Don Diego must not read it before I give it."

"*Sí,* Padrecito, *sí!*"

"*Muchas gracias.*"

"*De nada.*"

I thereupon repaired to my room to prepare for the resting of my eyes. I set my obnoxiously noisy, though necessarily so, alarm to wake me a half hour before the post-siesta news. My eyes settled into their resting position when I remembered one more obligation.

I called Joseph Murphy on his mobile phone.

"Joseph," he said briskly.

"What's going on?"

"What's going on is that my promised bride is negotiating, through translators, with LOT. We talked to the Russians this morning. These folks don't do siesta."

"She is enjoying success?"

"You gotta be kidding, Uncle Blackie. Of course she is.

Those Eastern Europeans are tough to read. Their facial muscles must have been frozen at birth. What's going on with you?"

"We are all invited to a wedding *pasado mañana* at the Church of Santa Catalina in Macarena and a dinner afterward at the Bar Giralda in Santa Cruz."

"Hey cool! I bet Marylou is really happy. She's been pushing it for a long time! We're not planning to leave till the next morning! Early! That all right with you?"

"Perfect. My best to the supersalesman."

"I tell her that it is good she is not selling encyclopedias."

I calculated the risks. My first loyalty is to Chicago and Sean Cronin. I would leave for Chicago tomorrow if necessary. On commercial flights which were less comfortable than on the Gulfstream 560. I would not be able to give the homily at the Mass, but Don Pedro could read it for me, doubtless with as much gusto and better pronunciation than I could. I called the Cathedral.

"Holy Name Cathedral Rectory! Megan speaking!"

Who could resist a church which could produce as much competent gusto in its gatekeepers!

"Megan Flores, I bet!"

"*Sí*, Padrecito Negro . . . where are you?"

"In Seville, I believe, though these days I can never be sure."

"Sounds like you're upstairs."

Even today the young view intercontinental phone calls as extraordinary events. They expect the caller to be shouting loudly so that their voices will echo on the winds and miraculously settle into the Chicago phone system.

"I don't think I am. Indeed, my best information indicates that I am in the Cardinal's palace in Seville."

"How wonderful . . . Hey, Cardinal Sean is doing real well. He'll be out in a couple of days! Isn't that great!"

"Indeed! Do you think Father Coyne would have a minute or two to talk to me?"

"Absolutely!"

They ran the rectory, heard all the news first, and decided how much time a priest had. Alas, we couldn't ordain them.

"Hi, Blackie. Herself says you're still in Seville. Siesta time, isn't it?"

"Eye-resting time, in fact . . . How is our mutual friend doing?"

"Fine, the doctors say. They've changed his medication which is what doctors do. They want to keep him for observation another couple of days. Nora is with him all the time. She has a room right next to his. My-sister-in-law, the witch, rides in on her broomstick and prays over him. Sometimes she brings my red-haired niece who is a witch in the making. She tells me that he's going to be all right eventually. It's that last adverb that worries me. Your sister drops in occasionally."

"Give them all my love! I have to preach at a wedding here the day after tomorrow which will be the end of my mission. We'll fly back first thing the next morning, Friday, I guess. . . ."

"Saturday."

"Really!"

"Really."

"I knew that. . . . Don't let the Megan move the rectory across the street on you."

"I look out the window a couple of times every day to make sure they haven't. Take care."

It was now time to sip the sherry I had taken from lunch and quiet the complaints of my weary eyes.

There was still that important clue I had forgotten. What was it?

The noxious alarm, a tool of the demons, awakened me violently.

"Why are you waking me early, evil machine?"

I realized that I had to watch a TV broadcast. I wondered

what mischief the people at the Municipal might be engaging in this evening. I would let them call me.

Don Diego and Don Pedro were sitting in front of the modest TV in their parlor.

"Don Pedro tells me that you have prepared a brilliant homily for the wedding, but I must wait to hear it."

"That is true."

"He adds that I will be pleased with it."

"I hope that is true."

"He suggests that after the Mass we should have copies to distribute to the press, if they so desire it and to those who will come to my little dinner at the Bar Giralda. In any event we will publish it in our Catholic weekly, if you do not object?"

"*Cierto* no . . . I am happy to report that your brother Sean Cronin seems to be recovering and will be out of the hospital the day after the wedding."

"So you must leave us?"

"A coadjutor bishop must coadjutorate."

"You must return to al-Andalus. If you do not promise we may hold you captive in the dungeons of the Inquisition."

"I will miss Seville and your unfailing courtesy and welcome."

"You have been a delightful guest. We will await your return."

Such is the formality in which churchmen must engage, so they will not weep at farewells.

The television screen came alive. The scene was the entrance to Blessed John XXIII Hospital. A crowd of medical men and women, security guards, onlookers, and reporters crowded around the doorway, held in check by uniformed Civil Guards. My friends Don Manuelo and Don Pepe lurked in the background.

"Doña Teresa Maria, Duchess of Seville y Huelva, who was subject to a murderous assault is about to answer questions concerning the assault and the police investigation. Thus far no arrests have been made."

La Doña emerged on the arm of her promised one. She was wearing a white pantsuit with a brilliant red and gold sash around her waist. Enough to hide any bandages which might still protect her from infection. She also wore a scarf of the same color around her neck and a white lace mantilla that neatly obscured a bandage on her head. Her eyes were bright and her smile radiant. Flanking the couple were Maria Luisa and Don Isidoro de Colon. The two Santiago children, grinning impishly, were holding the hands of Maria Luisa for dear life. That young woman was wearing a similar pantsuit, though the sash and scarf were blue and gold.

Wonderful picture for the European fashion magazines.

"Can you hear me?" she asked the crowd as she fingered the lavaliere microphone on her scarf. "Good!

"First, you will wonder about my health, especially considering my second announcement.

"I am recovering rapidly from my injuries. The doctors and nurses and medical technicians and the cooks here at John XXIII have been very good to me. Their care has made it possible for me to recover more quickly than I would have thought possible. However I still experience some soreness. I will need a little more time for complete recovery. As to the police investigation, I have nothing to say but I am quite certain that the Investigating Judge and the police are making progress and will soon be able to announce arrests."

She was talking without notes, but confidently and clearly. Don Diego gave a thumbs-up sign to me.

"Before I make my announcement, I wish to say that I have consulted with my doctors and they have no objections so long as I lead a quiet and restful life for a few more days.

"Therefore it is with great joy that I announce with Don Leandro Santiago y Diaz that we will be joined in holy matrimony the day after tomorrow in the Church of Santa Catalina in Macarena."

She leaned against her lover, temporarily weak. She had ventured beyond the point of no return.

The crowd, stunned by the surprise announcement, cheered deliriously. La Doña smiled and waited patiently to continue her statement.

"Don Diego," she continued . . . as the crowd calmed down, "the Cardinal Archbishop of Seville, will preside over the liturgy." She lost her train of thought and clung more diffidently to her promised groom. "The groom's man will be Don Isidoro de Colon, Admiral of the Ocean Seas."

Cheers for Izzy, who grinned and waved.

Well, he could drive a launch to Gibraltar and back with great skill.

"The woman of honor will be my extraordinary daughter, Señorita Maria Luisa. She will be assisted by Don Leandro's two daughters, Señorita Justa and Señorita Rufina . . ."

Maria Luisa carefully folded her mother into her strong athletic arms. The teenagers clung to her sobbing happily. Now all four women were weeping. So were most of the women in the crowd. Romances are even more romantic when there is a happy ending.

"I am so happy to have new daughters, especially two such lively and sensitive young women. I want to tell you, my new children, that you need treat me with no more diffidence than does your older sister!"

More cheering, more cameras flashing, a tour de force. Splendidly choreographed, Don Diego!

I raised two thumbs and saw that El Moro was weeping.

"After the nuptial Mass my husband and I will go to a place where we will begin our married life together and I will receive the remaining medical care I may need. We will return to our beloved Seville before we leave on our *luna de miel*."

A discreet hint that they might not quite engage in marital relations immediately. It would reassure the women who were watching that Don Leandro was not a brute.

"Finally you may wonder why this wedding is taking place now. I have not had a husband for a long time. At this stage of my life with everything that has been happening, I want a husband and need a husband. On the desk in my office are two black and white pictures, one of my mother, a sweet young woman, I am told, who died at the age of twenty along with my unborn baby brother. The other is of a gentle young man I knew when we were both in the University. We loved each other from a very great distance but were too shy to exchange anything but a cursory good morning when we passed one another in the corridor. Those two photos remind me to pray for lost love." Her voice stopped for a moment. "When Don Diego found me an *abrogado*, a widower, to assist me in the legal problems I was encountering I discovered the same smile I had fallen in love with in the corridors of the old cigarette factory when I was a child. I told myself that I had found a husband with whom I could spend the rest of my life. Fortunately for me he feels the same way."

The two of them embraced. He kissed her on the forehead. She brushed her lips against his. They clung to one another briefly. The crowd became hysterical.

"I assure you that when we return soon to Seville before our wedding trip we will answer all your questions. I must make one more comment to a question you wouldn't ask today but would think of tomorrow. My dazzling daughter, Maria Luisa, will move in with her two sisters and they will be in charge of her while we are away."

Loud cheers from the two girls as they embraced their new sister.

The cheering continued. La Doña and Don Leandro waved happily. A woman doctor moved toward her.

Then I saw the clue I had forgotten. Someone dressed in dark clothes and a kind of cloak emerged from the crowd, jumped the police barriers, and with a long knife in hand raced toward La Doña. Even on live television time seemed to stand still. There was no one to stop the assassin. The love story would end with more death. Then, it seemed out of nowhere, a man in a blue suit literally flew through the air and made a block that would have been a credit to an NFL fullback. Columbus's descendant had saved the life of a woman with the blood of Isabella the Catholic in her veins. Nice symbol.

The woman doctor snatched the knife. Doña Candida fell on the man in black and held him on the ground. Don Isidoro de Colon rose from the ground, casually brushed the dust from his jacket, and accepted the embraces of La Doña and Maria Luisa. He smiled modestly and waved once to the crowd, like Tiger Woods touching his cap after he had walked off the eighteenth green.

17

Our threesome in the office of the Investigating Judge was in a very gloomy mood.

"It was an inexcusable blunder," Manuelo confessed, taking off his coat and hanging it on the back of the chair.

"We knew about him," Pepe admitted, "and we didn't think he mattered."

"It is at least useful that no one knows of our error," Manuelo argued.

I said nothing at all.

"But we know. We knew of his existence."

"He claims that he's a gypsy, but that is not necessarily true."

"And he claims that a tall woman in black give him a hundred euros to follow Don Leandro."

"He asserts she gave him a thousand euros to stab the woman at the press conference."

"He says she was tall and haughty. It sounds very like Inez."

"But he would not persuasively identify her in court. An attempted murder charge against him would be dismissed as a weak attempt by the police to find someone to blame for the crimes against La Doña."

"However," I pointed out, "as we search for someone who

209

could be the person with the knife, we have at least some confirmation in our own minds that Inez is the prime suspect. Alas, there are no fingerprints on the knife and it was not among those on the walls in her quarters. Rather its mates were on Don Marco's walls."

"Therefore," Manuel concluded, "we interrogate Don Teodoro Guzman because we have not done so yet. Perhaps we can find some explanation in his responses."

"He was the one who put the barbiturates in the sherry, that is clear. You could accuse him of attempted murder and attempted rape and that might force him to tell you more than he wants to."

"We do not know"—Pepe shook his head—"how he got into the room."

"But we do," I insisted. "I will tell you how he did it."

I did.

They listened skeptically at first then with increasing interest as I proposed a solution to the simplest mystery in the case—how someone entered La Doña's apartment when it was supposedly locked while both of the keys lurked next to their respective miraculous medals.

They glanced at one another for a moment of thought.

"It is really so simple. Anyone could have seen that explanation. But, as you might say, Padrecito, you did and we didn't."

"I have no desire to claim credit."

"The honorable Miguel Casey said that you never failed to solve a locked-room mystery."

"Not so far. There could always be a first time."

"It is then most likely that he opened the door and poured the pills into her sherry and then came back later to torture her."

"Most likely but not proved, Pepe," the Investigating Judge said.

"That he opened the door, I think we can prove," I said. "What happened next perhaps he will tell us if he is frightened enough of his own fate."

210

Don Teodoro was a criminal beyond any doubt, a weak man, a Peeping Tom at least. Perhaps a would-be rapist and arguably an accessory to murder. But he was above all a sneak. Such men panic under pressure as he had with his fraud against the Army. A murder charge could destroy what was left of his courage, especially if he knew that he was, perhaps unintentionally, partially responsible.

"Bring him in," Manuel ordered. "He has been told of his rights to an *abrogado?*"

"He dismisses that. He is a military officer, a hero indeed. He has fought ETA for years. He has no fear of ambitious prosecutors."

The police officers who had arrested him escorted him into the room. He wore his uniform and cap. He kicked his heels together and bowed.

"Gentlemen, I am at your service."

He had seen too many movies about the foreign legion. The tight fit of his uniform hampered his scripted attempt at jaunty indifference.

"Don Teodoro Guzman, we are considering a charge of the attempted murder of Doña Teresa Maria, Duchess of Sevilla y Huevla. You may refuse to answer our questions or you may choose an *abrogado* to protect your rights under the criminal code of the Spanish state during our questions. What are your wishes in this matter?"

"I didn't try to kill the whore." A sly smirk crossed his round face. He had no respect for his interrogators.

"If you refuse to answer our questions we will charge you and suggest that you be imprisoned unless you can post substantial bail."

"Ask your questions."

"Will you please sit down, sir?"

"I'd rather stand."

"I hereby inform you that your conversation is being

recorded. This is both to preserve your rights and insure that the court knows our precise questions during this interview."

He shrugged.

"I take the shrug of your shoulders to indicate that you understand the recording."

He shrugged again and sneered at the prosecutor and his staff.

"Captain Guzman, would you look at this evidence bag please."

"I wish to make the point that in the Army, because of my rank as chief of quartermaster service in Andalusia, my proper title is El Jefe."

"Very well, El Jefe. What do you see in this bag?"

"A container."

"And inside the container?"

"Pills . . . some kind of medication I suppose."

His confidence was fading. He had not anticipated this.

Eejit!

"Can you read on the label the name of the medication?"

"It appears to be some kind of barbiturate."

"Would it surprise you to learn that it is the same kind of barbiturate that was found in La Doña's sherry carafe and in the bottle of sherry that was used to fill that carafe?"

"Coincidence!"

"Indeed!"

"They are not my pills. I don't need pills to do my job."

"So. I put it to you that our search found this container in Doña Inez's medicine cabinet."

"Then why ask me about it?"

"Because your fingerprints are all over it."

He lost all his steam.

"I never touched the bottle. It belongs to her, not to me."

"Her prints are on it too, but yours are more recent."

"I don't care. I never touched the container."

"Let me describe to you what happened. You have been observed many times in recent weeks lurking in the corridor outside of La Doña's apartment, hoping perhaps for a glimpse of either her or her daughter in their lingerie or less."

"I just have to look out of the window of my room to see them displaying themselves in their swimming pool in our courtyard."

"But you wanted to see more, did you not? So you tried to peek in the door when the housekeeper was cleaning the room. Maybe you did find the occasional peek at one or the other of them as they were dressing."

"I deny that."

"You admitted that you walked the corridors often?"

"It was our house as well as theirs. We had the right to walk anywhere we wanted."

"An interesting claim."

Sweat was pouring down his face and his hands were twitching nervously.

"It is the truth."

"You were often tempted to reach inside the door and reverse the emergency lock. You knew from observation that when Señora Vlad closed the door it automatically locked. La Doña never lifted the emergency lock when she admitted the housekeeper. Thus when Señora Vlad closed the door, the lock was still on. Only the two women had keys to open it and they both wore them around their necks next to their miraculous medals."

"I don't care about such nonsense."

"This particular day, your lust was so strong that you reached inside the door and released the emergency lock, then you retreated quickly. You were excited by your courage and success. Now these two women were without protection."

"The younger woman is my promised bride. I have some claims on her."

"She does not acknowledge that role."

"Don Marco Antonio and Doña Inez betrothed her to me. It is all in the family records."

"Records which have no legal force in the present Spanish state."

"They do in Spanish honor."

"Perhaps. But Señorita Maria Luisa has said publicly on many occasions that if you so much as touch her, she would castrate you."

"She does not understand the code of the family. Her father on his deathbed gave us the power to approve the marriages of both of them just as if he was still alive."

"So you had the right to enter their rooms at night and have your wishes with one or both of them in their rooms and molest them? That argument will not stand up in a criminal court of the Spanish state at the present time."

"The Army is ready at any time to bring down the Spanish state . . ."

"Such a statement is close to treason."

"I understand that," he said, struggling to recover his bravado.

"You went back to your own room and pondered your good fortune. You understood that the two women would fight you. Even one of them might do you serious damage. They would recognize you and report your molestations to the Civil Guard. You wondered how you could have them completely under your power. It occurred to you that some of these pills"—the Juiz lifted the evidence bag and shook it—"would make them unconscious. You were aware that Doña Inez kept such a container in her room. You were delighted at your insight. You went to her quarters, sneaked into her bathroom, removed this container, and poured half of it into your pocket. Then you hurried back to the other side of the *palacio* and poured some of the pills into La Doña's sherry carafe. If the two women would have their nightcap you would have both of them at your disposal. You knew, as everyone did, that La Doña spent some time each evening with her *amante* in Santa Cruz. You didn't know where Señorita Maria Luisa was. However, you did know that Inez's spy—yesterday's attempted murderer—would report to her when La Doña left her apartment above the Bar Giralda. Inez was keeping a record of her cousin's nights of sin. After waiting for some time so that the soporific would have taken effect you hurried over to La Doña's apartment to begin your amusements. You wore gloves of course. Maria Luisa was not in her bedroom. So you tiptoed into La Doña's room. Your brain was burning with a Peeping Tom's lust. You noticed that she had tipped over the sherry carafe. You carefully removed the key chain from around her neck and tore off her gown . . .''

"No! No! I removed it very gently." Our brave soldier began to weep. "She was so beautiful! I did not want to hurt her. I would not have hurt her. I just wanted to look at her."

I felt some satisfaction that he had repeated the outline of events I had provided. The locked-room mystery was partially solved. The issue now was whether he would repeat the rest of my outline. If so I could leave for Chicago almost at once.

"You lost your sexual arousal and ran from the room," Manuelo went on implacably.

"I left only when I realized she might be dying."

"You thought you might have murdered her?"

"Her breathing was very light. Her skin was cool. Her marvelous breasts were hardly rising. I was afraid that maybe I had killed her. I ran for help. We should get her to a hospital. We could say that she had taken an overdose like her mother had . . .''

"And you put the key in the inside lock! Why?"

"I don't know why! I wasn't thinking clearly! I discovered it was still in my hand! I had to put it someplace."

He slumped over the prosecutor's desk, a spent and useless man.

"And then?"

"I ran back to our apartments. Don Marco and Doña Inez do not go to bed until very late. They watch television and drink wine, a bottle each. I found them in their robes and fell on my knees and confessed what I had done. Don Marco called me a stupid fool. We might lose the money she had given us. He staggered to his feet and tottered into the corridor. Doña Inez rushed to her apartment and returned with gloves and a small gun. She put the gun in the pocket of her robe and grabbed a knife from a display on the wall of their parlor. I was still on my knees weeping.

"She ignored me and yelled at her husband, still staggering against the wall of the corridor. 'Put on your gloves, you stupid old fool!' She was not as drunk as he. She was always the more ruthless and careful criminal. Like when she tricked Teresa's father into granting us control of their lives. He resisted till the bitter end and gave her only part of what she wanted, but still she beat him down."

That was within the story line I had proposed. When they arrived at her apartment Don Marco would try to protect La Doña. Inez would want to kill her. Marco and Teodoro were accessories to attempted murder. Inez guilty of the crime.

"You returned to your own apartment?"

"I thought of killing myself. Then I realized it would not bring Teresa Maria back to life. I sat there on my bed for a long time. Then I heard a muffled shot from across the courtyard. I knew that beautiful wonderful woman was dead. I had killed her."

He sobbed hysterically and called God's wrath down upon himself. He told God that he deserved hell for all eternity.

"I begged God to spare her life," he cried. "God heard my prayer. I did not kill her. God be praised. I offer myself as a victim."

"Don Teodoro Guzman," the Juiz intoned solemnly. "I charge you with the attempted murder of Doña Teresa Maria,

Duchess of Sevilla. I will instruct a court to try you for this crime."

Pepe pressed a button. Two uniformed cops entered.

"Take this wretch away and lock him up."

The guards dragged "El Jefe" out of the room.

We sat around his desk, gloomy and silent.

"May La Doña never hear that story," Manuelo muttered.

"A pathetic creep," I agreed. "Incapable even of great evil."

God, I presumed, would find many reasons to exercise his mercy, which he usually did. Don Teodoro was a petty crook but not steeped in evil. Doña Inez? An insanity plea here on earth. In the beyond? Maybe that plea would hold there too.

"We need only confirm this story with an interview of Don Marco and the case is closed. We will bring him in tomorrow morning."

"He will appear here on his own initiative," I said.

"Why do you think that, Padrecito Negro?"

"He will report his wife's death from an overdose of barbiturates."

He stared at me.

"*Cierto.*"

"What will happen to them?"

"They will plead guilty. Teodoro will go to a military jail. Marco to a prison hospital. It will all happen very quietly."

217

18

El Moro was saying his prayers again, clad in his scarlet T-shirt and jeans, the complete postmodern Cardinal.

He raised an eyebrow when I came into his study.

"So."

"That's how Seamus Heaney begins *Beowulf*."

"A story more bloody than this one? It is said that the Gypsy isn't a Gypsy but a Catalonian gardener employed by Inez?"

"That is not improbable."

"The story is finished?"

"By tomorrow morning anyway."

"It will end, ah, cleanly?"

"I have reason to expect that it will, yes."

"Any more deaths to be expected?"

"One perhaps."

"Inez."

"Arguably."

"I have suspected for some time that she killed Anna Rosa."

"Patently."

"Your task here is finished then, Blackie . . . after you read that homily."

I sighed.

"Time to return to Chicago. A coadjutor is helper. Milord Cronin needs a helper."

"Indeed. You leave the day after the wedding?"

"Which is tomorrow! Probably, unless we hear bad news from Chicago."

He made the sign of the cross.

"If it pleases God."

"The Moors would like that."

"Means the same thing . . ."

"Patently you did a fine job persuading La Doña to accept your scenario."

"It was not easy. The good woman is not frightened by casual if passionate sexual couplings. They dull the memory and kill the pain. She is afraid of marriage which does not kill the pain without dangerous efforts. She is not terrified by a lover with whom you sleep at night and leave alone by day. She is terrified by a husband who becomes an integral part of her life."

"Not an unreasonable reaction."

"Yet she is deeply in love with the splendid Don Leandro and will wither without him as she well knows. This contradiction could not be tolerated."

"She did not want to go off to a sanatorium up in the Sierra Nevada?"

"That appealed to her, oddly enough. It would mean peace, kind of a nirvana . . . I told her that she had come back from the dead. I said that resurrections meant new beginnings, that God expected a new beginning from her. A new life which was a renewed life. She was still shaking with fear . . . and all the time desperately holding the hand of the husband of whom she was afraid."

"Resurrections are not supposed to be easy."

"Even for Jesus?"

"I have never been in a position to ask him. But for the rest of us new beginnings mean new terrors."

"*Cierto* . . . It was finally the children that trapped her."

"Children?"

"Justa and Rufina . . . I cannot keep them straight, so I must not use first names with them."

"If they are like other young women I know, that would amuse them greatly."

"When it looked like she was going to leave our meeting, the two embraced her and said they wanted her for their new mamacita. When their first mamacita was dying, she promised them that she would send a new mamacita. Would she please, please, PLEASE be their new mamacita."

"Ingenious. And no one suggested such a strategy?"

"Not as far as I could tell . . . but Maria Luisa could easily have whispered it in their ears. They have somehow become very close to her."

"Thick as thieves."

"Then she organized the rest of the project, remembering to dutifully ask her promised groom's approval. He merely laughed. He laughs at her all the time. Somehow it seems to melt her resistance. I do not understand this . . ."

"The communication between lovers is sometimes obscure to those around them."

I did not feel it appropriate to suggest that it might have something to do with a certain propensity to excessive modesty—doubtless a remnant of the influence of her duenna, now alleged to have sent a gardener to kill her.

However, I did say, "Perhaps someone should explain to La Doña that the last two Popes compare spousal nakedness to the vulnerability of God."

"Of course . . . she seemed quite happy however while she was deputing responsibilities to people. I was told that it was not necessary that I be at the announcement and that it was necessary that I insist that you preach. Naturally I agreed."

"Naturally."

"It all revealed itself very well, except for the unpleasant incident at the end which was resolved by the impressive athletic skills of the current Admiral of the Ocean Seas."

"Don Pedro tells me that he plays soccer with Isidoro, as I take it the young man is called, and he is awesome."

"I like particularly the way he brushed the dust off his jacket."

"He might do well in the bullring with that sort of flair, but that would not be in his character. One can assume that Maria Luisa would not tolerate that."

"Not a chance."

"Well, if we can avoid any more trouble by this time tomorrow night they will be safe in their retreat up in the Sierra Nevada, and their new life begins."

"I am reasonably confident that my colleagues at the Municipal will prevent any more onslaughts from La Duenna."

"Please God."

"Oh, yes, La Doña wonders if she can read your homily beforehand so she can meditate on it."

"Tell her she can meditate on it after the wedding."

I called the Cathedral and the MIC (Megan in Charge, this time Megan Kim) read me a message from Father Pastor, "Tell Blackie when he calls that the Cardinal is in a very good mood and in no rush to turn the Archdiocese over to him."

Fair enough.

I turned on my baby computer because I suspected that there might be an e-mail from my spiritual responsibility. There sure was.

Padrecito Negro,

I will be given in marriage tomorrow, as you no doubt know, to my dear Don Leandro. I am terrified. I would escape if I could, but I know that I cannot. It is terrible to think like this because I love him so much, but as I keep telling everyone, I am not ready for marriage. Will I ever be ready, they ask me. The honest answer is that I am sure I will never be ready. I feel like I am a Christian woman swept up from the Costa del Sol by Berber pirates and that I am going to be sold on a slave block tomorrow. None of this is fair to poor Leandro, whom I love with all my heart and soul. Yet I am terrified of him. I was not afraid at all when we seduced one another. However, as I now learn, seduction and marriage are very different matters. To remove my garments for him now means a permanent sur-render of myself. Even to type those words makes me shiver.

He laughs at me all the time like I am a funny little child. Maybe I am. I delight in his laughter, but I know that my fears will not always amuse him. I don't know what I will do when that happens.

I am so very tired. I slept well last night and felt good all day. However, my argument with Don Diego and the preparation of the announcement has worn me out again. I sent Maria Luisa off with her little sisters to buy the bridesmaid dresses. Then I called her on my mobile and told her to buy my dress too. She has better taste than I do and far fewer inhibitions. It hangs here in my room, all sil-ver and white glow. It fits me perfectly because it fit Maria Luisa perfectly. It is modest technically, even poor Inez could not object, but it is made so that there could not pos-sibly be any doubt about the shape of my body. If I didn't value my body I would not exercise so fiercely to keep it attractive. Yet I am shamed when people admire it. Now there will be no choice.

Poor Leandro will not be able to make love to me, the doctors say, for perhaps two more weeks. I do not want to be a torment to him. I wish that I could jump into the Guadalquivir and disappear.

223

I remember the night before my first marriage. I had no idea what to expect, but I was fond of my promised groom. He was a good-looking man, elegant, slender, sensitive. I knew I could trust him. I was young and very innocent. I did not know there were men who desired other men more than they desired women. We tried to make love that night and I blamed myself for our failure as I did for a long time. I also learned how to give him some pleasure. Then a woman I met on the train to Madrid talked about such men and I understood. We continued to try. I was still fond of him, but I did not understand. Occasionally we completed the marriage act, though it was not pleasurable to either of us. However, we did manage to produce Maria Luisa, who was a wonderful event. My husband liked her, but shortly after she was born he took a new and important assignment in Madrid. So Maria Luisa and I had our apartment in the castle by ourselves, though Don Marco and Doña Inez were always there watching and disapproving of both of us.

I do not think anyone chooses to be like my husband was. They are humans like the rest of us. God, I am sure, loves them. It is wrong to hate them or persecute them.

I had a couple of brief affairs—in Paris and in London—they did not amount to much, but at least I learned how to do it. I decided that passion was not worth the effort. Then I met Leandro and rediscovered real passion. Now I must discover marriage for the first time. I am like a spinster preparing for her wedding night—one in which lovemaking is delayed for a couple of weeks. Do not worry, Padrecito, I will go through the marriage tomorrow with a smiling face. And listen to your homily with great attention. I will even meditate on it afterward.

With respect and affection,
Teresa

Doña Teresa Maria,

I am looking forward to the wedding because it will be a resurrection event. You came back from the dead the other day and you're coming back from a much longer death created by evil people. The only way you can accomplish that rebirth is to leap into it.

I wonder, given the pernicious influence the duenna has had on your life, if the nakedness between husband and wife may trouble you. Perhaps it even troubled you when he was only an **amante.** *Modesty is an important and necessary virtue but its dictates vary from time to time and place to place. You might want to reflect on the fact that both the last Popes teach that the vulnerability of naked spouses with one another gives us a hint of the vulnerability of God and humans in the love relation with God.*

I will see you tomorrow at the wedding. God bless you and your husband and your much expanded family. Feel free to write me from your mountain hideout. We will expect you in Chicago in early July.

El Padrecito Negro

The next morning I walked over to the Municipal for what I hoped was the last time. My colleagues were sitting at their desks and looking very glum.

"Today is the wedding," Manuelo said, smoothing down his hair. "You will be present?"

"Preaching."

"In Spanish?"

"*Cierto,* though you will think it Mexican. That's what we speak to our people in the United States."

"What will you talk about?" Pepe asked.

"Why God made *las fresas.*"

"That is a strange subject for a wedding."

"You'd be surprised."

"What will you say?"

"You will have to come to find out."

They both chuckled.

"We will be there," Pepe said. "We cannot permit another affair like last night. La Doña is now a worldwide celebrity. And a wonderful woman. Seville must defend her."

"A good point."

"Who do you think is the killer?"

"The one who stabbed her and shot her and sent the poor Catalonian to kill her? Don't we already know that?"

"Doña Inez?"

"Who else?

"You think she is the only danger?"

"No. There are always people out there who want to kill the good and the beautiful. You must be alert at all times. But if you have Doña Inez under control, there is no threat from the subjects of this investigation."

"We would like to think that is true. Why don't you tell us the last phase of your locked-room solution?"

"Surely it is patent. Doña Inez was driven to murder madness by her envy of La Doña. She needed to kill her just as she killed her mother. She would also have to kill eventually Maria Luisa. All have bad blood in her view. There is only one way to get rid of the person with bad blood. She killed Anna Rosa and the unborn Duke. Unfortunately it was the time of the Falange and no one dared to bring a charge against the wife of a prominent member of that party. This time she obtained the barbiturates, her favorite mode of poison as we know, and stored them in her medicine cabinet. She intended at the first opportunity to slip some of them into her cousin's food or drink. She assumed that, as in the old days, no one would search her apartment and find the tablets and determine who purchased them. It seemed very easy. She hired that young Catalonian gardener who worked on her roses as a fall-back weapon.

"When Teodoro dashed into their parlor with his hysterical story, she saw another opportunity. By this time, she was out of her mind. If she were responsible she would have realized the danger to the loan they had received from La Doña. But the bad blood had to be extirpated. She grabbed a gun, two pairs of gloves, and, as a final thought, a knife.

"Don Marco was drunk and fought to stop her, probably all the way from their apartment to the still-open door of La Doña's apartment. It must have been a comic scene as they stumbled across the stairs and the corridors of the old palace. It is a wonder that she didn't stab him by accident. They tumbled into the apartment, the husband clinging to his crazy wife. She lunged in and swung her knife, probably aiming for the vagina. Her husband pulled her back and the knife cut into Teresa's body but with less damage. Then, I speculate as I draw the picture, with superhuman effort he pulled her out of the bedroom and she pulled out the pistol in her pocket and fired. For the second time in a few seconds her aim was poor."

My colleagues were silent.

"That is a very ugly story," Manuelo said.

"No more ugly than sending that poor Catalonian misfit into the wedding announcement yesterday."

"Don Marco is guilty too," Pepe said, pounding the desk. "He should have called the ambulance immediately."

"I will not defend him," I said. "He failed in his duty as did Teodoro. However, that woman dominated their lives for years. They were certainly accessories, as our law would put it."

"Teodoro did more than that," Pepe said. "There was enough soporific in that sherry to kill a dozen people."

"We must arrest her," Manuelo said. "God only knows what she will do today if we don't stop her."

Pepe agreed.

"We cannot permit another demonstration."

My colleagues were spooked. An arrest at the *palacio* before

227

the wedding would cause a sensation that they would rather have avoided. But not arresting Inez could cause a far worse tragedy. They could ask that the wedding be postponed but that too would be a scandal. Could not the Civil Guard protect Seville from a madwoman?

"We can't expect the remarkable Isidoro de Colon to intercept a killer this time."

A woman staff member knocked on the door and entered.

"Don Marco Antonio Gomez wishes to talk to you, sirs."

The old man who walked into the office was a classic picture of an aging grandee. He was wearing a perfectly fitting gray suit, a fashionable white straw hat, a white shirt with a regimental tie (this one probably authentic), and white gloves. A single ribbon on his lapel suggested a military honor, probably for killing agricultural anarchists who were running wild in this city. He carried a cane that must have come from Spanish Morocco when there was a Spanish Morocco.

He accepted the chair we offered him, sat down on it, and rested both hands on the cane in front of him. A man of decency, honor, and respectability. A man who had also left La Doña bleeding to death on her bed.

"Señores," he began formally, "I have come to report that my wife committed suicide this morning. She used the barbiturates with which she killed Teresa Maria's mother and tried to kill Teresa Maria herself. I have also come to assume my full responsibility for these terrible events. I did not kill my wife. Nor did I try to prevent her killing herself. I will answer any questions you may wish to ask."

"Why?" the Juiz asked.

"It is a long story. I suppose I must tell it. As you know I wiped out the anarchist brutes here. I was a young officer, ruthless, brilliant. Then when we defeated the Reds in 1939 I held many important positions in Madrid. After the war in Europe the Generalissimo sent me back here to assure that there would be peace in Andalusia. The people welcomed me because they still feared the Reds. I had not married. The old Duke invited me to live in his palace. Inez Mercedes lived in the house too, a beautiful and lively young woman who had lost her parents during the Civil War. Her vitality captured my heart. At that age she looked much like Maria Luisa and enjoyed the same enthusiasm for life. Even though I was much older, she seemed to like my company. We were both lonely, outcasts we thought. She loved the young Duke, but he had eyes only for Anna Rosa. We fell in love and married. We were very happy together. I have loved her deeply ever since. She honored me and respected me and enjoyed me. We were not able to have children, a great loss for both of us. I suggested we see doctors about the problem. She refused because of her modesty. Yet we were happy together. There was only one problem in our life—Anna Rosa had married the young Duke and given him a daughter who was a sweet little child. Then she became pregnant again. If it were a boy, he would be the next Duke. I could not understand her obsession with these matters. I was a distinguished general officer in the Army. We had all the money we needed for a comfortable life . . ."

He paused in his quiet narrative, trying, it seemed, to control his sorrow.

"To be a Duke or a Duchess in those days meant something, but not very much. Now of course it is worthless. Even Catholics have little reverence for them. My beautiful gracious wife was obsessed with Anna Rosa's 'bad blood.' I was losing my lovely wife to that obsession. Thus I was relieved when the poor woman died, of an overdose of a soporific, the doctors said. I sorrowed for her and the little boy. It was a tragedy, but we had many tragedies in Spain. I had my lovely wife again. You can imagine my horror when I found barbiturates among Inez's medications. I thought that perhaps she had . . . but I didn't permit myself to think it. Yet it remained a tiny worm eating away at my happiness . . ."

He stopped talking again, dabbed at his eyes, sighed, and began.

"I must finish this story. I want you all to understand that I never stopped loving my wife. Never. Even when she was dying this morning I held her in my arms. Her rage against poor little Teresa was almost insane. She appointed herself Teresa's duenna and supervised her life. She reported the child's disgraceful behavior to her father with great glee. Teresa is of much stronger constitution than her mother. She learned to dismiss my wife as unimportant, a gnat buzzing around. Yet when she told the Duke about her scandalous behavior with the flamenco dancers over in Triana, the Duke removed her from the University and at my wife's suggestion arranged for a marriage with a man we knew was a pretty boy. That would be the end of Teresa, my wife said. We had no children so neither would she. But Teresa did have a daughter who drove my wife to a frenzy of resentment. The young Duke left all the financial affairs of the family in Teresa's charge when he departed from here for good. She had come to the marriage with money of her own. She was a shrewd investor and did many wise things with both the Duke's money and her own. She was interviewed often in the papers and on television. When the Duke was dying of the wounds from the Basque attack we persuaded him to give us charge of the family. It was in a way my wife's last effort to defeat her enemies. We controlled their rights to marry, but she still controlled the money and owned this house. She wrote very clever articles about life in Andalusia which became popular everywhere in Spain. Everyone in Seville adored her. She traveled to France and Italy and England. My wife was beside herself with rage. She insisted we betroth the daughter to Don Teodoro, who was a protégé of mine in the Army. That was a mistake. Maria Luisa dismissed him with contemptuous insults; La Doña had been patient with us all her life. She had endured my wife's constant interference with hardly a complaint. My wife was to her a wicked old woman whose blood had curdled with jealousy. Not worth bothering about. The betrothal was the last straw. It had no legal force. Nonetheless, she now perceived my wife as more than an annoying nuisance but a serious danger. She asked the court to revoke her father's will and took her *abrogado* as a lover. My wife spied on her and kept records of the times they were together in that wretched little hole in Santa Cruz. If Teresa Maria became pregnant and gave birth to a son, that boy would be the next Duke . . . May I have a cup of tea please? My throat grows dry."

One of the guards brought in tea and cookies, none for me. I was very deep inside my magic cape.

"I told her that even if that should happen," he continued with his agonized confession, "we would lose nothing. My wife said that the baby would take the place that belonged rightfully to our son. . . . That startled me. I thought now that her envy, which so disfigured her beauty, had turned into insanity. She also said that if the daughter should marry the Colon boy that would be the end of our opportunities. . . . I saw three generations of women ruined by my wife's madness. I still loved her, but I realized she was a very dangerous woman. Then, as you know, Teodoro and I found ourselves needing money. We were both faced with ruin and perhaps jail. I visited Teresa's lawyer, a nice young man I must say. I confess that I envied him. He called me the next morning and said that La Doña would lend us the money if we ceded the rights from the will and agreed to leave the *palacio* within a month. Leaving the house would be very difficult. We had lived here so long, my wife said while she wept. That was harsh but I understood Teresa's reasoning. She wished to protect her daughter and her new lover. My wife became hysterical. She swore on the blessed sacrament that she would kill Teresa just as she had killed Teresa's mother and would someday kill her daughter. I should have taken the threat more seriously. Despite all the evidence, I never believed that my lovely, loyal wife could do evil. Yet I was worried. I told myself that this fugue would go away in a few days. Then Teodoro, who has behaved very badly, rushed into our parlor and described Teresa naked and unconscious on her bed. My poor wife became a mad dog. I ran after her as she shouted that she would cut out her, uh, reproductive organs! I was able to restrain her so that the knife went into Teresa's belly. Then I dragged her away and threw her on the floor of the corridor! I threw my poor beautiful wife on the floor! Then I returned to Teresa's room! I don't know why! I was crazy myself now . . ."

Deep inside my cloak I feared he would have a heart attack. That reminded me of Sean Cronin. I realized how, long ago, I had found time to worry about him.

"I heard my wife behind me, turned and saw that she had the small pistol she hides beneath her undergarments in her dresser. I pushed her arm up. The bullet crashed into the wall above Teresa's head. I wrestled the gun out of her hand and struck her. I hit my poor, demented wife with all my strength. She looked at me with great surprise as she went down, a look that said you have always loved her more than me. I had never hit her before in all our years together. I dragged her out into the hallway. She pulled the door as I laid her gently on the floor."

"She locked you out of the apartment!"

"I tried to open it and only then did I remember that Teodoro—slimy idiot that he is—had left the key in the lock."

"You were locked out!"

"Yes, gentlemen. I believed she had killed Teresa with that last attempt and I was as responsible as she was."

He took the clean white handkerchief from his jacket pocket and wiped his face.

"Why didn't you call an ambulance and the police?" Pepe demanded.

"I know now that I should have. I didn't think about it. I had consumed a bottle of wine. I had seen the knife go into Teresa. I wished that hell would open up and consume me and my dear one for all eternity."

"You assumed," Pepe snarled, "that La Doña was already dead."

"As I said, I had seen the knife go into her. Then I heard the alarms. Maria Luisa had returned home . . . Perhaps she had saved her mother."

"Through no fault of yours, Don Marco."

"I know."

That was less than fair. He had at least prevented his wife from sinking her scorpion sting into Maria Teresa's reproductive organs. They had all they needed. They would report that the final assaults in her bedroom were the work of a mentally deranged woman as was the attack yesterday. The two men would plead guilty and receive relatively mild sentences.

"I thought that my wife had learned her lesson. Then there was the attack yesterday evening. I told her she would probably have to go to prison. She said she knew that and would not permit it. She left the parlor where we had been talking and returned in her finest robe. She had taken some of the pills which she always carried with her in her purse. She wanted to die in my arms. I held her until she went to sleep, as I had done many times during our forty years together. She was a wonderful woman, gentlemen. She had only one fault and it destroyed her. You will find her earthly remains on the couch in our parlor. I don't want to go back there ever again. You may put me in prison."

He shuddered and bowed his head.

I thought to myself that if once, just once, in his life he had said to her, if you do not give up this obsession I will leave you, this tragedy would never have happened. He had been a brave soldier—by his standards—destroying brutal Red farmers by the hundreds, maybe thousands, but he lacked the courage to draw a firm line on his wife. Well, leave them all to heaven which has its own standards of mercy and, on the record, doesn't want to let anyone escape its loving embrace. All of this was beyond me.

Don Marco wiped his face again, neatly folded his handkerchief, and put it back into his pocket. He stood up, leaned on his cane, and waited for the guards to collect him. He went without protest.

"What do you think, Padre?"

"My God," I said, "is in the forgiveness business, fortunately for all of us sinners."

"We will consult with Don Diego and ask him to speak with La Doña and her husband."

"You have an explanation, a murderer who is deceased and two prisoners who have cooperated in the crime and will plead guilty. No need to have trials unless you want to make a point."

19

It was like a Feria day, a great fiesta. The little plaza in front of Santa Catalina and the streets around it were filled with cheering people, everyone dressed appropriately for the festival—Civil Guards in their elaborate costumes, out of a Beaumarchais opera, spear-carrying soldiers in golden armor mounted on white horses, clerics and nuns in full robes, choirboys in red, ordinary citizens in their Sunday best, Don Diego overwhelmed in red watered silk, flag bearers representing their guilds in medieval uniforms, American tourists with their digital cameras.

It was a gloriously lovely day, blue sky, an occasional lacy cloud, a brisk wind blowing in from the ocean, moderate temperature.

The Spanish TV network had posted giant television screens all through the surrounding neighborhoods and one supergiant in front of poor little Santa Catalina. I thought of my mother and my sister. They would love the show and probably take credit for it.

There was also a small TV screen in the sacristy of the church where Don Diego, Don Pedro, the parish priest, the groom, and the ineffable Don Isidoro waited patiently for the promised bride. The church was dense with the scent of orange blossoms.

Would there be some mad person out in the crowd with a gun or a bomb, a jihadist demanding the return of al-Andalus to its rightful Muslim rulers? In fact, it turned out that there was one such and the Civil Guard caught him.

"You know," Isidoro said with his engaging grin, "this is all kind of cool. I think I'll marry a Duchess too."

"You'd better," Don Pedro whispered.

"Too true."

The choir, crammed in a side aisle, began to sing. Gregorian chant at first. The polyphony would come later. Don Diego at my suggestion had sternly limited the run time for the choir. Outside a band began a light opera military march. Then wild applause sounded somewhere outside and a white limo pulled up, surrounded by Civil Guard motorcycles. Six of the mounted knights climbed off their horses and created an avenue for the bridal party with their spears. The door of the limo popped open and the two junior bridesmaids, uneasy in their wraparound blue and gold finery, stepped out.

Cheers and more cheers!

Then Maria Luisa, pushing the envelope as always in a little blue and gold below-the-knees dress held in place by defiant spaghetti strings.

"Well," Don Isidoro observed, "she'll do nicely as a young Duchess until a better one comes along."

Everyone in the tense sacristy giggled, everyone except the unobtrusive American bishop whom no one even noticed when he slipped in the back door of the church. He was considering how he would read the manuscript that was neatly arranged in a Chicago Olympics folder. His mental model for that was how it would sound on the lips of Megan Flores from the Cathedral office in Chicago.

Then there was a fanfare of trumpets and the bride emerged on the tiny sacristy TV, glowing in her white and silver gown. When the fanfare stopped, she walked slowly up the steps to the door of Santa Catalina, there was a pause, a kind of collective gasp from the assembled crowds as a front view of her coming up the steps of the church appeared. Then she turned and waved at all of us.

Then the multitudes went manic with cheers which would overwhelm even the sounds of the soccer stadium or the bull-ring.

"You know, Isidoro," Don Leandro murmured, "she'll do nicely for a mature Duchess until a better one comes along."

There was a touch of sadness in his eyes. She had suffered more than most to get to this festival day. Now he wondered whether he could cure her sorrows.

Cierto, I said to myself.

A wedding march that I did not know, probably from some opera, had begun. I thought it was catchy but perhaps a bit suggestive.

Had she taken pain medicines before she had left the hospital? Being Spanish I'd bet she had not.

"We Sevillians know how to do a great spectacle," Don Diego, now wearing the fool's grin from a Goya painting, whispered as he walked out to greet the bridal couple. The two young bridesmaids had recovered all their confidence. They sat in chairs at the foot of the steps to the tiny sanctuary with an adult's defiant poise. Then the descendants of Isabella the Catholic and Cristobal Colon joined hands, winked at each other, and strode up the stairs as if they owned Seville, Spain, and the world.

I suspected that they winked at Don Diego too.

Then the bride and groom reached their kneelers. Don Diego shook both their hands together by way of welcome.

The choir provided a brisk Kyrie and Gloria.

All Spanish church music I had once observed sounds the same and if you can sing the first verse, you have no trouble singing the rest of it.

Most convenient.

Don Diego read the wondrous story of the Wedding Feast of

Cana from the pulpit high above the center of the church. He closed the Gospel book.

"The homily at this happy event will be give by John Bleakwood Ryan, coadjutor archbishop of Chicago, who has been helping here the last couple of days. The bride and groom have asked that he give the homily as a sign of their great respect and affection."

Bleakwood, huh!

I waited till he had come down the stairs and returned to his portable throne which had edged St. Joseph out of his rightful place in the sanctuary. Then I stumbled to a stand near the bride and groom, the only open place.

"I will begin by saying that this is a Native American story about why God made strawberries. In fact it is a Cherokee Indian story which I heard once on a tape by Gail Ross who is a Cherokee princess. I asked the ineffable Don Pedro who, as we know, does all things well to translate the story into Spanish. I will present it in the Mexican dialect that we use in the United States because it is the dialect of most of our people. I grant you complete freedom to laugh at my pronunciation. If, however, you do laugh, Don Pedro will write down your name and address and you will hear from us. I must also comment that though both Don Diego and Doña Teresa wanted to vet this harmless little story, I told them that you don't try to censor an Archbishop, even if he is only a coadjutor with right to succession."

They laughed. This ridiculous little bishop in his ill-fitting cassock with its dull purple buttons at least had a sense of humor. I channeled my memory to the emphases in Megan Flores's speech and plowed on.

WHY GOD MADE *LAS FRESAS*

Once upon a time, long, long ago, there was Earth Maker and First Man and First Woman. Earth Maker isn't God to the

Cherokee. Rather he is the one who has responsibility for organizing things. They lived in a whitewashed stone cottage on the edge of a green field with a silver lake and a road over the hills and out beyond. First Man and First Woman were very much in love and very happy together. Earth Maker was pleased with himself because it appeared that his experiment of creating male and female had been a huge success. Oh, they argued a few times a week, but never anything serious.

Then one day they had a terrible fight. They forgot what they were fighting about and fought about who had started it and then about what the fight was about.

Finally First Woman was fed up. You're nothing but a loudmouth braggart! she said and stormed out of the cottage and across the green field and by the silver lake and over the hill and out beyond.

First Man sat back in his rocking chair, lit his pipe, and sighed happily. Well, at last we'll have some peace and quiet around here. The woman has a terrible mouth on her.

But as the sun set and turned the silver lake rose gold, he realized he was hungry. Woman, he shouted, I want my tea. But there was no woman to make the tea. Poor First Man could not even boil water. So he had to be content with half of a cold potato. Then as a chill came over the cottage and First Man felt lonely altogether, he sighed again, let his pipe go out, and felt he needed a good night's sleep. He didn't light the fire because, truth to tell, he wasn't very good at such things. First Woman did all the fire lighting in their house because she could start fires in a second.

The poor fella shivered something awful when he pulled the covers over himself. Well, he told himself, she did keep the bed warm at night. He didn't sleep very well and when he woke there was a terrible hunger on him. Woman, he shouted, I want my tea! Then he realized that there was no woman and no tea. So he had to be satisfied with the other half of the cold potato.

Well, he was sitting in front of the cold fireplace, puffing on a cold pipe, wrapped in a thin blanket, when Earth Maker appeared.

Let me see now, said Earth Maker. This is earth and I made ye male and female. And you're the male. Where's herself?

She's gone, your reverence.

Gone?

Gone!

Why's she gone?

We had a fight!

You never did!

We did!

And she left you?

She did, your reverence.

You're a pair of eejits!

Yes, your reverence.

Do you still love her?

Oh, yes, your reverence, something terrible!

Well then, man, off your rocking chair and after her!

She's long gone, your reverence. I'll never catch up with her.

No problem. I can move as fast as thought. I'll go ahead of you and slow her down! Now get a move on!

Poor First Man, his heart breaking, trundled out of his chair and down the path across the green field and by the silver lake and out beyond.

Meanwhile Earth Maker caught up with First Woman. She was still furious at First Man. She walked down the road at top speed, muttering to herself as she went.

The woman has a temper, Earth Maker reflected. But that fella would make anyone lose their temper.

So to slow her down, Earth Maker said ZAP and created a forest. Didn't she cut through it like a warm knife cutting through butter.

Then Earth Maker ZAP created a big hill. Didn't she charge over the hill like a mountain goat?

So ZAP, Earth Maker created a big lake. That'll stop her, he said to himself.

It didn't stop her at all, at all. She charged into the lake and swam across it, Australian crawl.

I don't know where she learned the stroke because Australia didn't exist way back then. But she knew it.

Och, said Earth Maker, there are problems in creating women athletes, aren't there now? Well, the poor thing is hungry, so she'll slow down to eat. ZAP. There appeared along the road all kinds of fruit trees—peach trees, plum trees, grapefruit trees, apricot trees (no apple trees because that's another story).

What did First Woman do? Well, she just picked the fruit as she was walking and didn't slow down a bit.

Sure, said Earth Maker, won't I have to fall back on me ultimate weapon. I'll have to create strawberries!

ZAP!

First Woman stopped cold. Ah, would you look at them pretty bushes with the white flowers.

As she watched didn't the flowers turn into rich red fruit.

Ah now isn't that gorgeous fruit and itself shaped just like the human heart.

She felt the first strawberry. Sure, doesn't it feel just like the human heart, soft and yet strong and firm. I wonder what it tastes like . . . Sure, doesn't it have the sweetest taste in all the world, save for the taste of human love.

Well, she sighed loudly, speaking of that subject, I suppose the eejit is chasing after me, poor dear man. I'd better wait for him.

So didn't she pick a whole apron full of strawberries and sit by the strawberry bush and wait for First Man.

And finally, he came down the road, huffing and puffing and all worn-out.

This is called the strawberry bush, she said, pointing at the bush. And doesn't the fruit taste wonderful. So she gave a piece of fruit to First Man, like the priest gives the Eucharist.

Oh, says First Man, isn't it the sweetest taste in all the world, save for the taste of human love. So they picked more strawberries and, arm in arm, walked home to their whitewashed cottage by the green field and the silver lake and the hill and out beyond. 'Tis said that they lived happily ever after, which meant only three or so fights a week.

"Now I want all of you here, especially Leandro and Teresa" (and I put my hands on both their heads, carefully avoiding her wound) "to remember every time from now on when you taste *strawberries*, that the only thing sweeter is the taste of human love. And remember too that love is about catching up and waiting and true lovers know when to catch up and when to wait."

I stumbled away from my makeshift pulpit and withdrew to the empty sacristy to unwind. I had noted with some satisfaction that there were many tears in the church, most notably from Teresa who was weeping profusely as her promised husband held her close.

Well done, if they cry, they've at least heard you.

The next step was the actual exchange of vows which was done briskly in the sanctuary. I watched it on the television in the sacristy. You keep taking these terrible chances and someday you're going to fall over yourself.

The exchange of vows, which is what the whole spectacle is all about, took only a few minutes. I watched in from the door of the sacristy. La Doña seemed solemn and depressed as the ritual began. She was imagining herself on the slave block in Algiers. Perhaps her wounded body was hurting. Perhaps she was exhausted from the strain. She had come too far to turn back. Nor would she turn back if she could. Yet she might well be scared. I didn't blame her. Don Diego might well have gone too far in orchestrating the

Feria. Yet it was a fitting and perhaps essential experience for her resurrection experience. Resurrection isn't supposed to be easy.

Bride and groom recited their pledges clearly and confidently. After Don Diego's final words, they collapsed in each other's arms, clinging desperately to one another, La Doña a limp form in her husband's arms. An enormous cry of celebration from the crowd. Don Diego smiled benignly over the couple and embraced both of them. He then turned and bowed to me. What did he want? Ah I should congratulate them too. Idiot, too many sleepless nights.

I offered my hand first to Leandro who grabbed it fervently and leaned against me.

"*Mucho gracias,* Padrecito Negro. We will never forget you! Never!"

Better not.

Then the bride embraced me. Same scent. Same womanly feel to her. Well.

"Hang in there," I told her.

"I will, Padrecito Negro, I will. *Siempre.*"

Ah, she had overcome, temporarily, her fears. That would have to happen many times. In time it would be automatic, please God.

I decided as Don Diego and I continued the concelebration of the Eucharist that I could at least provide some congratulation to Himself.

It was a near thing, I reported, of course you know that. I claimed just a few days ago that there was no more mystery or romance in Seville. I couldn't have been more wrong, could I? This poor woman has had a miserable life. She has many happy days ahead of her. Protect her and her husband and her new family, and if you don't mind, grant peace and forgiveness to those who have tormented her. May they all find eventual joy with you. Me too. Forever and ever Amen.

Then it was Communion time. I assisted and indeed placed

the Body of Christ on the tongues of my stalwart nephew and his valiant promised bride.

It was but a brief walk down to Santa Cruz from Santa Catalina. However, it would not be safe for the newly married to try to cover that distance on foot. The armored white limousine waited for them at the door, surrounded by the Civil Guard and the spear-carrying mounted soldiers.

They waved to the crowd and to the cameras from the steps and hopped into the protection of the limo. Don Diego, Don Pedro, and I slipped out of the back door of the church and into the Cardinal Lexus which was innocent of any distinguishing markings. We however had two Civil Guard motorcycles to lead us through the back streets to the Bar Giralda.

"I will receive complaints this evening and all day tomorrow from my colleagues."

"Cardinals?"

"Cardinals, bishops, priests, the nuncio, maybe the Secretary of State.

"They will all wonder why they weren't invited. Some will ask why you of all people were asked to preach. They have never heard of you, it would seem."

"May it stay that way."

"I will tell them that because of injuries to the bride and the attention to the attempts on her life that it was necessary to achieve the matter quickly and convey her husband and her to a safe retreat where her recuperation may continue. They won't like that, but what can they say. You are on television, enough, I daresay, that it is not something you seek so that people will see you?"

"Chicagoans would say that they see me too much."

"Not one of those who call me will have a kind word to say about your brilliant homily. Nor will they say an unkind word about your homily. It did not exist. I for my part will put a copy in my file so I can borrow it."

"Priests never congratulate other priests on their preaching," I said. "It is against the rules."

"I will break that rule now. It was brilliant, but I said that didn't I? Nonetheless I will say it for the third time. It was brilliant."

"Totally," Don Pedro said, his eyes still glued to the narrow path ahead of us.

"Thank you," I said. "Cardinal Cronin likes it too. That makes it unanimous."

"What happened at the Municipal this morning?" Don Diego asked.

I told him.

"Sad," he said, "terribly sad."

"Don Marco ought to have been giving away the bride today," I agreed.

"I think most of us realized that she was a bit mad," the Cardinal said. "All very sad. It is a wonder that our bride survived it all, if indeed she has."

That was a lead for her spiritual director.

"She is a very strong woman."

We pulled up at the Bar Giralda. The Civil Guards in their fancy uniforms were lined up in front and across the street from them, the soldiers with their spears and armor. The front of the café was festooned with the yellow and blue colors of Seville.

When Don Diego entered, there was a wild cheer from the people. They knew that this was his production. His predecessor might not have permitted the marriage in Church. I disengaged myself from him and Don Pedro and began to walk around, my eyes blinking in the dark. Anytime there is a space with celebrating people, a priest is almost genetically programmed to work the room. I wandered about greeting people, especially my nephew and his promised bride.

"Nice homily, Uncle Blackie," Joseph said. "It gets longer every time you do it."

"The quality," I said, "improves like good wine with age."

"You totally must give it at our wedding."

"If the bride wishes it, that is my command," I said with a bow.

"We couldn't stop you if we wanted, which of course we don't."

"What time do we leave tomorrow morning?" I asked.

"Ten thirty, eleven unless you want to start earlier," our pilot replied. "Looks like good weather all the way across. I think I'll fly over the Azores rather than the glacier, head winds a lot weaker down here than up there."

"I don't want to know the details," I said. "I'm sick already."

"We have a lot better pressurization than the commercial jets," she replied, proud of her Gulfstream 560.

"I rejoice at that."

"We'll make it a smooth flight, Uncle Blackie, I promise. I told the crew to be ready for a seven o'clock call, just in case. I'm going to fly it all the way home, as the copilot.

"Don't tell my mother."

The good Mary Kathleen rejoices in the last of the marriages in the family and believes that Peggy Anne is an intelligent, proper, charming young woman—the ideal successor to herself in the final phases of civilizing Joseph. As family pilot of twin engine jets ("such *small* things") she wasn't quite so sure. She had permitted herself to understand that two *real* pilots on the plane meant that Peggy would do very little *real* flying. I was not permitted to express an opinion on the subject. I strolled over to the wedding table where everyone was laughing. La Doña pulled me down next to her.

"Feeling OK?" I asked.

"My *husband* asks me that all the time. And he laughs at me all the time," she protested. "Padrecito Negro, make him stop laughing at me."

It was not a seriously meant protest. The laughter embarrassed her but she loved it.

"If he ever stops laughing at you, you should start to worry."

"As you said in your note," she whispered, "it makes me feel naked, which I kind of like."

"I did not say it, woman, I implied it."

"I know, Padrecito, I'm a nervous wreck. We're going to some kind of retreat or something up in the Sierra Nevada. I'll need to catch up on a lot of sleep."

Holding her hand, which I don't think he had released since they joined hands in the sanctuary of Santa Catalina, Don Leandro leaned over to me.

"That was a wonderful homily, Padrecito. Everyone seems to want a copy of it."

"I believe Don Pedro is selling copies now," I said.

"Is it true, Padrecito, that Inez killed herself this morning?"

She should have been protected from that news.

"I'm afraid that it is, Teresa."

Her scent was as powerful as every other time—different this time, but still discreet, subtle, and powerful. Lucky Leandro would always be absorbed in it.

"Did Don Marco kill her? They say that he is in jail."

"He is in custody, as is Don Teodoro. He did not kill his wife. However, he did hold her in his arms as she died."

"Poor man, he loved her so much . . . I had hoped that he might have presented me to my groom in church this morning. Will he be in jail for long?"

"I don't think so."

"Leandro, will you remind me when we come back from the mountains to see what we might do to help the poor man?"

Her husband nodded solemnly.

"*Cierto,* dearest one. That you would think of that is one of the reasons I love you so much."

He brushed his lips against hers.

"We had better dance now, Leandro, while I'm still awake. No one else will dance before us."

They rose out of their chairs and moved to the open space that the proprietor had created in the middle of the café. Guitars began to strum, young men and women began to hum, and the dance began. Flamenco it was not, but lively and vibrant it was. I spent the time autographing copies of my homily. Maybe I should open a store.

Isidoro and Maria Luisa danced by me. She was wearing a blue mantilla over her shoulders.

"She is terribly tired, Padrecito Negro. She should leave soon."

"I'll tell Don Diego."

I told him.

"No pain medication during the ceremony, I suppose?"

"Her name isn't Teresa for nothing."

A mobile phone was ringing somewhere. Arguably it was mine.

"Father Ryan."

"Nora, Blackie."

"Oh, no."

"They're doing all they can . . . I don't know what's happening. The nurses act like he is dying. Nuala says I shouldn't worry."

"One is never far from being right when one believes her."

"I'm all right. I've been through these things before. Don't rush home, Blackie, sounds like a wedding party."

"I'll talk to my pilot who is here . . . What time is it in Chicago?"

"Eleven in the morning."

"I'll be there in twenty-four hours."

"Thank you, Blackie. I need you here."

"Sean?" Don Diego asked.

"Right . . . must leave early."

"Don Pedro and I will drive you to the airport."

"Thank you," I said and began searching for my pilot and her promised groom in the melee of dancing bodies. I found them, moving more slowly than the locals, in a dreamy pas de deux from which the rest of the world was excluded.

"What's the earliest we can leave tomorrow?"

"Cardinal Sean?"

"Dead?"

"Massive heart attack. Touch and go."

"We can get out at seven thirty without pushing anything. I'll call my crew and get them back from the beaches. You be there at seven. We'll get you through the formalities and will be airborne before eight at the latest . . . Joseph, are you game to drive me out there at six?"

"Will Cardinal Jimmy drive you out?"

"Cierto."

"That will be a help."

"We better say good-bye to the bride and groom."

I got there first.

"We must leave early tomorrow morning," I told them. "My Cardinal has had a massive heart attack. God bless and protect you both. Always remember strawberries."

"We'll be in Chicago in the summer. I promise."

She threw her arms around me.

"We'll never forget you, Padrecito." Her husband squeezed my hand.

I found Don Pedro and told him about our early departure.

"I will arrange to drive you to the airport . . . Should I awaken you? Shall we concelebrate before we leave?"

"By all means."

Don Diego had been listening to our conversation.

"I will go with you tomorrow," Don Diego promised. "Perhaps I can overcome any procedural problems . . . Should I take you home now?"

"No, I can walk. It's just around the corner."

"That's true. I should know that. It is my city after all."

Joseph and Peggy Anne were waiting for me at the door. I thanked the proprietor for a wonderful evening and left the party with a very heavy heart.

Sean Cronin's death would be like losing a parent.

20

"*We will take off in a* minute and a half," said the woman in her flat professional voice. "We will fly over Seville and you'll be able to see Santa Cruz and the Giralda and the Cathedral. Then we will pass over the Santana Park, wetlands and dunes, and then the Atlantic. Please make sure your seat belts are securely fastened and your luggage properly stored."

Margaret, as she was at the controls of an airplane, had temporarily banished her exuberance, a loss in the drab and weary gray-colored world.

"These marshes were created by several earthquakes. The most recent one diverted the course of the Guadalquivir River. Some archaeologists say that an earlier quake wiped out a great civilization along the river between here and Cadiz, though much of it of course remained to absorb the best of every new immigration. The legend of Atlantis, the fabulously rich land beyond the Pillars of Hercules, may be based on these memories."

Once a schoolteacher, always a schoolteacher, even if you are taxiing out to a runway.

"Here we go!"

Peggy Anne again.

The plane came alive, roared down the runway, and poked its

slim silver nose into the sky. I remembered the "little engine that could" from my childhood. The Gulfstream 560 was a small plane that didn't realize it was small. It could easily fly 7,000 miles and achieve a Mach .8 speed. Its cabin was roomy with wide and comfortable seats. I'd be in Milord Cronin's room at Northwestern Medical Center before noon, marginally less wiped out than if I were flying Iberian Air Lines.

Across the aisle Joseph Ryan looked for Seville. I didn't bother. I'd seen enough of it. What had been the point of the trip? Well, I'd been involved in freeing a magic princess from demons and dragons. She had strong allies, men and women who loved her. She would have made it anyway. I had perhaps added a touch or two to the comedy. I had solved one more locked-room puzzle, this one rather easy compared to some of the others. I had witnessed some of the agony and the ecstasy, the cruelty and the faith, the despair and love which have tormented Spain, quite literally from time immemorial. I had seen love triumph over despair. I had helped a strong and beautiful woman through a resurrection experience which she would now shape herself, imperfectly but vigorously. I would never forget her. I had met some excellent people and some nasty people. Now I was flying home to stand at a bedside—and perhaps the deathbed—of one of the most important persons of my life. I would, one way or another, gain new responsibilities that I did not want. I would have to struggle to avoid the corruption of power, power which I had not sought and did not want.

Dismal.

"Because of very strong headwinds north of us, we are not flying over the ice cap today. Rather we are flying across the North Atlantic and over the Azores Islands. In terms of distance this is longer but in terms of time it is shorter. Our landfall will not be in Labrador but near Boston. The computer projects an arrival at Chicago's Midway Airport at approximately ten thirty

Chicago time. The weather at Midway is good at the present time. There may be some overcast when we arrive, but we expect no delays in an on-time landing. I will notify you when it will be appropriate for phone calls to America. There won't be many sights to observe on this trip. What you see now is the Atlantic Ocean. It is what you will see for the next seven hours. I will not distract your sleep with any more chatter. Enjoy your breakfasts."

The two cabin attendants, trim matrons who much preferred working for Avion Electonics than a commercial airline, brought us our breakfasts, orange juice, tea, blueberry pancakes soggy in maple syrup, and bacon. The two women served three of us—Joseph, the "real" copilot, and one spaced-out little cleric.

I managed not to spill too much syrup on my wrinkled clerical shirt.

"She's really good," the "real" copilot said. "One of the best young pilots I've ever seen, steady, confident, and reliable."

"Just what a man wants in a wife," Joseph said with the perfectly straight face which marks all his madcap ironies.

The pilot, like most such men, was innocent of irony and wit. "It was her decision to fly the southern route. The right one naturally."

"The route of your man, Christopher Columbus."

"I guess it is."

"A lot of ocean down there," my nephew remarked.

"Don't worry, we won't get lost. We have three redundancies in our guidance systems and we could also follow the radio signals manually. As it is now, the computer is flying the plane."

"I hope she punched in the right numbers," Joseph said, stretching out his long legs.

A cabin attendant removed my tray. I covered myself with a more generous blanket than a commercial flight might have provided and curled up for a sustained eye-resting period. My sleep had been tormented by images of the dramatis personae of the romance, particularly La Doña and her springtime scent. No, I would not forget her.

From a long distance I heard the promised bride singing the Galway Lullaby, "Blow winds blow . . ."

Peggy Anne, I thought, is still Peggy Anne.

Then the world with all its ambiguities and regrets slipped away. At one point I thought Peggy came back to the cabin and kissed her promised groom more intensely than I had ever seen her kiss him. Pilot shouldn't do things like that. Then, a couple of moments later, she spoke again.

"That's Cape Cod down there . . . Boston the home of the bean and the cod, where the Cabots speak only to the Lodges and the Lodges speak only to God. . . . It's also the home of a university that calls itself Boston College. Less said about them the better . . . Uncle Blackie, if you want to call the rectory you can do it now. Just like a long-distance call . . ."

Saturday morning, a little early to call.

"Holy Name Cathedral Rectory, good morning, this is Megan."

Megan Quinn, the "real Megan" as she called herself.

"Good morning, Megan. Father Blackie over Boston."

"Father Blackie! Come right on home! They need you here. . . . Father Coyne left a message for you . . . The Cardinal had a restful night. His condition continues to be critical, but stable. His vital signs are good. What time should Father Coyne pick you up at Midway?"

"Around ten thirty, Megan. If it changes I'll be back to you."

"Cardinal's going to get better, I just know it."

"Fersure, Megan."

Then Peggy Anne called Joseph.

"Better tell them you've made it safely across the Atlantic."

"Only attacked once."

"You seemed to have survived."

"First time I was almost raped on an airplane."

"You haven't seen anything yet. Don't tell your mom I flew the plane across the Atlantic and still found time to attack you."

"She wouldn't mind the latter. She thinks it time we marry."

He dialed the number on Longwood Drive.

"Dr. Murphy . . ."

"Hi, Dad, your last born here. The pilot thinks we're over New England but she's not sure. It may be Curacao."

"I'll tell your mother that."

"Good idea . . . We'll land at Midway at 10:28. Central Avenue terminal. You can park right on the tarmac."

"You guys will want to go to Grand Beach for the weekend? It's lovely weather."

"Why not?"

"Pete and Cindasue will be there too, with the kids of course."

"We don't mind kids."

I tried to go back to sleep.

My organism tends toward depression after a plane flight. What a waste of time! Even if I had been hugged and kissed by La Doña.

"We will land precisely on time," the alleged copilot informed us, "10:28 Central Daylight Time. We will land from southeast to northwest and taxi to the Central Avenue Terminal. The weather in Chicago is good, high now in the sixties, mid-seventies during the day. There's a front passing through, so we will encounter some cloud cover on landing. Nothing serious. Maybe a few bumps. The ceiling is about five hundred feet. Chicago will become visible in a hurry as we descend. Please tighten your seat belts and prepare for landing."

The attendants scurried about collecting glasses. I desperately wanted a Bailey's but there was no time for that.

There were a few bumps, nothing that the Gulfstream

couldn't shrug off. We plunged deeper into the darkness. The landing gear went down, the flaps clicked into position. No Chicago yet. Maybe we *were* landing at Curacao. Through the clouds a hint of the city—the University blinking in and out in breaks in the cloud, an appropriate posture for it.

Then the city—the Dan Ryan Expressway in all its elegance, State Street, the golden knight on what used to be St. Martin's Church, the ground racing up to meet us, parking lots at Midway, the terminal rushing by, the aircraft hesitating, floating, and then bumping into the ground and then grinding to a halt.

Not bad, I thought.

"Midway Airport," she informed us, "Chicago, Illinois, USA, Richard M. Daley, Mayor."

Applause from the five of us.

"Thank you."

"Let's fly back," Joseph cried. "This is fun."

"Be sure you have your passports at hand and fill out the landing cards, Uncle Blackie, if you have not done so already."

I scribbled my vital information on the card. I had bought nothing, not even trinkets for the Megans. Shame on me. I wanted to go back to bed.

An immigration officer came on board, glanced at our passports and landing cards, and waved us off with a smile.

Nice to be part of the establishment. There were two cars on the tarmac, the Ryan Lincoln Continental, all black and shiny and nineteen seventyish, and the Cardinal's limo, a nondescript Buick with bulletproof windows. I was ushered off first on the drop-down staircase.

George Coyne greeted me at the bottom along with my sister the valiant Mary Kathleen Ryan Murphy.

"I just talked to Nora at the hospital this morning. She says that he's a lot better. Talked to the Pope."

"My sister-in-law, the good witch," George said, "sees bright auras around him. That makes it official."

"That young woman flew the plane all across the Atlantic, didn't she, Blackie?"

In her crisp khaki AVEL uniform and baseball cap, "that young woman" was leaving the ship with her promised groom in tow.

(When flying her Cessna 310 Bravo, she wore a Notre Dame uniform.)

"Patently, though in fact technically she was only the copilot."

"She is truly a remarkable person. Probably too good for Joey John (Joseph's original name when he was still a galoot). But I think we'd better let her in while we can still get her."

I winked at the ever-patient Joe Ryan.

Either of us could have said that this was a dramatic policy change. Mary Kate would have denied it vigorously.

"Congratulations, Peggy," she said, embracing her promised daughter-in-law, "I hear it was a perfect flight."

Margaret Nolan navigated the change perfectly.

"Thanks, Mom, it was fun."

I climbed into the Buick in the front seat next to George.

"You must excuse my sister."

"What the hell, Blackie, she's a doctor. Nuala is only a witch . . . He's in a good mood this morning, even before the Pope called him. I think he's decided that he's not tired of life anymore and wants to live a little longer. Apparently the Pope accepted his resignation, reluctantly and with the promise that he would still call on him for advice . . . which he'd get plenty of anyway. Poor Sean ought not to have to sit through meetings of the Priests Council anymore. They're incapable of a discussion toward a conclusion. You'll have fun with them."

"I may resign after the first one."

"Good vibes about the succession. Lots of phone calls to the rectory asking about your work style."

"And the reply?"

"From Megan Quinn . . . He works terribly hard and he is always kind, even to reporters. He's a very sweet man."

"I'm not sure this will happen."

"Well you can never tell with those assholes over there in the Vatican. Priests are OK, though some picked up a line from the media, Chicago needs a change of style. You know what stupid bastards priests are."

We were hurtling down the Adlai E. Stevenson Expressway toward the Drive. There was almost no traffic on a Saturday morning in May. My stomach went into a firm knot. I did not want to preside at Sean Cronin's obsequies. But I didn't want to replace him either. I did not want in particular to struggle with a priesthood whose culture was defined by mediocrity and envy. There were many, many good, hardworking priests in the Archdiocese—until you brought them together. Then they collectively sank to the lowest common denominator. It was that way with the apostles probably.

Then we turned into Lake Shore Drive and the Chicago skyline leaped up ahead of us—a black and silver tracing against an increasingly dark sky and irritated lake. Not exactly the Merry Month of May.

I was in a very bad mood. Airplane trips did that. So did hospital rooms. I must mind my tongue or I would say something I would later regret. Like "My style is very different from Cardinal Cronin's. I suffer fools much less gladly than he does."

True enough, but not something I would say until I was over jet lag.

We turned off the drive at Chicago Avenue and edged our way through the side streets in the medical center area. The media waited—a mass of TV cameras and a bee swarm of reporters.

"I have come to visit the Cardinal," I said, trying to slip through them. They were however an impenetrable mass.

"Do you expect you will succeed the Cardinal?"

"Do you agree with those priests who say the Archdiocese needs a new style?"

"Why were you out of town when the Cardinal had a heart attack?"

"Do you think a bishop has the right to choose his own successor?"

"What were you doing in Spain anyway?"

I replied to all of these questions that I would have no comment until I had a chance to speak with Cardinal Cronin and learn his condition in greater detail.

A group of hospital guards appeared and, with some considerable difficulty, cleared a way for me.

We rode up to his room. Nora was waiting at the door.

"You look terrible, Blackie. You must take care of yourself. For our sake."

Nuala Anne appeared, rosary in hand.

They both looked terrible too, though on them terrible was better than it was on me.

"The doctors say that he is critical but stable. They hold out hope. He's in amazing good humor. I don't understand that. All we can do is pray that he makes it."

Behind her Nuala gave a sign with her hands that said all was well.

I make a point never to argue with someone who reads auras.

"Do you want to see him, Blackie?" Nora asked. "What a stupid question! Yes, by all means go in and see him. Put on one of those gowns inside the door."

Milord Cronin was propped up in bed, various lines and wires protruding from his body, almost like a laboratory designed by the late Dr. Frankenstein. Monitors behind him were buzzing and flashing. He did not appear as sick as reported. His color was better than I had seen many times when he hadn't had a heart attack.

Two doctors and a nurse stood by, though the nurse was probably a doctor. They stepped aside.

"Holding his own," said the nurse, who was now patently a doctor. "Maybe a little better than that."

Milord Cronin opened his eyes.

"Blackwood," he said, moving a hand in my direction. "How good of you to come! It didn't take you long!"

I touched his hand in greeting.

"I have seen you look worse when you didn't have a heart attack."

He laughed.

"I keep telling these wonderful people who are taking care of me that I'm going to make it. . . . I called your friend over in Rome yesterday. He called back this morning."

"Ah."

"I told him that I knew I would survive but that nonetheless I wanted to retire formally because Chicago deserved something better than an invalid. He accepted my resignation, as he said with the utmost regret, and hoped that I would continue to advise him with my usual vigor. He said we could announce that you can do it when you go downstairs. He said the nunciature would confirm your succession tomorrow morning. There's no question about that. I suspect there was some last-minute desperate conniving. He saw you doing a homily on Spanish television yesterday. I said the strawberry one? He said it was charming. So tell them downstairs that the nuncio will make an announcement tomorrow . . ."

"And let them guess?"

"Yeah . . ."

A red light began to peep.

"Slow down, Cardinal."

"OK . . . don't leave, Blackwood."

I looked at the woman in charge.

She nodded.

"I'm going to move into the house by Lincoln Park . . . if you don't mind?"

"Why should I mind? I had on record many times that it looked like a Victorian funeral home."

"Nora will move in with me . . . Nuns will still be around, so it will be all right . . . I've got work to do."

The doctor frowned.

"OK," I said.

"Come back again," she said. "Remarkably he does continue to improve."

I dumped my gown in a container in the outer room.

"How does he seem?" Nora asked anxiously.

"The young woman who seems to be in charge used the word 'remarkable.'"

"Yes, that's what they're saying this morning. Last night they were telling us to prepare for the worst."

"Blatherskites," Nuala said, still tolling her beads.

"Blackie," Nora said, hesitating for words. "I don't know how to tell you this, but he told me this morning that when he almost died last night, his family came to him—his mother and father and his brother Paul. They were all young and happy. They told him how proud they were of him and that he had to stay on earth a little longer because there was work to do."

Nuala nodded her head up and down as if in approval.

"I don't know what to think. He hated them all, you know. Why he would imagine them . . . And yesterday he wanted to die. Now he wants to live. I don't know. Nuala thinks I should believe him. We've been through so much . . ."

"His anger is all gone now. The colors are bright again.

Death doesn't stop reconciliations. Now you, your reverence, should go home and rest. We don't want to have to pray two Archbishops through a crisis, do we now?"

Her brother-in-law rolled his eyes.

"My best to Dermot and the brood."

"Sure, isn't me Dermot a living saint altogether?"

I rode down in the elevator in a state of confusion.

"I never said she was a bad witch," George Coyne protested.

I emerged from the door into the driveway and waited for silence.

"The Cardinal's condition is still the same, critical but stable. But he looks good, I thought. There seems to be agreement that he is making some progress. I heard the word 'remarkable' a couple of times. We continue to pray.

"He asked me to make an announcement. He spoke with his Holiness this morning and submitted his resignation. The Pope accepted with great reluctance and affirmed his hope that the Cardinal would continue to send him advice. I assume that this is official."

"What about a successor?"

"The Cardinal told me to announce that there would be a statement sometime tomorrow morning from the nunciature."

"Do you think that you will replace him?"

"No one replaces a giant like Sean Cronin."

"What do you think?"

"Our Rome correspondent reports that there was a last-minute campaign to derail your train."

"I have not heard that rumor but it wouldn't surprise me."

"Do you want to be Archbishop of Chicago?"

"No."

"Have you heard that some priests in Chicago think that there should be a change in style in the governance of the Arch-diocese?"

"Yes. It is unfortunate that in the present state of things, local priests and laity are not given much chance to provide input on these matters."

"How would you characterize your style in comparison with Cardinal Cronin's?"

"I wouldn't . . . One more question, please."

My old friend Mary Alice Quinn asked, "Blackie, is the Cardinal going to recover?"

"I think so."

And that was that.

21

He did recover and moved into the house on North State. Nora Cronin moved in after him. She and the nuns got along just fine. I was invited up once for supper. She told me later with wide open eyes that she had come to believe that his family had visited him. I wouldn't deny it.

I was named Archbishop of Chicago the next day, an appointment which stirred little comment in the city. So what else is new. My first act was to attend a meeting of the Priests Council. The subject was what to do with old Holy Days of Obligation. It was sick making. Less than a discussion, it was an occasion for making statements, assertions of opinion which were fervently presented but without any evidence to support them. There was no progress toward consensus and apparently no need felt to achieve it.

When they ran out of bullshit (excuse the expression) the experience wound down.

"I do not detect any consensus emerging from these exchanges . . . Does anyone?"

Silence.

"Nor any clearly expressed alternatives which we could perhaps vote on?

"This is very unfortunate. None of us can afford to wander aimlessly in discussion of such a critical issue (I didn't think it was all that critical). Therefore I propose to adjourn this meeting and schedule another one a week from today where we can gather again to work toward consensus. I'll look forward to seeing you."

They left unhappy about the loss of their precious time. However, we had established a precedent. If you waste Blackie's time, he doesn't like it.

And to the question of what I should be called now that I had new responsibilities, I replied constantly in those days with a variant of my usual line, "As far as I know, my name is still Blackie!"

Epilogue

Caro Padrecito Negro,

I am very happy to learn from Don Diego who came to visit us this morning that you are now the real Archbishop of Chicago and that your dear Cardinal has recovered from his illness. He too has had a resurrection experience, no?

We are up in the Sierra resting, relaxing, trying to regain our sanity. It was very wise of Don Diego to provide this interlude before we start our wedding trip to America. My husband said that since we had begun our affair we were always rushing. There was never time to talk, to learn about one another once again, to simply enjoy one another's presence. We were always running, running, running. I was pleasantly surprised to learn so much about my husband. I think he is surprised by me too. These conversations in which we reveal so much about one another must go on through our whole life together as we try to discover who the other is. We must find time to talk about one another. We both are very grateful to have found the spouse that we have. And we must permit greater knowledge to improve our love. My husband continues to laugh at me with much, much affection.

My health is improved. I am eating more than I have and put on some of the weight I lost. I no longer need pain pills and I swim every day. I feel strong again. So we are able to resume our lovemaking which is so sweet and gentle and slow. No more rushing to get it over with and get on to our next task. The only work we have done is to design the changes in our apartment, now that the palacio is ours. We must make room for my new daughters and my husband and any other family we might acquire. Eventually we will redo the whole place and find useful things to do with it. It is a landmark to a very bad time for the Spanish nobility.

I know more now than I did about the attempts on my life. I need not know all the details and when I do my reaction will be the same. I forgive all of them. How can I be a Catholic and not do that? I especially worry about poor Don Marco. I have told Don Diego to convey to him that I will have a place for him when he is released. Both Don Diego and my husband agree that this is as it should be.

Once a week there is a call from Maria Luisa and the little ones. They are having a grand summer. They want us to hurry back and spend time with them before we go to America. Don Diego will find a place where we can all live together for a week or two. Then we will be off on our real wedding trip to America. We expect to be in Chicago in late June. What hotel would you recommend we stay in?

Sometimes my husband and I get on each other's nerves. We both are very intense people and we have lived and are living through intense weeks here, rewarding, exciting, and exhausting. And as he says it is so fortunate that we have passion to ease the strains of the common life.

I am very happy just now, caro Padrecito. I did not think I would ever be happy. I am grateful for your guidance.

I hope I can continue to rely on it now that you have such an important new job.

Teresa

P.S. It would also appear that there may be another marriage in our family soon. Maria Luisa tells me with a smirk that she enjoyed the last wedding so much that she may arrange another one next year. I am very fond of Don Isidoro. He makes my daughter laugh, which is what my husband does for me. I do not encourage her in her plans because my support might make her think she ought to reconsider.

I replied by return message.

Congratulations on the remarkable achievements you and your husband have made. When a newly married couple are as young as, let us say, your daughter and my nephew, the adjustments are easier because young people are so much more flexible in their ways. We will be looking forward to seeing you in Chicago. The Four Seasons Hotel is around the corner from the Cathedral as well as the Peninsula Hotel. Make your reservations now because Chicago is filled with tourists in the summer.

God bless all,

Blackie

P.S. I will always have time to guide you.

I thought that there was a scent on the e-mail from her that I had printed out. But you can't scent e-mail, can you?